CHARLOTTE GREIG worked as a music journalist in print and radio before becoming a folk singer and songwriter. She has made five critically acclaimed albums and written a book on girl groups (*Will You Still Love Me Tomorrow? Girl Groups from the 50s On*). She lives in Cardiff with her family. *A Girl's Guide to Modern European Philosophy* is her first novel.

Praise for *A Girl's Guide to Modern European Philosophy*

Shortlisted for the *Good Housekeeping* Book Award

'This is one of those rare novels that manages to be sparkling and funny as well as intelligently thoughtful. A young woman coming of age is trying to expand her mind and live inside her body both at once: her difficulties are imagined with comedy and delicate sympathetic insight' Tessa Hadley

'A tender portrait of a feisty little girl lost... honest and intelligent, and Susannah's resourceful courage is both funny and poignant' *Observer*

'Intelligently written and engaging, *A Girl's Guide to Modern European Philosophy* brilliantly evokes 1970s university culture, with ....d that you can almost taste h.........................*carlet*

'This is a solid, enjoyable debut... memorable and engaging'
New Statesman

'A compelling read' *Mail on Sunday*

'[A] charming, funny book' *Image*

'Fresh and modern... so well constructed that you cannot stop turning the pages to find out what happens next' *Aesthetica*

'A funny, provocative coming of age novel' *Sainsbury's Magazine*

'Packed to bursting point with ideas... deeply satisfying' *New Welsh Review*

A GIRL'S GUIDE

to Modern European Philosophy

Charlotte Greig

Copyright © 2007 by Charlotte Greig

First published in this edition in 2008 by Serpent's Tail
First published in 2007 by Serpent's Tail,
an imprint of Profile Books Ltd
3A Exmouth House
Pine Street
Exmouth Market
London EC1R 0JH
www.serpentstail.com

ISBN 978 1 85242 994 2

Designed and typeset in Plantin by Sue Lamble
Printed in the UK by CPI Bookmarque, Croydon CR0 4TD

10 9 8 7 6 5 4 3 2 1

For John

acknowledgements

I would like to thank Pete Ayrton and everyone at Serpent's Tail.

Thanks also go to Helen, Carol, Anna, Tessa, Jennifer, Ellen, Paul, Simon and Julie for reading and commenting on my work from the start.

I would like to acknowledge the award of a writers' bursary from the Academi for the purpose of completing this book.

I would also like to thank Marie Stopes International for their help in researching it.

Thanks to my family for their support over the years.

And finally, thanks to John Williams, for everything.

She needs no worldly admiration, as little as Abraham needs our tears, for she was no heroine and he no hero, but both of them became greater than that, not by any means by being relieved of the distress, the agony, and the paradox, but because of these.

Søren Kierkegaard, *Fear and Trembling*

MODULE 1

Friedrich Nietzsche:
Human, All Too Human

chapter 1

I WOKE UP LATE THAT MORNING. It was because I kept getting stuck in a dream. It used to happen to me all the time, and it was a bloody nuisance. In the dream, I'd wake up, switch on the bedside light and walk over to the window. I'd draw the curtains and look outside, and then I'd see that everything out there was in negative: white trees against a black sky, a white road snaking into the distance with black cars travelling up and down on it. Seeing that would make me realise I was still in the dream. So I'd walk back to the bed, get in, and try waking up all over again. But each time, however hard I concentrated on every little detail, the little beaded chain on the lamp, the wood grain on the bedside table, I couldn't wake myself up. And each time I walked over to the window, I'd still find myself staring at that landscape in negative.

I knew the only thing for it was to scream my way out. I wasn't very keen on this idea. It just didn't seem right, screaming your head off as you woke up every day. It was weird behaviour. But I didn't have much choice. If I wanted to wake up, there was nothing else for it. So I summoned my voice, which seemed to have disappeared somewhere far down in my chest, and with a huge effort I called out. At first I knew I was only dreaming I was screaming, but then I managed to make my voice break into reality, and I was.

I stopped as soon as I could. I was making a hell of a

racket. I was pretty sure I was awake, but I looked out of the window to double check. The curtains were slightly open and outside I could see a watery blue sky, with dull, soggy looking trees against it. I didn't need to get out of bed and go over to look out. I knew I was wide awake now. And I was all right. I turned over to see if I'd woken Jason up, but when I did, he wasn't there.

I wish he had been. All I needed was to hold on to his sleeping body, his back towards me, just for a few minutes before I got up. After that, I always felt better. With Jason, you could wake up screaming and he'd just shift a bit and groan and go back to sleep, and then you could cuddle up to him for as long as you wanted with his back towards you and it wouldn't disturb him at all. And later, he wouldn't ask you anything about why you'd been screaming. He'd have forgotten all about it. He wasn't the kind of person to ask himself what was going on in your mind, or his. That was one of the things I liked best about him.

But anyway, this morning he wasn't here. That wasn't anything unusual, he often stayed up in London instead of driving back to Brighton. I just wished he had been, that's all. And it gave me a sick, sinking feeling that he wasn't. As though everyone had forgotten about me, even my boyfriend. As though I could wake up and scream myself to death one morning and nobody in the world would give a shit.

I got up, went to the bathroom and cleaned my teeth, looking in the mirror. The sight of my face always cheered me up, however bad I felt. I looked completely normal, like one of those girls you see going off to work at their job in an insurance office or something. Long brown hair, a roundish face with a pleasant, mild expression on it. Nothing out of the ordinary at all.

When I went back into the bedroom and put my new jeans on, I felt even better. They were FUs from Jean Machine that I'd bought the week before in London. They were uncomfortably tight but a nice shape, with flares from the knee down to the ground, over my platforms. With the jeans looking so good, I didn't have to spend much time thinking about what else to wear. I found a T-shirt, slung on my jacket, and packed my files in my shoulder bag. I was running late, so I didn't have time for breakfast. I let myself out of the flat.

It was a wet day outside, mist hovering over the sea and a dull, rhythmic sucking noise coming from the beach as the waves rolled in and out. It was the kind of morning that could turn out either way, with the sun breaking through the mist or staying behind it. The big Regency houses on the square looked impressive in the mist, but close up you could see they were all falling to pieces. It was the same with the grass in the middle; it looked clean, but if you walked across it you'd get half a ton of dog shit on your shoes. So I walked around it, up to the bus stop, and took a ride to the station. On the way, I looked out at the guest houses with their lopsided, rusting balconies and 'Vacancies' signs in the front windows. It started raining.

At the station, I could see the Falmer train still at the platform, so I ran over and caught it just as it was pulling out. I got a seat by the window and lit a cigarette. I liked the Falmer train. It was small and scruffy, and the windows were filthy. Everything rattled as it went along, even though we were only going at about two miles an hour. Normally the only people on the train were students, but as it was nine in the morning, today there was no one at all. It felt snug in there, as though you could forget about the whole world, and the whole world could forget about you.

I was late for my tutorial, but only by about ten minutes. I ran out of the station and nipped over the dual carriageway through a hole in the hedge instead of taking the underpass. By the time I got there, I was out of breath and sweating a bit, but I thought, well, even if my face is all shiny, at least it will seem as though I've made an effort.

That said, the shiny face was a bit of a worry, because I wanted to look good in the tutorial. The tutor, James Belham, was one of the trendiest guys at Sussex. He was quite famous, actually. Modern European Mind, the course we all had to take in our second year, was his idea, and a journalist had written an article taking the piss out of it in a Sunday paper. Belham didn't seem bothered though. He was a serious person, even though he was very good looking and could have acted the star and flirted with all the female students. He had brown curly hair and was into Nietzsche, which I was as well. We were reading *The Birth of Tragedy*, and writing these essays about Dionysus and stuff. It was all very intense, what with it being nine in the morning and Belham being so serious and handsome, and there being only two other people in the tutorial this term: Dennis and Rob.

Dennis wasn't the sort of guy you'd fancy. He had wishy-washy blond hair and pink skin, and a neck covered in spots. Every week, he wore the same clothes: a sickly green jumper and some dark blue jeans that looked stiff and new. His shoes were a horrible tan colour. You could see his socks between the bottom of his jeans and the shoes, which was not a good sign. Only a very determined girl would want to take someone like Dennis on: you'd have had to completely change him, starting with the jeans. But he was incredibly bright, in an over-keen sort of way. You could see Belham loved teaching him. The pair of them kept the whole tutorial going, and all Rob and I had to do was sit back and listen.

At that time of the morning, it was hard for me to think, so I usually didn't say much. Neither did Rob. Belham didn't seem to mind too much because we'd done some essays for him in the first week of term and he knew how much we loved Nietzsche. And also, the situation with Dennis was interesting.

A few weeks into the term, Dennis had taken his jumper off in the tutorial. And underneath, his chest had been bare.

He'd sat there, talking very fast, naked from the waist up. I'd sensed there was some kind of Dionysus thing going on with him. Belham didn't seem to mind. He wasn't an uptight sort of guy. He'd just let Dennis talk on, and so had we. After the tutorial, Dennis had put his jumper back on and walked off, but over the next few days I kept seeing him wandering around campus wearing a sleeveless red vest, even though it was October and freezing cold and raining most of the time.

The following week, Dennis had come to the tutorial wearing the vest and his jeans but with no shoes on. He'd been waving a copy of Nietzsche's *Human, All Too Human* and was very agitated about something he'd read in it. He'd started talking about it to Belham, and in the heat of the discussion, he'd taken the vest off and bared his chest again. Then he'd opened the book and started reading from it, stabbing his finger in the air and shouting out, 'Cannot all values be overturned? And is Good perhaps Evil? And God only an invention, a nicety of the Devil?'

Once again, Belham hadn't reacted. I think he'd decided it was best to let Dennis get whatever was bothering him out of his system. But we all felt a bit uncomfortable, especially when Dennis walked off half-naked into the rain at the end of the tutorial, muttering something about 'a great separation' under his breath. We were all wondering what he was going to do next.

When I came in this time, I noticed immediately that Dennis wasn't there. I apologised for being late, and then I asked where he was. Belham looked embarrassed and said unfortunately Dennis had suffered a mental breakdown and had left Sussex for the time being. Then he changed the subject and started talking about Husserl, who was next on the list for Modern European Mind and was a bit of a drag, especially after Nietzsche.

Without Dennis, the tutorial didn't go with much of a swing. Rob and I spent most of our time looking down at the floor. It was partly that we didn't have much to say about phenomenology, and partly that we'd become self-conscious now that we were left on our own with Belham. And conscious of each other. I found myself glancing at Rob as if I was seeing him for the first time, which I was in a way. I wondered whether I fancied him. I did a bit. He had brown curly hair like Belham's, only it was longer and more tangled. His jeans were the right length, and he wore a silver bangle around his wrist. His eyes were brown and soft, and there was a downy moustache on his upper lip. He had a kind of innocent look about him. He was my age, about twenty. Just a boy really. But anyway, I put my head forward so my hair fell across my face and peered through it, which I always did when I wanted to look at someone without them looking at me.

Eventually Rob and I got out of the tutorial and decided to go and have a coffee together, which we'd never done before. We both wanted to talk about Dennis. So we went down to the European Common Room, which was full of people smoking and stubbing their cigarettes out in plastic cups and talking about politics. We saw Paddy in there, so when we'd got our coffees, we went over to talk to him. Paddy was a tall bloke of at least twenty-five who'd never finished his degree and just hung around campus with all the students. He'd had a serious accident by driving into a tree when he was drunk, and had nearly killed himself. Afterwards, he'd had a pacemaker fitted in his heart which he'd let you listen to, if you were a girl that is. You had to press your ear against his chest. Everyone on campus looked up to him. He knew everything that was going on.

Paddy leant back in his chair and began the story of Dennis. You could tell he'd told it a lot of times now, and he was enjoying it more and more each time.

'Dennis finally flipped,' he said. 'Two nights ago, he started wandering round campus, completely starkers. In the end this girl reported him because he jumped out at her from a bush as she was going up to West Slope. She thought he was going to rape her or something but he just started babbling at her. When she got in he went on babbling at her, kneeling down and talking through the letterbox in the door, so her flatmates completely freaked out and called the police.'

'God!' said Rob.

Paddy warmed to his tale.

'So then a couple of policemen come down, and when they ask Dennis what's going on, he just looks at them and says, "The more unintelligent a man is, the less mysterious existence seems to him." The policemen think he's stoned or taking the piss, and call the Vice Chancellor. While they're waiting, Dennis starts talking to them about Schopenhauer, which cracks everyone up.'

'So what does the VC do, then?' said Rob.

Paddy went on: 'When the VC gets there, he keeps Dennis talking about Schopenhauer and tries to put a blanket round him. But Dennis keeps taking it off. Then the VC says, "Thank you, officers, I'll handle this." The fuzz are only too keen to get away, but as they leave, Dennis turns to them and says in this really serious voice: "In individuals insanity is rare, but in groups, parties, nations and epochs it is the rule." One of the policemen looks well pissed off, and leans over to Dennis and says, "You watch it, sonny boy," but the other one goes, "Come on, let's get out of this madhouse." Then the VC leads Dennis outside to his car. Dennis gets in the car meek as a lamb, and that's the last anyone's seen of him.'

'So has he gone off to the loony bin or what?' I asked.

'There's a rumour his parents came to get him,' said Paddy. 'Or he could still be living in the VC's house.'

'Aren't there some students camping on the VC's lawn at the moment?' Rob said.

Paddy laughed. 'Yeah. That guy's got problems. Exam strike, I think.'

'What do you mean, exam strike?' said Rob.

'Well, exams are part of the hierarchy, aren't they,' replied Paddy, as though this was blindingly obvious. Then he turned away, lit another cigarette, and went back to talking to his friends. We sensed Paddy had had enough of us and our second-year questions. So we moved away and continued the conversation.

'God, poor Dennis,' said Rob. 'Maybe we should have done something.'

'Done something?' The idea of doing something about Dennis had never occurred to me. 'How do you mean?'

'Well, I don't know. Helped him a bit. Tried to calm him down. Asked him if he wanted to have a coffee with us.'

I thought about this. I couldn't really imagine socialising with Dennis. He was too odd. And to be honest, if it had turned out that he was lonely or upset instead of just super-intelligent, my instinct would have been to avoid him like the plague. That kind of thing was embarrassing.

'Don't be stupid, Rob,' I said. 'What could we have done? Told him to put his woolly on before he went out in the cold?'

Rob laughed.

'He's probably all right,' I continued. 'A bit of a rest and he'll be fine. *In individuals, insanity is rare.*'

Rob laughed again. 'I suppose so.'

'It was too much Nietzsche, I reckon. You need to be careful with that stuff.'

Rob looked at me. As he did, I started feeling a bit panicky. What I'd just said had come out more serious than I'd intended. The hairs on my head started prickling and a wave of fear went through me. Just for a second, I remembered screaming myself awake that morning. Then the feeling passed.

I hoped Rob hadn't noticed, but maybe he had. There was an awkward silence. Then he said, 'Shall we go down to the library basement?'

I didn't have a lot to do on campus that day, and I wasn't

in a hurry to get home. I wanted to pay Jason back for not being there in the morning, even though I knew whatever time I turned up, it wouldn't bother him. That was the problem between us. He knew he had me, but I didn't know I had him. So I hesitated for a minute, just to give Rob the impression I was usually quite a busy person, and then I said, 'OK.'

On the way to the basement, we stopped off at the library and I went off to the short loan section to get a copy of *Human, All Too Human*. I was intrigued to find out what had upset Dennis so much. There was only one copy left, so I took it out and queued up to get it stamped. Then I put it in my bag and went downstairs to meet Rob.

The library basement was a filthy place that served disgusting coffee from vending machines, but it was the most popular spot on campus for socialising, mainly because people went into the library to study and came out after about five minutes for a break that lasted all afternoon. There were loads more people to talk to in there, and we told and retold the story of Dennis and the policemen until a crowd had gathered round us and were all hooting with laughter. The smoke in the air got so thick we could hardly breathe, so after a while we moved on again.

This time, we went over to the crypt where some Buddhists had set up a café called Atlantis. The food looked horrible. There was cold, sticky brown rice and some red mush they called 'refried beans'. But the way they did the tables was nice. They were low on the floor, and beside them were big yellow and orange floor cushions you could sit on. There were joss sticks burning everywhere and a tape of Indian music was playing in the background.

We found a table in a quiet corner and sprawled out on the cushions. We didn't order any food, just cups of jasmine tea. A girl next to us had just eaten, and kept burping loudly in a pointed way, as though to show she was not bothered with social conventions. We tried to ignore her. We talked about philosophy for a bit, and after a while Rob said, 'So where do you live?'

'In Brunswick Square,' I replied, not adding, 'with my boyfriend.'

'You've got your own flat then?'

I hesitated. 'Not really. I'm sort of... sharing.'

Well, it was Jason's flat. And I was sharing it with him. I changed the subject before he asked me anything more.

'And what about you, Rob?'

'Oh, I'm living over by the London Unity in a communal house.'

I knew that area of town. It was full of run-down little houses and scruffy corner shops, and half the rooms up there had blankets instead of curtains in the windows. You could tell just by looking at it that it was student land.

'Right.' I couldn't think of anything more to say. I found all that student stuff a bit depressing, which was one of the reasons I lived with Jason in Brunswick Square. At least he was an antique dealer and not a student. But when I was on campus, I didn't go on about Jason too much. I thought people might think I was a bit straight if I did. And anyway, I wanted to keep my options open. Jason was a lot older than me and sometimes it was a relief to be with people my own age, like Rob. Even if they were a bit studenty.

After a while the joss sticks started to make me feel sick, and Rob got fed up with the Indian music tape, which was beginning to wear out and make those sliding sounds, so we went over to the union bar. It was completely different in there: noisy, with chart music blaring out of the jukebox and everyone shouting over it. By now it was late afternoon and we were starving, so we filled up on beer and crisps and cheese sandwiches. After we'd eaten, we stopped trying to talk and just sat there watching the alcoholics playing on the fruit machines. Then the rugby club came in from a match and started getting rowdy. Not long after, a bunch of feminists arrived looking for them, and they all started yelling insults at each other. Everyone in the bar started cheering as the row escalated, and we joined in. The next thing was, chairs were being hurled around and Rob and I were laughing and holding on to each other and ducking out of the way. In the end the barman got fed up and chucked us all out, even though most of us were only in there trying to have a quiet drink.

Outside in the rain, I said: 'I think I'd better be getting back now.'

Rob said, 'OK. I've got to meet someone later, so I'm staying on campus.'

There was a pause. I wondered who he had to meet.

'See you around.'

'See you around.'

He hesitated. Then, just as I was turning to go, he said, 'Are you going to the gig tomorrow night?'

'What gig?'

'John Martyn. He's playing here on campus.'

I thought about it. I'd never heard of John Martyn, but I wasn't going to say so. 'I might,' I said. 'Depends what I'm doing.'

'OK. See you there then. If you come.'

'OK. If I do.'

Then I turned round and walked off quickly, heading back to the station.

chapter 2

WHEN I GOT IN, THERE WAS still no sign of Jason. The flat was exactly as I had left it in the morning, the washing-up in the sink and bed unmade. I thought, he probably phoned when I was out and he'll call again this evening. Nothing to worry about.

I put the kettle on, did the washing-up, and made the bed. Then I sat down with a cup of tea, took out *Human, All Too Human*, switched on a lamp, and began to read.

The book wasn't anything like *The Birth of Tragedy*. It wasn't as confident, or as entertaining. It seemed to have no structure to it, and the writing was jerky, muddled, at times almost insane, as though Nietzsche was having a brainstorm, or a nervous breakdown. Even so, there were moments when I recognised what he was talking about, though I wished I didn't.

Loneliness surrounds him, curls round him, ever more threatening, strangling, heart-constricting…

I looked up. The room seemed to have grown very dark and quiet. This wasn't the kind of stuff you wanted to read on your own, I thought, waiting for someone to come home. I should have got something else out. But I carried on, although it was heavy going, until I came to the bit about the great separation that had freaked Dennis out so much.

…the great separation comes suddenly, like the shock of an earthquake: all at once, the young soul is devastated, torn loose,

torn out – it itself does not know what is happening …

I sighed, stuck a pencil in the book as a marker, and put it down beside the lamp on the table. I couldn't concentrate, not at the moment anyway. I'd have to try again tomorrow, during daylight hours. Maybe it would make more sense then.

I glanced up at the phone, expecting it to ring, but it didn't. It was one of those old black bakelite phones with a big silver dial and a twisted cord like you'd see in a forties' film. Jason had found it in a house clearance and got it done up so it worked. Everything in the room was like that. The lamp was one of those art deco jobs with a dancing nymph holding the light in her hands. The chair was a battered leather one with little brass studs in lines round the edge, only some of them had fallen out. And there were quirky things on the wall, like a row of forties' plaster women with red lips and wavy black hair wearing coquettish little hats.

When I'd first seen the room I'd thought it was gorgeous, but being there alone now I realised I didn't like it. It didn't seem homely. It looked like a museum. When I'd started living with Jason, I'd realised that this stuff came and went all the time. One week a particular lamp would be there, the next Jason would have sold it to somebody and there'd be a different one. If you looked up on the shelves, you could see about ten of the nymphs dancing about in various stages of decay, waiting to be done up and sold. When you first came in you looked at all these lovely things and thought what a beautiful room, but when you got to know it you realised it was just a warehouse.

The phone went on not ringing. I started looking around me, thinking about the objects in the room in a way that I never did when Jason was there. The more I looked at them, the more I realised I couldn't stand them. The plaster women with their cupid mouths looked ugly and stupid. The nymphs were silly and sentimental. The leather chair was uncomfortable, with a spring that poked into your bottom unless you sat in a certain position. There was nothing in that room I could ever get attached to. It was all just stuff to be bought and sold. And it was all Jason's, not mine.

I hated staying in on my own in the evening. That time when the night starts coming down and it gets blacker and blacker outside till you can see nothing when you look out of the window except your own reflection looking back at you. I wondered what Rob was doing. It had been nice being with him during the day. I didn't have his phone number, but I thought, he's bound to be in the Unity. Maybe I should go over there and see if I can find him. The trouble was, the Unity was over the other side of town. I couldn't be bothered to take a bus. And not only that, it wasn't a good place to go on your own, looking for somebody. It was one of those little pubs with only one door on to the street. When you went in, everyone looked up, and then if you couldn't see anyone you knew, you had to turn round and come back out the same way. By that time, everyone knew you were on your own. And didn't have any friends. So it was no good going to the Unity unless you definitely knew the person you were going to meet would be there. It was too embarrassing otherwise.

Then I had an idea. I thought, I know, I'll go over to the Brunswick. The Brunswick had two doors, so you could go in one, pass through both bars looking around you, and then get out the other. That way, you could look as though you had just left one bar and were on your way somewhere else, instead of feeling like an idiot who had just been stood up. And they also did food in the Brunswick, so there were usually a lot of people milling about queuing up and not paying attention to who was coming in the door next. That was a big advantage. There were always students in there – the pub was right next to Brunswick House, an old hotel donated to the university to house students because it was a fire risk.

On the way up there, I started feeling really hungry. I

thought, I'll get one of those dishes where you can load up on potato salad at the counter. By the time I arrived, my mouth was watering. I took a deep breath and walked in, looking around but trying not to look as though I was. Nobody in the first bar. In the second, there was a big group of students at a table in the corner, smoking and laughing, but when I passed I couldn't see anyone I knew. Damn. Now I wouldn't be able to eat. No potato salad.

Outside in the street, I stood around for a bit wondering what to do. None of the shops were open. On the way home, I passed by Brunswick House in case anybody I knew was on their way out. I didn't want to go inside. It was too depressing. All dirty kitchens with people drinking cup-a-soup and writing their name on their eggs before they put them in the fridge and arguing about the washing-up.

Nobody came out of Brunswick House, so I carried on to the square. There was nothing else to do but go back home. I felt pathetic. When I got back in, I thought, well, Jason might have rung while I was out. He might have just missed me. If I hadn't gone out I would know he hadn't rung, so it wasn't a complete waste of time. The thought cheered me up, so I heated up a can of beans and made a couple of pieces of toast for my supper. Then I lay on the floor and looked up at the ceiling and smoked a cigarette.

In all evening, on my own. It had been quite a long time since this had happened to me. I wondered what people normally did in this situation. Watched TV. Well, that was out, because we didn't have one. The only time I ever watched TV was in one of the student houses, usually after closing time, when people would turn the lights out and cram themselves into rows and switch on *Outer Limits*. Everyone would stop talking and we'd sit there in the dark watching the screen. I'd try to take an interest because all the others did – well, the blokes anyway – but to tell the truth I couldn't see the point of it. One minute we were all talking and laughing and having a good time, and the next we were all sitting there silently in the dark watching some nonsense about flying saucers. It didn't make sense to me.

Reading a book was another possibility. But I'd tried that already, and I couldn't. Not with the phone sitting there silently watching me in the corner. There was only one other alternative. Listen to some music.

As a rule, I didn't have anything to do with the record player. Jason had a quadraphonic stereo, which was his pride and joy. I wasn't allowed to touch it. I wasn't even allowed to touch any of the records in case I did something to them that would upset the stereo. Every time he put a record on, he would dust everything with a little brush, and then he would have to sit in exactly the right place between the four speakers to listen to the music. I couldn't see what all the fuss was about. After all, I thought, you've only got two ears, what do you need four speakers for. But I didn't say anything. It didn't seem worth arguing about, and after all, it was his flat. He could do what he liked in it.

He played records all the time when he was in. He liked jazz mostly, stuff like Duke Ellington and Billie Holiday. His taste in music went well with the flat, and I liked it, but to be honest I'd never taken the slightest interest in it. It was just there, like the plaster women and the nymphs.

I went over to his record collection and flicked through the LPs. There was only one I recognised, a boxed set of Grover Washington albums, which he'd given me for my birthday. I'd never listened to it. Or perhaps I had. He might have put it on one night after dinner, I couldn't remember. Anyway, there was nothing there that meant anything to me. Then, towards the back, I noticed a name that rang a bell. John Martyn. The guy Rob had mentioned. The one who was playing on campus tomorrow night.

I walked over to the stereo. I put the record on and twiddled a few knobs until the sound came through. It didn't seem all that difficult. Then I took my boots off, lay down on the floor again and listened.

At first I thought the record was on at the wrong speed, because his voice sounded all low and mumbly, but then I realised it was supposed to be like that. You had to concentrate to make out the words, and they kind of wove in and out between the instruments, which wove in and out between each other. The music wasn't like anything else I'd ever heard. It was slow and spacey and it drew you in. It sounded like a person starting to fall asleep, where everything starts going a bit weird and distorted, but at the same time you're being wrapped up in a delicious, warm haze so you want to stay there and start to dream.

I listened to the whole of the 'A' side lying there on the floor. I didn't move until the needle started bumping round at the end. Then I got up, put the sofa cushions on the floor and dragged some bedding on top of them. I turned the record over, switched off the lamp and lay down again under the covers. It was so comfortable I decided to stay there for the night so after a while, when I'd warmed up, I took off my jumper and jeans and threw them out on the floor.

After that, I lay there for ages looking up at the darkness, with John Martyn singing to me. Sometimes tears welled up in my eyes when he sang words like *Curl around me like a fern in the spring*, which reminded me that Jason wasn't here alongside me, and in a way, never would be. But most of the time I felt comforted and I didn't mind so much about being alone.

By the time the needle got to the end and started bumping again, I was too tired to do anything about it. The last thing I heard as I fell asleep was the sound of it going round and round.

chapter 3

NEXT DAY, I HUNG AROUND the flat but I still didn't hear from Jason. By now, I was getting worried. I felt sick and I couldn't eat anything, which was just as well because there was nothing in the flat anyway, and it saved me going out to the shops and having to talk to people about the weather, which I couldn't do in this kind of mood. So I stayed in all day and drank cups of tea and smoked cigarettes. And waited.

It wasn't that I thought something bad had happened to Jason. He didn't seem to be the sort of person that would have a terrible car accident or a sudden heart attack or be robbed or get stuck in a lift. He seemed to go through life without any worries about that kind of thing. And as a result, nothing bad ever seemed to happen to him. That was the trick, you had to ignore the possibility of things going wrong. Then nothing did. It was a trick I hadn't mastered yet.

No, the problem wasn't Jason. It was me. I couldn't stand being all on my own here in his flat, surrounded by the nymphs and the plaster faces, thinking and waiting and worrying. What if he didn't come back? What if he'd left me and gone off with someone else? What would become of me? Where would I live? I'd have to face the fact that I was just another student. I'd have to get a room on campus, and hang around with those girls who were Christians and drank cocoa in the evenings, and had pillow fights, and put stuffed animals on their beds. Or I'd be one of those lonely, weird people like Dennis that everybody laughed about behind their back. I'd wake up screaming every morning, with the rest of my life yawning ahead of me. On my own.

As the day wore on, I got more and more tense. I had to get out of the flat. I couldn't think of anything to do during the day, but I decided I would definitely go to the gig on campus in the evening. There was no point in staying here worrying, there was nothing I could do. It was no good phoning the police, Jason would have thought that was stupid, I knew he would. He'd be irritated with me and think I was a fool. No, it was best to leave him to his own devices. He'd never needed my help in the past, and I was pretty sure he didn't now. He wasn't the kind of person who needed anyone's help. He liked to do his own thing, and he didn't like people getting in his way or bossing him about. He'd come back sooner or later, but in the mean while he'd probably prefer it if I just got on with my life without him.

To pass the time, I lay on my makeshift bed on the living-room floor, listening to John Martyn and reading *Human, All Too Human*. This time, in the grey light of a rainy day, it seemed to make more sense. Nietzsche seemed to be describing a terrible emotional crisis that had overtaken him, and that he was only just beginning to recover from.

Another step onward in convalescence. The free spirit approaches life slowly, of course, recalcitrantly, almost suspiciously. It grows warmer around him, yellower as it were; feeling and fellow-feeling gain depth; mild breezes of all kinds pass over him...

I kept going, and after a while, I began to get the hang of what he was saying. A lot of the book was taken up with little homilies, or aphorisms as he called them, giving nonsensical advice about this and that, as though he imagined himself to be a kindly uncle you might go to with your problems instead of a half-deranged hermit you'd steer well clear of if you had any sense; but towards the end, I realised he seemed to be describing something I recognised.

If you were a free spirit, as Nietzsche called it, you went through a 'great separation' when you suddenly became aware that everything – family, values, religion – meant nothing to you. It usually happened in adolescence or early adulthood, like it had with Dennis. At first, you'd almost lose your mind, but after that you'd somehow get used to the situation. After you'd been through the great separation, you knew you were always going to be lonely; that you were always going to suffer; that you were never going to feel secure about anything. But as time went on, you'd begin to realise you weren't mad; you were just outside the ordinary social world, saddled with an inescapable task, a destiny, that you couldn't help following, even though you didn't understand what it was.

The secret power and necessity of this task will hold sway within and among our various destinies like an unsuspected pregnancy, long before we have looked the task itself in the eye or know its name.

Because of this task, you were going to have to go through life without getting too involved with anything, or anyone.

He who has come in part to a freedom of reason cannot feel on earth otherwise than as a wanderer – though not as a traveller towards a final goal, for this does not exist. But he does want to observe, and keep his eyes open for everything that actually occurs in the world; therefore he must not attach his heart too firmly to any individual thing; there must be something wandering within him, which takes its joy in change and transitoriness.

Perhaps that explained why I felt so weird, so disconnected, most of the time. Maybe I wasn't mad; maybe I was just a wanderer, like Nietzsche, Dennis, and countless others who had drifted their way through human history. Of course I was going to be lonely, and have nightmares, and wake up screaming, and feel I was going mad sometimes; ̶ ̶ ̶ ̶ ̶ ̶e would be glorious moments as well.

To be sure, such a man will have bad nights... but then, as recompense, come the ecstatic mornings of other regions and days...

I went on reading, and after a while I looked up. Outside the window, the sky was growing dark again. Almost a whole day had gone by, and I hadn't even noticed. Normally that would have made me feel weird, and embarrassed about myself, but somehow, as I finished the last page of *Human, All Too Human*, it didn't seem to matter. In fact, I felt elated. I may have spent the whole day lying on the floor half-dressed, reading Nietzsche and smoking and drinking cups of tea, but that didn't mean I was a dosser, or that my life was empty and isolated. It meant that I was a free spirit, and like the free spirits of the past, I had a secret destiny, a task to do. I just wasn't sure what it was yet.

In the late afternoon, I had a bath and washed my hair, putting the ends in a cupful of conditioner and then rinsing it in the basin. I combed it out wet so it dried flat and straight down my back. I put some make-up on, very carefully, so it didn't look as though I was wearing any make-up at all. When my hair was dry, I put on clean white pants and a clean brown T-shirt. The T-shirt had long sleeves and a low neck with a string you tied together in the middle, casually, so it looked as though you just happened to see the shape of your breasts underneath it. I put my new jeans back on and wore my highest platforms under the flares. Then I slipped on my old dark blue velvet jacket, which was very tight and coming apart at the seams and had a button hanging off a thread at the front.

It all took hours. By the time I'd finished, it was time to go out. Before I did, I glanced in the hall mirror. I looked fine. I'd got it right. The main thing was, I didn't look as though I'd tried too hard. I looked as though I'd just thrown my clothes on to go out for the evening. I looked cool, but as though it came naturally to me. I looked like a free spirit: someone with something to do, somewhere to go, possibly even a secret destiny to fulfil.

When I got to campus, the Falmer bar was buzzing. I fought my way to the bar and got myself a drink, which I didn't like doing – normally, I got some bloke to do it for me. Then I wandered upstairs to the hall, looking for Rob, or anyone else I knew. Inside, it was jam-packed with students sitting cross-legged on the floor blowing out clouds of smoke and kicking over plastic beakers of beer by mistake. I peered about in the gloom, recognising a few people on my course but no one I much wanted to talk to. If things got bad and nobody better came along, I'd go and talk to one of them. But for now I'd wait and see if Rob and his crowd turned up.

I went back downstairs and then up again, so I'd look as though I'd come in after him. This time, he was there, in a group on the floor near the door. I could tell he'd been looking out for me, because he jumped up immediately as soon as he saw me, and came over.

'Hi, Susannah. How's it going?'

'Fine. You OK?'

'OK. Good. Yes. Fine.' He seemed nervous. 'I didn't know if you were coming or not.'

'Nor did I. But I really like John Martyn, so I thought I would.' I said it as though I had been a fan for years.

'Great. Are you with anyone? There's some space over here if you like.'

I didn't answer his question about whether I was with anyone or not. I just walked over with him and nodded to his friends. One of them was a good-looking, dark-haired girl I'd seen on campus before. She ignored me as I sat down next to Rob, trying to avoid the beer puddles on the floor. The group were all passing round a joint. When it came to me, I took a quick drag, held it in my mouth rather than taking it down to my lungs, and passed it on. I didn't want to get stoned. In this kind of mood, with people I'd only just met, I knew it would make me paranoid.

The lights went down, the talking stopped, and John Martyn came on stage. He was older than us, maybe in his late twenties, with curly hair and a red scarf tied round his neck. He was holding a bottle of beer and looking confused, as though he'd wandered on stage by accident and suddenly found himself under the bright lights. He went over to his guitar, swaying slightly, and sat down on a chair. There was a feeling of tension in the hall as he fiddled with his leads and his electronic boxes. He seemed not to notice us sitting there watching him. I wondered if he was pissed. There were a few crackling noises. Then he plugged the guitar in and started playing.

The guitar wasn't like a normal guitar. All these loops of sound were coming out, layer upon layer, as though he was playing ten guitars at once, and a load of other instruments as well. You couldn't quite follow what was happening. There was only this one guy on stage, sitting there with all these little boxes around him, weaving all these complicated patterns on just one guitar. After a while, I stopped trying to work out how he was doing it and just listened. And as I did, I stopped thinking about me, about Jason, about the flat, about Rob, about what was going to happen tonight. I stopped thinking about anything at all.

The hall went dead silent as we all drifted off with John Martyn's guitar. It went on building up, layer by layer, until I felt dizzy. Then he started singing. His voice came in waves, like on the record. He slurred his words, maybe because he was drunk, but I got the feeling he would have done the same thing sober. *Curl around me...*

'I love this one,' I whispered to Rob before I could stop myself.

'God, so do I,' he whispered back. Then he put his arm around me, squeezed my shoulder, and let go again. Out of the corner of my eye, I noticed the dark-haired girl get up quietly and leave.

As the singing went on, a huge relief started to come over me, like it had the night before when I'd been in the flat on my own. Tears started rolling silently down my face, so I put my hair forward to hide them until they dried. It wasn't that I felt paranoid. I wasn't really stoned, but the dope was having an effect. And the music seemed to be loosening my mind. I felt as though I'd been in danger, but now the danger was past, and everything was going to be all right. Without thinking, I laid my head on Rob's shoulder and closed my eyes. Then I realised what I was doing and jerked my head back up. He put his arm round me and this time, he left it there. And I laid my head back down on his shoulder. And left it there.

We stayed like that for the rest of the gig. At the end, when the lights came up, we let go of each other quickly. John Martyn was trying to get off the stage while everyone was clapping but he couldn't find the exit and came through the audience instead. He passed right in front of us, still looking confused. He didn't seem to know where he was. And, for a moment, neither had we.

'Do you fancy a drink, then?' asked Rob, as everyone was getting up to leave.

'Where?' I said. 'There's nowhere to go. The bar'll be closed by now.'

'Well, I've got a car. Everyone's coming back to ours, we've got some cans in at home.'

'OK,' I said. At least I could get a lift in to Brighton. Then maybe I could take a cab back to mine.

We went out to the car park, with a bunch of his friends. Rob's car turned out to be an old A40 with those little orange indicators that popped up out of the roof when you wanted to turn left or right. It had leather seats inside, and a wooden dashboard. We managed to get four people in the back, and one in the front, besides Rob, who was driving. I

sat on this bloke's knee in the back, with my head bent over
to one side under the roof. The car groaned along the road
really slowly. It probably wouldn't have gone very fast at the
best of times, but with six people in, it hardly moved at all.
To make matters worse, the bloke smelt a bit. His hair and
clothes had that musty smell of men who don't wash much
but aren't naturally that smelly. It could have been worse, I
suppose. But on the way, I thought of Jason and his yellow
Morgan, with just the two of us in it bombing up to London
in the fast lane.

When we got to the house by the London Unity, it was
just as I had expected. Cold, tatty rooms with blankets
instead of curtains in the windows and red light bulbs
screwed in to the ceiling sockets. We all huddled round the
gas fire in the living room and drank beer. Then out came
the joints and the cups of tea. After that, it was slices of toast
and margarine and squares of Cadbury's milk chocolate for
the munchies.

I'd relaxed a bit by this time and started taking a few
drags of the joints. I didn't want to go back to the flat in my
normal frame of mind, and have to face all those red plaster
lips pouting at me. I thought maybe it would be a good idea
to get a little bit stoned after all. Besides, Rob's friends were
nice. They weren't threatening at all, apart from the dark-
haired girl who had left during the gig. There was Dino, who
was good-looking and worked as a postman, and Mark and
Jan, who were a couple, and Hervé, who was French and
doing International Relations, and sat playing the guitar
along with the music on the stereo, not very well as far as I
could make out.

Mark and Jan eventually went off to bed, leaving me with
Rob, Dino and Hervé. I sensed they were all interested in
me. Dino, I knew, wouldn't make a play for me. He had long
fair hair and a pretty face, and was used to women making
the first move, you could tell. So he just sat there watching
me for a while, to give me a chance to show some interest,

and when I didn't, he went to bed. He had to be up at five in the morning for his postman job, he said. That left Hervé and Rob.

Rob went into the kitchen to make some more tea. While he was in there, Hervé took the opportunity to play me a song he'd written. The minute he started, I realised he was hopeless. I didn't know much about songwriting, but it sounded terrible. The chords all seemed wrong and his voice wandered about over them, with no recognisable tune. It seemed to be a love song of some kind with a chorus that went, *I'll be your lover man, any way that I can. Any way that I can, I'll be your lover man. Yeah!* The words sounded wrong, the way you'd write if you couldn't speak English very well. But when he'd finished, he sat back looking very pleased with himself.

'So what do you think?' he asked. 'Be honest.'

I didn't know what to say. 'Very nice,' I lied.

'You liked it?' he persisted.

I wasn't prepared to go that far. So I mumbled something and looked down at the floor.

'Don't be shy,' he said. Then he leaned forward over his guitar, as though he was going to kiss me.

It wasn't that he was a bad-looking guy. In fact, he was better looking than the average student, dark-haired with an earring in one ear and a French, gypsy sort of look about him. It was just that the song was so awful. There was no question of fancying anyone who could write a song like that.

'Excuse me, I've just got to go to the loo,' I said, and jumped up. I went out to the hallway, which was freezing, and climbed up the wooden stairs, which had no carpet and made a banging noise, even though I was trying to tiptoe. On the landing I found a small toilet, separate from the bathroom. Inside it was lit by a very bright bare light bulb. You could see layers of dust on the pipes and in the corners of the floorboards. There was a pile of newspaper on the floor instead of loo paper, and the window was jammed open.

If it had been warm in there, and clean, I could have sat down for a moment and collected my thoughts. I could have decided what to do next. Go downstairs, call for a taxi, drink my tea and go. As it was, I stood there and started shivering. I didn't know what to do. Hervé was down there in the living room, limbering up to kiss me or to sing me another of his songs. Rob would be in there as well, waiting for Hervé to go to bed, which he obviously wasn't going to do in a hurry. And I was waiting it out up here, I wasn't sure why.

I started feeling very sick. I turned the light off because the brightness was hurting my eyes. I crouched down on the floor, hoping the nausea would pass. But it didn't. So I stayed there, with my back against the wall and my arms around my knees, in the cold and dark. And, as long as I didn't move, I felt better.

I stayed there for a long time. I don't know how long. But after a while, someone started banging on the door. It was Rob.

'Suse?' He sounded worried. 'Are you OK?'

'I don't know.'

'Can I come in? I mean, can you come out?'

'OK.' My eyes had adjusted to the dark and I could see the door, so I unbolted it and stepped out into the corridor. Rob tried to peer into my face, but I kept my head down with my hair covering it.

'What's the matter?' he asked.

'I don't know.' We were whispering so as not to wake up Dino and the couple.

'Well, come and sit down a minute. I'll get you a glass of water.'

He led me to his room down the corridor and sat me down on the bed. Then he nipped off and came back with the water. I drank it but I still felt dizzy. He put a coat round my shoulders and then sat holding my hand, saying nothing.

Eventually, I said, 'Where's Hervé?'

'Gone to bed, I think. Why, was he hassling you?'

'No, no. Well a bit, maybe.' I paused. 'It must have been the dope or something. I just started feeling weird.' I paused again. 'And there are some things going on… that are a bit … heavy.'

I waited for him to start asking questions, but he didn't. He just went on holding my hand.

'Try to breathe slowly,' he said. 'Take a deep breath through your nose and let it out through your mouth. Like this.'

He took a deep breath in, held it for a few seconds, and then gradually let it out. As he showed me, I thought, how ridiculous, but to humour him I fell in with his breathing. I shut my eyes and concentrated. Then he told me to tense and relax each part of my body in turn, from my toes up. I did what he said, feeling a bit of an idiot. But after a few minutes, I started feeling better. The sick feeling had passed, and I could think straight again.

I didn't say anything, but he seemed to sense that the worst was over. He let go of my hand. We sat in silence for a few moments. I knew I should make a move to leave, but I felt too tired.

Then, as if he could read my thoughts, he said, 'Do you want to stay here? You could sleep in my bed. I can stay downstairs on the sofa if you want.'

I looked around the room, noticing it for the first time. It was completely different from the rest of the house. Rob had hung Indian fabric with a red and brown pattern on it around the walls and ceiling so that the room looked like a cosy tent. In the middle, over the light fitting, hung a Chinese parasol. The bed had a thick eiderdown on it, and the pillows were fat and white. By the bed was what looked like an old-fashioned hurricane lamp, which cast a soft light over the bed.

Then I looked at Rob. He looked beautiful in the light of the hurricane lamp, his face framed by his long, dark hair. He had a big, holey sweater on, with sleeves that were unravelling at the cuffs. Underneath, I could see his silver bangle. I thought, I do fancy him. But he hadn't made any move towards me. Perhaps he wasn't interested in me. I wondered for a moment whether he was a poof, what with the Indian fabrics and the silver bangle and everything. Or maybe it was just that he was an unusual kind of person. Or very young. Or something.

I lay down on the bed and closed my eyes. I couldn't think any more. I couldn't imagine getting up and going home now. All I knew was, I wanted to sleep.

'All right,' I said. 'Thanks.'

Rob got up to go. He stood hovering by the bed.

'OK, then. Goodnight.'

'Night.'

'Is there anything you need?'

'No thanks. I'm fine.'

I waited for him to go, but he didn't.

'Will you be all right on your own?'

'Yes, of course. Really, I'm fine now.'

There was a pause. He still didn't go.

'Are you sure?'

I lay there looking up at him, and he stood there looking down at me.

Then I said, 'No, I'm not sure. I'm not sure at all. I think you'd better stay.'

chapter 4

I WAS IN THE DREAM AGAIN, trying to get out. I was in bed, and the room was pitch black, so I stretched my arm out to turn on the bedside light, but then I remembered it was a hurricane lamp, and I didn't know how to light it. So I got up and moved about the room, knocking into the furniture like a blind man, feeling my way towards the window. When I got there, I pulled open the curtain and saw the white road snaking into the distance again, with the black cars travelling up and down it. When I saw that, I knew I had failed and I'd have to try to wake up again, so I felt my way back to the bed, got in, and summoned up my voice. But this time, I couldn't find it. I couldn't scream my way out. It was hopeless. This time, I was stuck.

Then I heard someone else's voice, a man's voice, calling my name. It seemed to be coming from far away, down a long corridor. I knew I had to call back, so I took a deep breath and tried to shout, but nothing came out. Nothing, except a silent shudder, but to my amazement it did the trick, and there I was all of a sudden, wide awake. In Rob's bed. And it was broad daylight.

Rob was propped up on one elbow beside me, naked, his hair tangled and his eyes wide, leaning over me and looking at me intently.

'What is it? What is it?' he was saying.

'What is what?' I replied, once I'd realised where I was.

'You were thrashing about as though someone was strangling you or something. Look, you're covered in sweat. Are you all right, Susannah? What the hell's going on?'

'Nothing's going on,' I said. I never had this trouble with Jason in the mornings. 'I just had a bad dream, that's all. I sometimes do.'

'What's bothering you? What's going on?' he repeated. 'Are you in some kind of trouble? Tell me.'

'For God's sake, Rob, it was just a nightmare,' I said, my voice rising. 'People have them all the time, you know. No, I'm not in trouble. There's nothing wrong with me at all. Stop going on about it, I've only just woken up. Bloody hell.'

My words came out harshly. I didn't mean them to. I was just embarrassed about lying in Rob's bed the first time I'd ever slept with him, sweating away and thrashing about like a lunatic. And scared, because being with Rob made me realise it wasn't normal to wake up like this in the mornings. Not that I did every morning, but lately it had been getting worse.

Rob looked upset. 'Sorry, it's just... what with last night, and everything...'

He looked into my eyes. I could see at that moment how vulnerable he was, how much he wanted me to reassure him. I had a dim memory of what had happened in the night. We had woken up and made love, me pretending to be only half awake, and it had been strange and intense, like a vivid dream. Now he wanted to know whether I still liked him, whether we would stay together, become lovers, or whether I'd just get up out of bed in a minute and go.

His eyes seemed to darken as he looked at me. With tenderness, or pain, or both. He began to stroke my hair. I couldn't stand it. I moved my head and looked away.

'You don't need to worry about me, Rob,' I said. 'I can take care of myself. Really, I'm fine.'

Once again, my words sounded harsher than I wanted them to. He looked down, miserably. I tried to break the tension. I said, as brightly as I could, 'I'll tell you what, though. I'd love a cup of tea. I'm dying of thirst.'

He sighed and got up to put his jeans on. I looked at his body. It was slender, almost like a girl's, but with smooth muscles under his skin, and a wisp of downy brown hair running down the base of his back. It seemed a sweet, childish spot. I put my hand out and rested it there for a moment, in what I hoped was a gesture of reassurance. He didn't respond. Instead, he stood up, buttoned up his jeans, and went downstairs to get the tea.

I lay there thinking about what to do next. I'd have to get up soon and get back to the flat. If Jason had come back by now, he'd know I'd been out for the night. I could say I'd slept on campus. Where, though? The best idea would be to say at my friend Cassie's. She was on my course, and she had a room on campus which she didn't use much, because she was living at her boyfriend's and only went back there occasionally to have it off with her tutor, who was married. We were always using each other as alibis.

Of course, Jason would be suspicious. He wasn't one to think very hard about my comings and goings, but he seemed to sense it when there was someone else in the offing. Once, I'd gone out for tea with a bloke on the course, and he'd never stopped going on about it. A bun and you're anyone's, he'd said. This time, his antennae would pick up a lot more. I wasn't very good at lying, or at covering my tracks, not where Jason was concerned, anyway. He could get anything out of me in the end, if he wanted to. He might just let this pass, but if his suspicions were aroused in any way, he wouldn't let it drop. My best bet was to get back to the flat before he appeared. I'd have to get a move on.

By the time Rob came back with the tea, I'd got dressed and was sitting on the bed, putting my boots on. He started as he came in the door, a cup of tea in each hand.

'God, you're not going already are you?'

'Sorry, Rob, I've got to get back.'

I took the tea, blew on it, and began to sip it even though it was boiling hot.

He looked crestfallen. 'Why?'

I started feeling irritated with him again. I was beginning to get sick of all these questions. 'Because. Just because, that's all. I've got things to do.'

'What things? Sorry, I mean, OK, fine. Shall we meet up later, then?'

'I don't know.' I sighed. I searched for something else to say, but I couldn't come up with anything much.

'... It depends,' I added.

'Oh.' He sounded hurt. 'So... when... when will I see you again?'

There was a pause and then we both started laughing. It was a line from a song we'd joked about together in the Falmer Bar, the day we'd been in there and the fight had broken out. We'd been sitting there with our beers talking about what Wittgenstein meant by saying that 'all swans are white' and we'd suddenly noticed all these other heavy philosophical questions coming out of the jukebox at us.

'When will we share precious moments?' I carried on.

'Are we in love, or just friends?' he remembered.

I knew the final line, but I didn't want to come out with it. Not in the circumstances. Then I did. I couldn't resist it.

'Is this the beginning or is this the end?'

It had cracked us up at the time. It was the sort of question that Wittgenstein, along with the Three Degrees, was for ever asking. But now, it didn't seem so funny, and I wished I hadn't said it.

Rob looked upset again, so I tried to cheer him up. 'Everybody was Kung Fu fighting,' I said.

He laughed. 'Those cats were fast as lightning.'

'In fact it was a little bit frightening...'

We started giggling and he sat down on the bed next to me, took my tea out of my hand, put it on the floor next to his, and pushed me back. I pulled away, jokingly, but he grabbed me and held me tight, and soon we were kissing and pressing our bodies up against each other in a way that took us straight back to where we had been the night before.

I wriggled out from under him and sat up. 'Rob, I'm sorry, I've really got to go.'

He sighed. 'Go on then. Bugger off if you must.'

The way he said it was half moody, half playful.

'I'll phone you.'

'You do that.' This time, there was a bitterness in his tone that made me wonder if he knew about Jason. Maybe someone had told him I already had a boyfriend. Or maybe he'd remembered that he hadn't given me his phone number. I'd been thinking of asking for it, but I wasn't going to now, with the mood he was in.

He didn't say anything else. He just lay there on the bed, looking up at the ceiling, as though he was waiting for me to go. So I got my things together as quickly as I could, and then I went over to say goodbye. He was still looking up, away from me.

'Rob?'

'What?'

'Just one thing. Were you calling me this morning?'

He sat up. 'What do you mean, calling you?'

'You know, when I woke up. I heard somebody calling me. Was it you?'

'No,' he said. He lay back down again. 'It wasn't me.'

Then he turned over on his side with his face towards the wall.

I walked over to the door. 'Bye then. See you around.'

He didn't reply, so I left the room.

I walked quickly down the stairs, stopping off at the dusty toilet on the way, and let myself out of the front door, hoping I wouldn't bump in to Hervé or any of the others. As I stepped out into the street, I saw the dark-haired girl from the gig the night before coming towards the house. I turned and walked quickly the other way so she wouldn't see me, wondering who she was and why she was coming here. As I turned the corner, I glanced back and saw her letting herself into the house with a key. I carried on walking fast, but as I did, I thought of Rob as I had left him, lying upstairs on the bed looking at the wall. Maybe that's how she'd find him when she went in to his room. Maybe... I stopped my train of thought right there. I didn't want it to go any further. But, ridiculous as it was, I felt a pang of jealousy.

When I got back into the flat, the phone was ringing. I ran over to it with my coat on, leaving the door open behind me, and picked it up. It was Jason.

'Where the hell have you been?' he said. 'I've been ringing you all morning.'

I was just about to launch into an explanation of how I'd spent the night on campus in Cassie's room when I remembered it was him who had been missing for several days, not me.

'I could ask you the same question.'

He laughed, and I realised I wasn't going to be subjected to an interrogation as to my whereabouts the night before. This time it was him who was in the wrong.

'Sorry, Susie, I should have phoned before.' So he hadn't phoned before this morning, I thought. I had the upper hand now.

'Where are you? What are you doing? I've been worried sick about you,' I said. An image of me and Rob lying on the bed kissing flashed through my mind. 'Worried sick,' I repeated.

'Sorry, Susie Q.' He called me this when he was trying to be nice to me. If anyone else had done it, I would have thought they were a creep. But with Jason, it didn't seem to matter.

'I'm in London,' he went on. 'I've had to stay up here to do a bit of business. Can you come up tonight?'

'Why? What for?'

'I just thought it would be nice to see you.'

There was a pause. 'I love you,' he added, as though that explained everything.

I could hear the clink of glasses and laughter in the background. He sounded as though he was phoning from a bar or somewhere, even though it was a bit early in the day for that. Wherever it was, it didn't seem like a good place to have a conversation.

'Are you drunk?' I said.

'Of course not, Susie,' he said, slurring his words slightly. 'I just want to see you.'

I could feel my resolve weakening. Jason was sweet when he was drunk. He was phoning me because he was happy and he wanted me to be there, it was as simple as that.

'I can't, Jason,' I said. 'I'll miss my lecture tomorrow.'

'Oh, for God's sake, Susie, missing a few lessons won't kill you. They'll never notice. Go on, please. For me.'

'But Jason...' I said, making one last effort to resist.

'We're having a great time here. We're at this new drinking club. There's a party on here tonight and I don't want you to miss it. I'll meet you off the train at Victoria. Get the 6.30. All right?'

I gave in.

'OK then,' I said. If I got up early the next day and got the train back, I could probably get to my lecture on time.

'But I can't stay long,' I added.

'Don't worry, we won't. We'll be back to sunny Brighton in a flash. See you at the station, Susie Q. Bye.'

He put the phone down before I could reply.

chapter 5

I GOT THE SIX-THIRTY TO VICTORIA that evening. I found a window seat on an empty table near the buffet car, and put my shoulder bag down on the aisle seat next to me. I hadn't brought much with me, just a few books, a notepad, a pencil, a toothbrush, and a pair of clean knickers for the next day. I rummaged about in the bag and, as the train pulled out of the station, I began to read, mainly to put off anyone asking me to move my bag so they could sit beside me.

I'd taken the book out of the library to mug up on my lecture next day. The lecturer was a famous Austrian professor called Paul Feyerabend who'd outraged everyone by saying that science wasn't very scientific, which didn't sound all that outrageous to me, but apparently it was. Anyway, the rumour on campus was that all the scientists who normally stayed in their labs in the 'B' block and never came out were going to be there, having apoplectic fits in the front row.

The book was called *The Structure of Scientific Revolutions* by Thomas Kuhn. I got into it straight away, looking up occasionally to think, gazing out of the grubby window at the frozen brown fields passing by under a colourless sky. Kuhn seemed to be saying, in a roundabout way, that scientists are more interested in their careers than in finding out the truth. Again, this didn't surprise me very much. But the way he wrote about it was persuasive. He was saying that, in science, belief systems or 'paradigms' evolve around certain ideas – for instance, Copernican astronomy or Newtonian physics – and then, suddenly, for no apparent reason, they're dropped. None of the paradigms fit together, and there is no rational progression from one to another. They change mainly because of social and financial pressures in what he called 'the scientific community'.

As I read, I realised why this idea had caused such a furore at Sussex. You could see why the scientists were incensed by the notion that one theory was no truer than another, and that academics just came up with stuff to keep their mates happy and hold on to their jobs. It was the kind of thing everybody knew, but nobody ever said, that is until Kuhn and Paul Feyerabend came along. I made a mental note not to miss the lecture, whatever happened in London.

After about half an hour, I went to the buffet car and got a cup of tea and a piece of fruitcake. British Rail fruitcake was so horrible that, once you'd eaten a piece, you didn't feel like eating anything else, however hungry you were. I was starving and I didn't have much money, so it was just what I needed. I carried the tea and the cake back to my seat, looking forward to getting back to the scientific revolutions, but when I got there I found a bloke sitting opposite my seat by the window.

He was very far out, this guy, a complete freak in fact. The sort of person Jason and his friends would have called a hippie. He had long, curly blond hair and a beard, strands of which were plaited together. He was wearing a long, electric blue woolly cloak of some sort and had a large brown felt hat on his head. Under the band of the hat he had stuck some ears of corn, which bobbed as the train moved. I took all this in at a glance, and sat back down, pretending to ignore him.

I started reading again, but it was hard to concentrate. On the other side of the table, the guy was laying out some tarot cards. He was arranging them in rows and murmuring to himself. I noticed that he was referring to a crumpled, handwritten instruction sheet in his lap. I put my head down so my hair fell forward and peered out through my hair. I could just make out the heading at the top of the sheet: 'Aleister Crowley's Thoth Tarot'. The muttering continued.

I took a swig of tea and a bite of fruitcake. I didn't know much about Aleister Crowley other than that there were loads of freaks in Brighton who were into him and that they practised something called sex magick. A girl I knew on my course had once slept with one of them, and had told us how he'd started praying in the middle of it. He'd explained to her later that, according to Aleister, if you prayed during your 'nuptive moment', you'd get what you wanted, but that it was no good her praying, it only applied to men. We'd had a good laugh about it at the time. The Crowley heads were ridiculous and most students took the piss out of them, but to tell the truth I was slightly scared of them as well.

I carried on reading my book.

We may have to relinquish the notion that changes of paradigm carry scientists closer and closer to the truth…

Opposite me, the freak went on turning up the cards.

Under normal conditions the research scientist is not an innovator but a solver of puzzles…

The mumbling grew louder and a card landed in the middle of the table, just above my book.

Individuals who break through by inventing a new paradigm are almost always very young or very new to the field…

At the edge of my vision, I could see that the card's face was turned towards me.

These are the men likely to see that those rules no longer define a playable game and to conceive another set that can replace them…

At the bottom of the cards were two words: 'The Lovers'.

I looked at the card, without moving my head. It was drawn in the style of William Blake, but not at all well. At the bottom of the picture were two babies, one dark and one fair. The lovers were a king and queen, and over them stood some kind of god figure with a long beard, his arms outstretched. I kept my face expressionless. If this was the freak's way of chatting me up, it wasn't going to work. The lovers. Not bloody likely.

I remained glued to my book all the way to Victoria, only raising my head as we came into the station. I got up before the train stopped, intending to stand in the corridor and wait. I'd had enough of staring at pages and trying to concentrate with the lovers hovering over the edges of them. I felt annoyed, and a little unnerved as well. I walked into the aisle without looking at the freak, but as I passed him, he touched my arm to stop me, and handed me a card. I was so surprised that I took it, glancing at it without taking it in, before closing my hand over it. I nodded quickly at him and moved away into the corridor before I looked at it again.

On the back of the card was a design of mystical curling snakes and yin and yang symbols. I turned it over and there, on the front, was a picture of a red-haired man with massive thighs, bulging eyes and a bristling moustache. There were two small horns sticking out of his head, and a silly little triangular hat perched on top of it. He was dressed in a medieval costume with a green tunic and tights and pointy yellow shoes, and there was some sort of lion next to him that seemed to be biting his leg. In the background was what looked like a bunch of grapes, with butterflies and fairies and whatnot flying about. At the bottom of the card were the words: 'The Fool'.

The train pulled to a halt, and as I got out on to the platform, I stuffed the card into my bag. A mass of people were pouring off the train, so I walked along with them and tried to get lost in the crowds as quick as I could in case the freak came after me, although now he'd given me the fool card instead of the lovers, I wasn't sure that he would. In fact, I felt a bit embarrassed now about the way I'd assumed that he'd been trying to chat me up, when all the time he'd probably been sitting there thinking what an idiot I looked.

I went straight to the ladies', and when I thought the coast would be clear, I emerged again on the platform to wait for Jason. We'd arranged to meet by the barrier, but he wasn't there. I wasn't surprised. Jason was always late for everything. But as I stood there, I started to get angry, mainly with myself. This whole evening was going to be one big hassle, and I'd be lucky to make it to my lecture next day. I knew already how things would pan out. Jason would say he'd drive me down to Brighton in the morning, and then he'd oversleep and I'd have to get the train at the last minute. I should never have come.

After half an hour I was in a foul mood, but then I saw the tall figure of Jason walking towards me through the crowds, his fair hair flying out around his head. He came up to me and breathed brandy all over me as he kissed me. He was wearing his old leather RAF flying jacket, with fur inside, and I put my head against it and smelt its reassuring, familiar smell. As I did, my anger evaporated.

'Sorry, Susie,' he said. He put his arm around me as we began to walk off together. 'I just didn't realise the time. I've been drinking all afternoon with Bear.'

Bear was Jason's best friend. They'd been at public school together, and they were still inseparable. Bear's real name was Rupert, but nobody called him that. The nickname Bear had stuck from his schooldays, and it was a kind of joke now, because he didn't look in the least like a bear, being slight and rather elegant. I liked Bear. I wasn't quite sure why, but there seemed to be a bond between us.

'Bear's waiting in the car,' said Jason. 'We're going for cocktails at Madagascar, OK?'

'What's Madagascar?'

Jason laughed. 'Oh, I thought I'd taken you there, Susie Q.'

'No,' I said. 'It must have been someone else.'

Jason laughed again, ignoring the sarcasm in my voice.

'Sorry, Susie, I thought I had. Anyway, it's this new members-only bar that's just opened. You'll see. It's great.'

Jason's yellow Morgan was waiting outside the station with Bear in the passenger seat. I climbed in and pecked him on the cheek, squeezing myself in between the two seats, over the gearstick. Bear grinned at me, pushing back his floppy dark hair and peering through his National Health specs, and put his arm round me, mainly because he didn't have anywhere else to put it. Jason got in and we took off at full speed, the tyres squealing, dodging between the cars.

'We're meeting Flick and Toby there,' Jason said as we hurtled along.

My spirits sank. Flick was Jason's older sister. She worked in advertising, and she made it clear that she thought I was an idiot. She had a business with offices and studios over the market at Covent Garden, managing a team of artists to draw storyboards for the big agencies. I'd worked there as a temp in the summer holidays, which was how I'd met Jason.

It was the year after my father died, and I'd come up to London to get away from my mother and Swansea, and the relations, and all the people I hardly knew who were still coming up to me on the street and being sympathetic and asking me how I was in a meaningful way. Jason hadn't been sympathetic at all: when I'd told him, he'd just changed the subject. I'd met him on the anniversary of Dad's death, although I hadn't been aware of the date until I thought about it afterwards. There'd been no one in the office when he'd walked in, and I'd been reading *The Birth of Tragedy* between telephone calls, and then I'd looked up and seen him grinning at me over the desk. He had a wide mouth, and his eyes were a glittering, luminous blue, with small black pupils in the middle that seemed to draw you in like vanishing points. I don't know what it was that he saw in me, but whatever it was, we couldn't take our eyes off each other, so we just went on staring at each other and saying nothing. It was like that French thing, *coup de foudre*, a bolt of lightning, love at first sight. I'd never felt like that before. Then he asked me what I was reading, so I showed him the book, and he said, Oh yeah, that Nazi guy, and I said he wasn't a Nazi, and then he asked me out to this wine bar in Covent Garden called Brahms and Liszt, and then we went to see *The Night Porter* which was showing in Leicester Square, and that was how it had all started.

It had made that time around the anniversary almost bearable, going out with Jason in the evenings and working in Covent Garden during the day, coming in through the market stalls on those sunny mornings, with the barrow boys calling me love and offering me peaches. A peach for a peach, they used to say. But Flick hadn't been happy with my work. My task was to phone the agencies and harass them to see our artists, but I wasn't very good at it. When they told me no, I just politely thanked them and hung up. Flick told me to try harder, but I didn't seem to be able to get the hang of it. After a few days we had no new appointments, so she told me to stop calling the clients, as she called them, and just answer the telephones and open the post.

Her boyfriend Toby wasn't so bad. He had two Dalmatians that went around with him everywhere. He left everything to Flick and concentrated on the dogs. He was quite interested in mysticism, and sometimes in the office he'd tell me about Gurdjieff or Carlos Castaneda, or whoever it was he'd been reading, but then Flick would come in and start glaring at me and we'd have to stop. Flick was a hard-nosed businesswoman. She didn't have any time for mysticism, or for Toby sitting about in the office doing nothing, or for me. When I started going out with her brother, she was horrified, although she tried not to show it. She couldn't understand why we were still together now that the term had started and I was a clueless philosophy student at Sussex University. I could see why she didn't like me, but then again, it was hard to imagine her liking any girlfriend of Jason's. She doted on him, and she seemed to want him all to herself.

We managed to find a parking space at the top of Long Acre and headed down towards the bar. You couldn't see into it from the street, all the windows had slatted wooden blinds pulled down over them. When we walked in, Flick and Toby and the dogs were already there. Flick was dressed in her usual Biba stuff, her blonde curls cascading over a short fur cape draped over her shoulders. Underneath she was wearing a forties' style maroon dress with a big fake flower in the buttonhole. She wasn't wielding a cigarette holder, but the way she smoked her cigarette, she could have been. Toby was beside her, reading the newspaper, wearing a pinstriped suit and a Homburg. Both the dogs were lying at his feet, wearing red leather collars and leads. They looked as though they'd been hired by an advertising agency to do publicity for the bar. Perhaps they had, for all I knew.

Toby jumped up and put the newspaper away when he saw us, but Flick didn't move. She kissed her brother, taking care not to spoil her lipstick, and nodded at me and Bear.

'What do you want to drink?' Toby asked. 'We're having daiquiris.'

I looked at the drinks on the shiny black-lacquered table. They looked pretty in their frosted triangular glasses with a slice of lime wedged on one side and a pink glacé cherry on a toothpick balanced over the rim. In the centre of the table was a white orchid in a delicate red and black vase. I suddenly felt thirsty, as though I was in Brazil on a hot summer's night instead of in London on a wet October evening.

'They look lovely,' I said, pointing to the drinks. 'I'll have one of those.'

Flick shot me a look as though to say, I bet you don't even know what a daiquiri is.

'Whatever they are,' I added, just to annoy her. Then I felt embarrassed and wished I hadn't.

The others ordered daiquiris as well, and Jason went off with Toby to get the drinks. I looked around. The place was impressive, all black shiny lacquer and silver chrome, and everyone in there was good looking and well dressed. I had on my blue velvet jacket, so I didn't feel too out of place, but my scruffy shoulder bag with the books in it looked awful against the chrome, so I wedged it out of sight under the table.

People were coming in and out of the bar and the place was filling up fast. They were all older than me, sophisticated London people with jobs in advertising and film, people with plenty of money, people with nice cars and nice clothes, people who wouldn't have given a toss about the things that interested me, like Nietzsche, or John Martyn, or the structure of scientific revolutions. I envied them, and I wished I was as well dressed as they were, but at the same time I wasn't sure I wanted to be part of that crowd. I knew my friends at Sussex would think they were bourgeois.

While Jason and Toby were at the bar, Flick started talking to us in the patronising tone of voice she normally adopted to speak to her brother's friends.

'So how's it going, Susannah? Still searching for the meaning of life?'

She meant philosophy.

'Yes.' I kept my tone steady and polite. I thought how hard she'd laugh if I told her about what I'd been reading in *Human, All Too Human* about being a philosopher and a wanderer and having a secret destiny, so I changed the subject.

'How's the business going?' I tried not to sound sarcastic.

'Great,' she said. 'Our turnover this year has been fantastic. We've got a great track record now,' she continued. 'Everyone knows us.'

'Good,' I said. I resisted the temptation to add, bully for you. But something in my manner told her I wasn't interested in her turnover or her track record, so she stopped talking to me and turned to Bear.

'So, Bear, what happened to that girl you were going out with... what's her name? The Australian nurse.'

Bear looked sheepish. 'Oh, you mean Steph.'

I'd never met Steph, but I'd heard about her. She was the first girl Bear had gone out with since I'd met Jason, which was a couple of years back now.

'Steph, that's it,' said Flick.

Bear shifted uncomfortably and cleared his throat. It was a nervous trait he had.

'Well, it didn't really work out,' he said. 'She didn't really approve of my job.'

Bear was some kind of city guy, a property developer of sorts, working for his father's firm. It wasn't a good job for him, Steph had been right about that. He wasn't the right kind of person for it. Bear was small, sensitive and sweet. He was good looking, with dark hair and delicate features, but he didn't have that thing that makes women fancy men. He didn't like pushing other people around. He didn't have much confidence. He had no interest in the job either, and made no effort to pretend he did.

'What do you mean, didn't approve of it?' said Flick.

'Well, she thought it was morally wrong,' Bear replied. He paused. 'She said I was a cancer on society.'

Flick guffawed. 'Oh, too much! Too much.'

Toby and Jason came back with the drinks and Flick started telling them about Steph and the cancer on society. Bear joined in the laughter, but I could see he was upset. Flick didn't seem to notice. Then she saw some people she knew at the bar and dragged Jason off to meet them. Toby followed, leaving me and Bear at the table with the dogs.

We sat in silence for a while, and then I said, 'Do you mind about Steph, Bear?'

'Not really.' He sounded miserable. 'I liked her but...
well, you know, we were so different. We just had nothing in
common.'

There was another silence.

'Don't worry,' I said. 'You'll find someone in the end.'

It was a stupid remark but I couldn't think of anything
else to say.

'It's all very well for you,' he replied. 'You've got Jason.'

I looked into his eyes. He looked back into mine, and
then both of us looked over at Jason standing at the bar,
chatting to his new friends. Flick stood beside him, tossing
her curls and laughing. Of all the women there, she was the
only one who seemed to be a match for him. But I noticed
that, from a distance, her chin had a hard set to it that was
almost ugly.

'Let's have another drink,' said Bear, finishing up his
daiquiri.

I was only halfway through mine, and I felt pretty drunk
already. I didn't really want another drink and I couldn't
afford one, but I didn't want to seem stand-offish.

'I'm completely broke,' I said. 'You'll have to buy me
one. They probably charge a fortune in here. Get me a coke
or something, otherwise you'll have to cart me off at the end
of the evening.'

'Don't be ridiculous, Susannah,' said Bear. 'The night is
young.'

Bear waved at a waitress and she immediately came over.
He ordered two more cocktails. Although he was so
insecure, he had a way of behaving in bars and restaurants
that always impressed me. He was never rude, but he always
got the staff's attention. It must have been his family
background. His father was a lord or something and the
family were absolutely loaded.

Bear and I spent the evening drinking at the table, while
Jason and the others flitted round the bar, mixing and
mingling. Jason came back from time to time to check we

were all right. I was drinking as slowly as I could, but Bear was knocking the daiquiris back so fast that eventually Jason decided it was time to leave. He got us back in the car and drove us over to a trendy café that served these great American hamburgers. It was a bit like Brown's in Brighton. In both of them, they had the best-looking waitresses I'd ever seen, the kind of girls with incredibly long legs that you'd imagine would be film stars, not waitresses. I watched them, mesmerised by their glamour as they glided around the room from table to table, bending from the knees as they served the customers, their faces impassive. It was depressing, really, and made me feel that life was impossible.

While we were eating our hamburgers, Bear started crying. He was obviously very drunk, but it wasn't just the booze. Maybe it was Steph, but I didn't think so. Jason was pretty drunk as well but he sobered up quickly and called the waitress over to pay the bill, and then we all got back in the car again to go to the party. On the way, Bear had to be let out to be sick on the side of the road. While he was heaving up, Jason decided that we should skip the party and get back to Bear's flat, where we were staying that night. Bear wasn't very keen, but it was obvious that he was in no condition to go anywhere, so in the end we just drove home.

Bear lived in a strange little flat off Kensington Church Street. It had art nouveau carvings on the outside of the building and must have cost a fortune to rent, but inside the noise of the traffic was a constant irritation. In all the rooms, you could hear the sudden squeal of taxis slamming on their brakes to stop at the traffic lights on the street below. The noise went on pretty much all day and night, which made it impossible to relax.

When we got in, Bear seemed to perk up. He put a Pointer Sisters record on and the drinks came out again. He and Jason started playing cards together, sprawled out on the sofa. I could see it was going to be a long night so I went off to the spare bedroom, took off my clothes, and got into bed.

I was exhausted, but every time I nearly drifted off to sleep, I woke up. Whenever I closed my eyes, I found myself in a white car, travelling along a black road. I recognised the car. It was one of the ones I'd seen in my morning dreams, when I got up out of bed and looked out of the window to see if I was awake. But now, instead of looking out at the cars, I was inside one of them. It was hurtling down the road at breakneck speed. There were white lines in the middle of the road that seemed to be coming at me faster and faster. Ahead of me, there was only a long straight road and nothing else but darkness on either side. I didn't think I was going to crash, but the car seemed to be speeding faster and faster. The only way I could stop it was to open my eyes.

I lay there all night, nearly falling asleep and waking up in a panic each time I did. Jason didn't come to bed with me. If he had, I might have been able to snuggle up to his warm body and get some sleep. But he didn't. Once again, I was on my own.

Eventually, I saw the first light of day edging round the curtains and I knew that in a couple of hours it would be time to get up and get back to Sussex.

chapter 6

I LET MYSELF OUT OF THE FLAT quietly before the others woke up, and walked down to Notting Hill Gate tube station. A grey mist hung in the air and the streets were wet with rain. You could see the blurred lights of taxis and buses and cars looming through the mist, and their wheels made a swishing noise as they went past that was oddly comforting. There was a newspaper seller outside the station, sitting in his booth wrapped up against the weather with a polythene bag over his flat cap, uttering a strange cry that he must have devised over many years to mark out his territory. People were scurrying about the streets with their collars up and their heads down, trying to get to wherever they were going before the next downpour, ignoring each other and clinging on to their private worlds for as long as they could in the first few hours of the day.

I took the tube down to Victoria. The carriage stank of fags and sweat and urine, and there were cigarette butts all over the floor and burn marks on the seats. The passengers were all jammed up against each other, hanging on to the straps under the strip lights in their ill-fitting grey suits, trying to open and fold and refold their newspapers as discreetly as they could. As we went along, the smell of wet wool and stale sweat and bad breath grew stronger and the windows got more and more steamed up. Each time the train went round a corner, the man who was standing next to me pressed himself up against me, all the while intently reading his newspaper. My nose was so close to his hand that I could smell the nicotine on his fingers. After a while I began to feel nauseous, so I turned my head away and started to breathe in deeply, the way Rob had taught me, letting my breath out slowly and shutting my eyes to calm myself. By the time we reached Victoria I was starting to feel better, so I trod hard on his toe and didn't stop to pretend it was a mistake and apologise before I got off.

When I reached my platform, the eight-thirty train to Brighton was just about to pull out of the station, so I ran on to it without buying a ticket, and found a seat near the buffet carriage. I bought a cup of tea but I couldn't face the fruitcake at this time of the morning, so instead I lit a cigarette and stared out of the window.

To be sure, such a man will have bad nights... but then as recompense, come the ecstatic mornings of other regions and days.

Nietzsche's words didn't seem so reassuring now. There was nothing ecstatic about the grimy woodlands and dirty fields along the edge of the railway bank, out there in the morning mist. They looked like the kind of places where small children might be taken to be murdered. I turned away, opened my book, and tried to read, but I was too tired to concentrate, so I went on staring out of the window at the grubby landscape all the way down to Brighton, then changed trains, lit another cigarette, and stared out of the window all the way to Falmer as well.

When I got to the European Common Room on campus, Cassie was waiting for me. She was drinking coffee out of a plastic cup and smoking a cigarette, trying to look haughty and unapproachable. I could see why. All the men in the room were glancing at her surreptitiously and as I passed one of them I saw him look over at her and whisper something to his friend.

When she saw me, her face relaxed into a smile.

'Thank God, Suse. Bloody hell, I feel like Daniel in the

lion's den in here.'

Cassie was prone to using biblical expressions. Her parents belonged to a religious sect called the Plymouth Brethren. They were always writing her long letters about fire and brimstone and Armageddon and something called the rapture, when all good Christians would ascend into the air and be taken into heaven. It could happen at any time. If it happened now, for instance, while she was smoking a cigarette and drinking her coffee, she'd be left behind with the rest of us heathens. She seemed resigned enough to her fate.

'Who's been hassling you?' I asked, looking around.

She indicated a dreary-looking bloke with greasy brown hair wearing a grey army surplus overcoat.

'Ooh, Cass, he's gorgeous,' I said.

She laughed, showing her perfect white teeth. I could see why all the men fancied her.

Then she stopped laughing and looked at me. 'God, Susannah, you look shattered. Are you all right?'

'I'm fine. I just haven't slept much, that's all.'

I told her about my evening out with Jason, and how he'd stayed up all night with Bear and hadn't come to bed and how I'd lain awake by myself until morning and then tiptoed past the pair of them crashed out in the sitting room, surrounded by bottles and glasses and ashtrays. Cassie listened politely, nodding now and then, but I knew she wasn't all that sympathetic to my problems with Jason. She didn't understand why I was so obsessed with him. Her own approach had always been to keep her options open. Her parents thought she was living on campus, but she spent most of her time at her boyfriend's flat in Brighton. She was also having an on-off affair with one of her tutors. Now and again there'd be someone else as well. She kept them all at arm's length and she didn't seem to suffer any pangs of conscience, which, given the fire and brimstone warnings, was pretty impressive.

Before we could discuss the matter any further, Fiona arrived.

'Come on you two, get a move on,' she said as she approached. 'We'll be late.'

Fiona didn't stand on ceremony. She was bossy – phenomenally bossy. But she did all the things Cass and I couldn't be bothered to do, such as find out which lecture theatre we were due to be in that morning, so we let her order us around. Occasionally she irritated me. Once I'd tried to discuss Jason with her, and all she'd said was, Get rid of him. End of conversation. So now I shut up about him and changed the subject.

We did as Fiona told us, finished our coffees, and got going. When we got to the lecture theatre, it was already full but we managed to squeeze in at the back, the three of us jammed up against the wall. Down at the front you could see the scientists. They were all dressed the same, in shapeless tweed jackets, with long hair and beards and glasses. In the middle and further back were the arts students, wearing tight-fitting velvet jackets and long scarves. I spotted Rob among them, sitting next to the dark-haired girl; and once more, ridiculously, I felt a pang of jealousy.

Then Feyerabend burst through the door at the front of the packed hall, accompanied by a pretty girl of about my age with red plaits, who appeared to be his girlfriend. He was a tall man of fifty, sixty, or so, wearing a black beret, a red scarf and a long, dark blue overcoat. He looked pale and was supporting himself on a metal crutch, limping over to the blackboard slowly as if in pain. When he got there, he picked up a piece of chalk and wrote on the board, painstakingly, in enormous letters: ARISTOTLE. Then, below it, in tiny, almost illegible letters, he scribbled: 'Popper'.

A roar went up.

'For heaven's sake!' said Fiona in my ear.

Karl Popper was the scientists' last hope. His argument

was that a theory could only possibly be true if there was some way of showing it to be false. Ideas like God, according to Popper, were meaningless. You couldn't prove them either way. Whereas ideas in science were falsifiable: you could test them. Popper wasn't claiming much for science, but even so, Feyerabend wasn't having any of it. As far as he was concerned, ideas in science weren't verifiable, and they weren't falsifiable either.

Feyerabend started talking in a strong German accent about witchcraft and science, and the shouting died down. But as he went on, some of the scientists at the front started getting restless and then two of them jumped up from their seats and marched up the aisle, looking furious. The door at the back of the hall was open, but when they got there, some of the arts students blocked their way. A scuffle broke out and the students started pushing each other and shouting. Everyone in the lecture hall was turning round, craning their necks to see what was going on, until at last Fiona strode over to them, pushed them all out of the door, and slammed it shut.

We turned back round to Feyerabend, who was standing at the board grinning at Fiona.

'Thank you,' he said. There was an unmistakeably flirtatious tone to his voice. All the students turned round, including the girl with the red pigtails, as Fiona blushed and looked down at the floor. Then they turned back and Feyerabend went on talking.

After the lecture, I spent the rest of the day socialising on campus with Cassie and Fiona, going from the European Common Room to the Falmer Bar to the Gardner Arts Centre, taking in the library basement and the crypt on the way. In the early evening, they went off together, so I decided to go home. I wasn't looking forward to spending another evening by myself in the flat, but I needed a bath and a meal and a good night's sleep. So I walked out of the university towards the station, feeling sorry for myself and noticing all the couples linking arms and kissing, until I came to the Meeting House just to the side of the main route out. It was lit up from inside and the stained glass windows glowed in the dark. For some reason, I turned off the path and went inside.

I'd never been in there before. I didn't know why I had come in now, except that my legs were aching and I felt like sitting down. There was nobody there but some candles were burning, casting a soft light over the brick walls and the wooden chairs. The stained-glass windows were modern ones, just rectangles of red, blue, yellow, and green arranged in random blocks of colour here and there, but the patterns they made were oddly soothing.

I sat down on one of the chairs and stared at the colours of the stained glass through the flickering candles, listening to the silence of the place. It seemed safe in there, and I felt as though I never wanted to move again. And after a while I began to feel a huge sense of relief, just as I had done that night at the gig listening to John Martyn sing, with my head resting on Rob's shoulder.

'Susannah?'

I jumped. Someone had come in behind me and was standing silhouetted in the doorway. For a few seconds, I couldn't make out who it was. Then I recognised him.

'Rob! What are you doing here?'

He came towards me, hesitant. 'I… well, I followed you down here, actually. I saw you walking through campus and I thought I'd catch you up before you got to the station and talk to you, and then I saw you come in here and…'

He was nervous and his words tumbled out. But when he got near enough to see the smile on my face, he relaxed.

'Come and sit down a minute,' I said.

He sat down on the chair next to mine and we both gazed at the stained-glass windows, not knowing what to say to each other. I was acutely conscious of his body next to mine, and I could smell the fresh, cold air from outside lingering on his hair and his jacket.

After what seemed like a long time, I finally broke the silence.

'Man, the colours,' I said.

He laughed. It was the sort of banal remark people made after staring into space for hours when they were stoned out of their minds. Among the students, it had become a shorthand way of describing someone who was always out of their tree.

'Yeah,' he said. 'Red is really far out, isn't it.'

We both laughed this time, and then silence fell between us again. I went on looking straight ahead, but I took his hand in mine and held it.

'Susannah...' His voice trailed off. 'I...' His voice trailed off again.

I turned to look at him. His head was framed by the lights in the windows, which formed a circle all the way around the building. With his long dark hair against the candlelight he looked like Jesus Christ, or the Angel Gabriel.

Then he bent his head slowly towards me and kissed me on the mouth. My heart started thumping. As his tongue slid into my mouth my stomach seemed to turn over and I felt my hands trembling. His hands were in my hair, and they were trembling too.

As we kissed, we could both feel ourselves beginning to want each other in that way you do when you've only slept with someone once and know that you are going to again, very soon.

'God, Susannah, I've missed you,' he said as we broke apart.

I wanted to ask about the dark-haired girl, but it didn't seem the time or the place. It would have spoiled the atmosphere.

He put his arms around me and kissed me again, pushing

his hands under my jacket, burrowing under the layers of clothing until he came to my skin. Then he began to feel his way up my body until he reached my breasts.

I took his wrists and pushed him away. 'For God's sake,' I said. 'Not in here. Anyone could walk in at any moment.'

We both started giggling like little kids, and he began poking his fingers into my clothing as I was wriggling about. Then I kicked one of the empty chairs by mistake and it skidded across the floor, making a noise, and we both stopped, slightly ashamed of the way that we'd been behaving in this holy place.

We looked up at the windows again and he began to stroke my hair as he had done the morning we were in bed together. This time, I didn't pull away from him. He looked into my eyes and spoke softly to me.

'I'm really into you, Susannah,' he said.

Once again, I felt like asking him about the dark-haired girl, but it seemed wrong to bring the subject up now. I didn't want him to think I was uptight and possessive. And anyway, I wasn't sure what I felt about him, beyond the fact that right now I wanted to be back in his bed again. So I said nothing.

'Susannah?'

He needed a response. I didn't know what to say.

'I need time to think, Rob,' I replied at last. 'It's a bit of a complicated situation.'

'Is there someone else?'

'Yes,' I said. 'I mean, no. I mean, I don't know.'

He heaved a sigh.

Then I said, 'And you?'

'What do you mean, me?'

'Well, I mean, you know… is there…' I paused. For some reason, I found it hard to say, even though he'd just said it. 'Someone else?'

'Umm, no,' he said. 'I mean, maybe. Sort of. But not if you… you know.'

'Right,' I said. I got the general idea. 'Well, that's... you know, how it is with me. Kind of.'

He sighed again. We didn't seem to be getting very far.

I got up and straightened my clothes, buttoning up my jacket.

'I've got to get home now, Rob. Shall we meet up tomorrow?'

He stood up too. 'Yeah, of course. Where?'

'Falmer Bar? About one?'

'Fine. Will you... you know?'

'What?'

'Well, will you... know by then?'

'I'm not sure,' I said. 'I really don't know if... if I'll know. But I'll think about it.'

He heaved another sigh. We walked over and stood in the doorway of the Meeting House. Neither of us wanted to leave. He kissed me again as we stood there, hard this time, biting into my lip with his teeth, as though he wanted to make a lasting impression on me before I went. Then, without saying goodbye, he walked off back into campus.

I thought about Rob all the way home. I looked out of the window on the train and ran my tongue over the bruise on my lip where he had bitten into the skin. On the bus, I put my fingers under my T-shirt and felt my stomach where his hands had touched it. As I turned the corner of Brunswick Square, the wind from the sea hit me hard, blowing my hair in front of my face, and I pushed it back, thinking of his fingers in it. My mind went back to the night we'd spent together, the night before last, and I replayed every moment of it, from when he had stood hovering over me, to when we had woken up in the night and made love, to when we had lain on the bed kissing fully dressed before I left next morning. Then I thought about what had happened last night in London, lying there on my own in bed for hours listening to the taxis braking and finding Jason asleep on the floor in the sitting room this morning. By the time I got to the street door of the flat, I'd made up my mind.

I let myself in. As I climbed the staircase, I was making plans. I'd make a cup of tea, have a bath, eat whatever I could find in the flat, and go to bed. I'd get a good night's sleep, get up early, pack my things, and leave a note for Jason. I'd explain that I was moving out for a while, that I needed some space, and suggest that we could meet some time if he wanted to talk. Then I'd ring Cassie and head over to her room on campus. She'd given me a key to the room and said I could use it any time as long as I let her know first – she didn't want me barging in on her and the tutor. I could dump my stuff and meet Rob for lunch and then stay in Cassie's room for a few days while I looked for somewhere more permanent.

As I came up to the landing, I noticed the light was on in the flat, shining through the glass in the front door. I took my key out and put it in the lock, but before I could turn it, the door opened, and Jason stood there, wearing a blue and white striped apron and holding a wooden spoon in his hand.

'Susie.' He leaned forward and kissed me on the cheek. The wooden spoon got caught in my hair. 'I'm making boeuf bourguignon.'

A delicious smell of rich stew wafted out into the corridor. I was tired and hungry, and it comforted me, as did Jason's big shoulders and chest under the apron pressing against my face. I breathed in the reassuring, warm smell of Jason and the onions and decided not to say anything for the moment. I could talk to him about our relationship over supper. I wanted to end it in a civilised way without hurting him. And I wanted to eat the boeuf bourguignon. After all, I'd had nothing but cups of coffee all day.

Inside the flat, I took off my jacket, hung it in the hall, and followed Jason into the kitchen. The stew was bubbling away on the stove, and on the table was an open bottle of red wine. Jason poured me a glass and started chopping some vegetables. I took a big gulp of the wine. It was smooth and warming, not like the rotgut stuff called 'Toujours' that the students always bought from the pub at closing time. Wine from the Toujours region, Jason called it.

I watched Jason cooking. His face was flushed from the heat of the stove.

'I'm really sorry about last night, Susie,' he said. 'Why didn't you wake me up when you left?'

'There didn't seem any point,' I said. 'We'd have been late if you'd driven me down.'

'I would have come to bed, but Bear was in a pretty bad way all night, so I had to stay and look after him. He's a bit down at the moment. He hasn't been going into work and his father's threatening to sack him and make him join the army. Teach him a lesson, and all that.'

I felt sorry for Bear. The thought of him joining the army was horrifying. But I felt a lot sorrier for myself.

'Well, I don't call getting pissed and staying up all night drinking with him looking after him, exactly,' I said.

Jason looked up, surprised. There was a bitter edge to my voice.

'I came all the way up to London to see you,' I continued, 'and you just bloody ignored me all evening.'

I hesitated. I could have added, at that point, 'I'm fed up with the way you treat me and I'm moving out,' but I didn't. Instead, I started crying.

Jason stopped chopping, put down his knife, and came round to my side of the table. In one movement, he picked me up in his arms, sat down on the chair, and put me on his knee. He murmured silly things in my ear, the way you do with a child, and held me close until I calmed down.

Then it came out, just like that.

'Jason, I want to leave you,' I said.

He didn't respond at first. There was a long silence.

Then he replied, 'No, you don't.'

He said it in a slow, firm, thoughtful way, as though he was absolutely sure he was right. It infuriated me, but at the same time I felt a kind of relief.

'What do you mean, I don't? I know my own mind, for God's sake, I'm not a child. I've had enough of the way you take me for granted. I'm going to pack my things tonight and leave in the morning.'

'Nonsense,' he said. 'Don't be silly, of course you're not. Susie, I'm sorry, I really am. I promise it won't happen again. I know I get carried away. I know I don't pay you enough attention sometimes. But I love you, you know that.'

I didn't know it. He hardly ever said it. The funny thing was, when I'd first met him, I hadn't really wanted him to. That day he'd walked into the office, I'd been reading a passage about Dionysus in *The Birth of Tragedy*. I'd looked up, and Jason had been standing there, grinning at me. I'd looked down and continued reading, then raised my eyes to his again, and smiled back. He'd asked me out, and then for the rest of that summer we'd gone out together, drinking in wine bars, eating in restaurants, and having sex in Bear's flat when he was out. During that time he'd never once asked me anything: about my father, my family, or my job, about Sussex, about how I was feeling, about whether I was happy. We'd never discussed any of it. He'd taken complete control of the situation from the outset, deciding every detail of what we did – from what dish he should order for me in a restaurant to what position he screwed me in when we were in bed. At the time, it had been a relief, and I'd been grateful to him for not prying into my life, but now I was beginning to want more: I wanted him to ask me what I liked, how I felt, to tell me that he loved me, to let me tell him that I loved him. But we never had that kind of conversation, and I was starting to think we never would.

But now that he'd said the words this time, I felt better, and I began to realise how difficult it was going to be for me to leave him. Jason was a good-looking, mature man of nearly thirty, who made boeuf bourguignon for supper, and knew how to choose wine, and how to make money, and how the straight world worked. I was only just twenty, and I didn't know any of these things. Neither did Rob. All we knew about was philosophy, and that wasn't going to get us very far, unless we wanted to live in a world of blankets in the windows, bare light bulbs and endless cups of tea for the rest of our lives. The more I thought about it, the more I realised that Jason was right. I didn't really want to leave him, not just at the moment, anyway. Maybe I wouldn't go tomorrow, after all. It might be better to leave it for a few days.

Jason looked at me quizzically. As though he could read my thoughts, he said, 'What have you been up to, Susie? You haven't met some hippie boy on your course, have you?'

My tongue slid over the bruise on my lip.

'Don't be ridiculous.' It wasn't difficult to lie. It was quite enjoyable, actually. 'Of course I haven't.'

Jason got up and carried on with the cooking. By the time we sat down to eat, he seemed to have forgotten our conversation. The meal was delicious, and he fussed around me, pouring wine for me and loading food on to my plate. Afterwards, we moved from the kitchen to the sitting room and sat among the nymphs and the plaster faces, listening to records. I wanted to hear John Martyn but I didn't ask him to put it on in case he got suspicious. Instead, we listened to Robert Palmer and J. J. Cale and Eric Clapton's 461 Ocean Boulevard, which I'd heard about a million times before.

I tried to stay awake, but I was so tired that I kept closing my eyes and drifting off. Each time I did, the music became more distant until I found myself in the white car again, with the white lines on the black road hurtling towards me as they had done the night before. I tried to jerk myself awake, but my eyelids seemed too heavy to lift, and all I could do was sit there with the car going faster and faster until at last the white lines began to blur into the darkness.

Oh God, this is it, I thought; this time we're going to crash.

chapter 7

I OPENED MY EYES. Everything around me was completely black. I could stretch out my arms and legs without touching anything, but I sensed that I was closed in, as if I were in a box, a box buried deep underground. I couldn't tell which way was up, and which was down. For a moment I panicked, the fear sitting like an invisible animal on my chest, squeezing the breath out of me, clutching me around my neck, trying to throttle me. I struggled against it, crying out for it to stop, to let me live, but as I did its weight grew heavier on my chest and its hands grew tighter around my throat. As my breath grew shorter, I began to feel dizzy, and little by little, my resistance began to fail. I thought, it would be so much easier now to stop fighting any more, to give up. Then I heard something far away in the distance, a voice calling out to me, very faintly. I listened for a moment and heard the voice, a man's voice, calling my name. Someone was coming for me, coming to find me. I just had to stay alive until he got here.

I took a deep breath in and then breathed out slowly, the way Rob had taught me. As I did, the hands around my throat seemed to loosen, and the weight on my chest grew lighter, leaving a sharp pain there instead. Then I heard voices above me, the clatter of boots and a spade, and someone was scraping the earth off me, pulling me up, and shaking me by the shoulders. The breath flooded back into my body and the darkness fell away. I woke up.

'Susannah!'

I was staring into Jason's face. He was as white as a sheet. I blinked at him.

'What's the matter?' He was holding me by the shoulders and shaking me.

'Er...' I couldn't think of anything to say.

He took his hands away from my shoulders and breathed a sigh of relief.

'Umm... Are you OK?' I said.

For a moment he looked angry, but then he started laughing instead.

'God, Susie, you gave me a fright.'

'What?' I said. 'What happened?'

He stopped laughing, and looked at me intently, suddenly serious.

'Don't you know? Can't you remember?'

'Remember what?'

'Susie, you were screaming your head off. You woke me up and I watched you lying there, trying to think what I should do, so then I started shaking you, and then you opened your eyes.'

The dream came back to me, but I didn't want to think about it now I was awake.

'Weird, isn't it,' I said. 'Anyway, it doesn't matter, I feel fine now.'

'Bloody weird,' said Jason.

For a moment I felt embarrassed, and then afraid. What if Jason gave me the push now he thought I was a weirdo? What if Rob did as well? Maybe I wasn't a free spirit and a wanderer and a philosopher like Nietzsche, with a secret destiny and a task to do. Maybe I was just a lonely freak like Dennis, screaming myself awake in the mornings. Maybe one day I'd be left down there for ever in my dreams, buried alive, and no one would call me and come and get me out, and the air would run out and I'd suffocate and never wake up again.

'I think you should see a doctor,' said Jason.

'Why?' I said. 'Honestly, I'm fine, Jason.'

'Susie.' He looked serious. 'You're damn well going to the doctor. Or else. I can't have you making this kind of racket when you wake up in the mornings. I've heard you do it before, but never as loud as this. Have you got one?'

'A doctor? There's probably one on campus, I suppose,' I said.

'Well, make an appointment today, OK?'

I thought about it. 'What am I going to say, though? Doctor, doctor, I can't wake up in the mornings? It sounds like one of those jokes: *Doctor, doctor, I feel like a pair of curtains. Well, pull yourself together.* He'll think I'm an idiot. I can't, it's too embarrassing.'

'Just tell him you scream when you wake up in the mornings. I'm sure they can give you something for it. Some kind of downers, mandies maybe. Get some for me as well.' He laughed, but he looked worried.

Jason told me to stay in bed while he went off and got a thermometer and took my temperature, which turned out to be normal. Then he ran me a bath, and while it was running we had a quick screw. I could hear the bath filling up, but I wasn't worried it would overflow because the hot water came out very slowly, so slowly that it was often almost cold by the time you got into the bath. And anyway, these days sex never took very long with Jason.

When I'd first met him we'd gone on for hours. He'd wanted to try out all sorts of things I'd never done before: from behind, sitting backwards on top of him, standing up against the wall, slithering about in the bath, dripping wet, or fully clothed, half clothed, wearing kinky underwear, and so on. Jason had obviously been with a lot of women, and he knew exactly what he wanted and how to get it. I'd never had a boyfriend like that before: in Swansea it had all been pretty straightforward: a kiss here, a fumble there, maybe going the whole hog once or twice before you got engaged.

It was a lot more of a blast being with Jason. I didn't really know why he fancied me so much, but he told me he liked my boyish body, and that seemed enough. There was usually something that turned me on during these sessions, but I wouldn't do anything about it, I'd just store it up in my mind and let him carry on and do whatever he wanted until he came, and then I'd think about it and rub myself up against him until I came. We never kissed each other during sex, or talked to each other. After a while he started wanting to try other things, like doing it up the arse, but I wasn't very keen, and I think it was then that he started to lose interest.

And I suppose I did too. Once the initial thrill wore off, I began to notice that Jason never tried to find out what turned me on, only what excited him, and I was getting fed up with it. I wanted more from him. We didn't discuss it, but lately, we hardly ever had sex, and when we did it had become a bit of a routine, something we both wanted to get over with as quickly as possible.

This time, it was over in seconds. Afterwards I got straight out of bed and got into the bath, while he went off to make a cup of tea. When he came into the bathroom, he was wearing his forties' silk dressing gown, which was black with dark green spots on it, and a pair of burgundy leather slippers. The colours set off his pale skin and blond hair, and he looked handsome and distinguished as he sat down on a cane chair in the corner, lighting a cigarette.

'I've got a surprise for you, Susie Q,' he said.

He took a necklace out of his pocket and handed it to me. I held it in the palm of my hand and looked at it. It was made of small amber beads, each one a slightly different colour, and in between each of the amber beads were some even smaller ivory beads. At the back was an ivory clasp shaped like a tiny flower.

'It's beautiful, Jason,' I said. 'Thanks.'

He came over and put the necklace around my neck, fixing the clasp at the back. Then he kissed my neck.

'Well, we're celebrating, you know,' he said, as he nuzzled my ear. Now that I was safely in the bath he seemed very affectionate.

'Celebrating what?' I said. 'Pass me a towel.'

I thought perhaps if I got out, he'd carry on cuddling up to me, but as he handed me the towel, he went back to sit in the chair. So I wrapped the towel around me, and went over to the basin to clean my teeth, admiring my new necklace in the mirror as I did.

'Look at this,' he said.

I turned round as he drew a small box out of his dressing-gown pocket. I walked over and perched on the edge of the bath to have a closer look, and as I bent forward the towel opened. Jason didn't seem to notice.

The box was small and round and made of ebony, with curly lettering on it picked out in white, shiny stones.

'*Dents de lait*,' I read. 'Milk teeth?'

I looked up at Jason. He nodded. His smile was wide. 'And look at this.'

He pressed a little button on the side of the box and it sprang open. Inside, there was a threadbare cushion of black silk. Laid on the silk were two tiny, blackened baby teeth. Above them, inscribed on the lid of the box, were two letters, C.A., and beside these a date: 1796.

'Who's C.A.?' I asked.

'Princess Charlotte Augusta of Wales, daughter of the Prince Regent. The guy who built the pavilion. Those are her teeth. That's what I think, anyway.'

I looked at the little black teeth. I couldn't decide whether they were sweet or disgusting. I put my hand out to pick one of them up, but Jason gripped my wrist, a bit more tightly than he needed to.

'Don't touch,' he said quietly.

Then he closed the box and slipped it back into his pocket, patting it as he did.

'Is it valuable?' I asked.

Jason laughed. 'Just a bit, Susie. Just a bit.'

'How much?'

'Fifty grand, at least.' He laughed again. Then he got up from the chair and hugged me. The towel fell off as he did, but he just picked it up off the floor and started drying the ends of my hair, which were wet from the bath.

'Susie, we're made for life, if I can pull this off I'll never have to work again. We can buy a house in Spain, get a yacht, sail the world... whatever we want.'

Buying a house in Spain sounded a bit bourgeois, I thought. But sailing the world on a yacht sounded OK.

'I'd have to finish my degree first,' I said.

Jason stopped drying my hair, wrapped the towel round me, and kissed me on the nose.

'You're priceless, Susie,' he said. 'Priceless.'

I walked into the bedroom, thinking about the tooth box. Jason often got excited about making a killing on one of his antiques, but I'd never seen him like this before. He'd never talked about Spain or yachts or sailing round the world before. I could tell this was different.

I started getting dressed, sitting on the bed. 'How much did you pay for it?'

Jason was dressing too, on the other side of the room. 'You won't believe this, Susie. Fifty quid. Fifty quid, and it's worth fifty grand. I can't believe my luck.'

'Where did you get it from?'

'That's the amazing thing. I was over at Bear's parents the other day, you know they've got this incredible place just behind Harrods on Cadogan Square, and I saw it there, stuffed in a glass cabinet in the nursery along with a lot of Victorian children's nonsense. I asked Lady Alicia if she could take it out so I could have a look, and when she handed it over I couldn't believe my eyes. It's definitely Regency, whether or not it's Princess Charlotte Augusta's, and the stones in the top are diamonds. So I offered Lady Alicia fifty quid on the spot, and she seemed happy enough with that. Told me to give the money to the butler.'

'But Jason, it's worth fifty grand. Didn't you tell her that?'

'Don't be stupid, of course I didn't.' Jason sounded irritable. 'You don't tell the person you're buying from how much you can make on the deal, do you? Anyway, I didn't find out until later exactly how much it was worth.'

'But they're friends, aren't they, Bear's parents? Surely you should tell them?'

Jason sighed. 'Susie, these people are absolutely loaded. The place is stuffed to the gunnels with antiques. They don't even know what they've got there. Fifty quid, fifty thousand quid, is nothing to them. They've got millions.'

'Yes, but even so...'

I turned round to look at Jason, who was winding a long brown and cream silk scarf round his neck.

'... I don't think it's right.' My voice trailed off, leaving a silence.

Jason ignored me. He finished dressing, putting on his jacket and adjusting his scarf in the mirror. Then he came over and sat on the bed next to me.

'Look, Susie,' he said, 'you don't understand. These people are shits. The whole time I was at school with Bear, they never came to visit him once. In the holidays, he'd go home and they would have gone off skiing somewhere, or to the Bahamas, leaving him with the servants. The poor kid never saw them. You know what he's like now. He needs looking after, and they still don't do a thing for him. Not a fucking thing. I don't owe them anything.'

He spoke quietly, but his voice was full of anger, and his eyes glittered as he looked into mine. I sensed it was time to let the subject drop.

Although it was Friday, Jason was heading back up to London that day to get the milk-teeth box valued. He wanted me to come with him, and maybe spend the weekend up there with Bear and Flick and everyone, but I said I couldn't, and that I had some things to do on campus that day. He drove me in and dropped me off, still in a state of excitement. I waved goodbye as he roared away in the Morgan, hoping none of my friends would see me, and then walked up towards the European Common Room.

On the way through campus I bumped into Cassie, and we stopped off at the crypt for a coffee. Once we got in there we realised they didn't do coffee, and you weren't allowed to smoke unless it was a joint, so we bought a couple of overpriced Red Zingers instead and settled down on the cushions, which stank of patchouli oil and joss sticks. We talked for a bit about the lecture and Feyerabend and Fiona, and then Cassie said she thought she recognised the girl behind the counter. There was a rumour going round that she wrote a column in a soft porn magazine called *Knave* under the name Lucy Valentine and that she was looking for someone else to take over now she was in her final year.

'Don't be ridiculous,' I said, glancing over at the girl. She was thin and tall with pale skin and lank, mousy hair, and she was wearing a baggy smock made of orange sacking. 'She can't be Lucy Valentine.'

'You'd be surprised,' said Cass. 'You can do anyone up for a photo and they'll look OK. It's the writing that's not so easy. You've got to have a talent for it.'

'But she's a Buddhist,' I said. 'You can't be a Buddhist and write a porn column.'

'Course you can,' Cassie replied. 'This lot are Bhagwans. They're all breadheads into tantric sex. They've got a new book out called *From Sex to Superconsciousness*, Taylor told me about it.'

'OK,' I said. 'But I still don't think that's her. And anyway, you're not thinking of taking the job, are you?'

'I don't know. The money's quite good. I mean, if they keep the photo of her at the top, who'd be any the wiser?'

I thought for a moment. 'I wouldn't if I were you. They'll

probably want a picture of you and then one of the brethren will see it and you'll be excommunicated.'

She laughed. 'Fair enough. But what if I wore a wig and called myself, I don't know, Mahogany Vixen or something...'

'That's terrible.'

'All right, Cleopatra Brown, then, or Melodica Jones.'

'Cass, there's something I need to talk to you about,' I interrupted. 'It's important.'

Cassie looked at me, surprised. 'Oh. Sorry. I was just...'

'Sorry, it's not your fault. I've just got a lot on my mind, that's all.'

'What's the matter?'

I picked up my tea and blew on it. It was still too hot to drink, so I put it down again.

'You know I'm going out with Jason?'

Cassie nodded.

'Well, I'm thinking of going out with someone else as well... I mean, instead.'

'Who is it?'

'This guy Rob. He's in my tutorial.'

'Have I met him?'

'Maybe. He's got kind of darkish hair and he wears a holey jumper...'

'Oh, I know the one. I think I've seen you with him on campus. Quite young, not bad looking.'

'Yes, well anyway, I'm thinking of splitting up with Jason and going out with him.'

'Have you...?'

Cassie tilted her head to one side and looked at me.

'Yes, we have. Once. But that's not what it's all about really. I just seem to have a lot more in common with him than I do with Jason. We're both into philosophy and...' I thought of the John Martyn gig. 'And music and everything. It's more of a laugh than with Jason.'

Cassie sipped her tea. 'Of course it is,' she said. 'It's always like that at the beginning.'

'He's really nice, Cass. It's not just a passing thing, I really like him. And he seems to be into me.'

'OK,' said Cassie. 'But that's not the point, is it?'

I didn't reply.

'Look, Susannah,' she went on, 'you've slept with this guy once. You don't have to leave Jason just because of that. Wait and see how it pans out.'

'But what if Jason finds out? He'll be so upset. He's incredibly jealous of me.'

'Just be careful, that's all. And I wouldn't worry too much about him, he's probably doing exactly the same thing behind your back.'

'Do you think so?'

'Well, of course. Everybody is, aren't they.'

I was about to say, 'Are they?' but I stopped myself and tried a different tack.

'But I'm not getting on very well with Jason,' I said. 'We hardly ever... you know.'

I picked up my tea and took a gulp. It burnt my tongue and the roof of my mouth.

'Is it him who doesn't want to, or you?' Cassie asked, tilting her head to one side again.

'Both really,' I said, but as I did I realised it was mostly him.

'Well, that's the way it is, Suse. It always gets boring after a while, and you have to start looking around. But there's no need to burn your boats. Stick with Jason, he's got a lot going for him. And keep Rob on the side, that's my advice.'

I waited for her to start talking about her own romantic complications with her boyfriend and the married tutor, but she didn't. Instead she finished her tea, set the cup down on the table, and asked, 'What are you doing tonight?'

'Not sure. Jason wants me to go up to London for the weekend, but I don't really fancy it. His bitchy sister is going to be there.'

'Well, why don't you come out with us instead?'

'Who's us?' I asked.

'Me and Fiona.'

'Where are you going?'

'Down to the Concorde. Girls' night out. D'you fancy coming along?'

'What's the Concorde?' I asked, feeling a bit of a fool for not knowing.

'It's a disco in town, just by the Dolphinarium on the seafront. It's a gas.'

Cassie had surprised me again. I'd never come across any students before who went out dancing in discos. Most people I knew stayed in at night and sat cross-legged on the floor, smoking joints and drinking cups of tea and listening to King Crimson records. The idea of a girls' night out was weird as well.

'Well, I don't know…'

'Oh, come on, it's just a bit of a laugh.'

I didn't have anything planned that night, and it did sound like a bit of a laugh. I needed a break from worrying about Jason, Rob, and the whole ridiculous situation. The more I thought about it, the more I felt like going out with Cassie and Fiona that night.

'OK,' I said. 'Where shall I meet you then?'

'We'll be there about nine or so.' She put on a serious academic voice. 'Time to get down and shake your funky tailfeather, Susannah.' She laughed and leaned over to squeeze my arm. 'See you there, then. I've got to split now, I'm late for my lecture.'

Then she got up and left, waving briefly at Lucy Valentine, who looked up and waved back as she went past the counter.

chapter 8

I SAT IN THE CRYPT FOR A WHILE on my own, wondering what
to do. I was due to meet Rob in a couple of hours, but I still
hadn't decided what I was going to tell him.

I knew I really ought to say it was all off, that I had a
boyfriend, that our night together had just been a one-night
stand. But I didn't want to. I knew I couldn't leave Jason –
not yet, anyway – but I wanted to see where things led with
Rob. Perhaps Cassie had been right: perhaps it was OK to
string them both along until I made up my mind. It didn't
seem altogether fair to keep lying to Jason, but I couldn't see
what else I could do in the circumstances. It was his fault
really – he was so straight and possessive, he'd never
understood the way things were at Sussex. He'd never been
able to see that you had to make your own rules here. It
wasn't worth trying to explain it to him.

I watched Lucy Valentine for a while scraping plates of
refried beans into the bin and then I walked up to the library
to drop in some books. They were all on short loan, with a
yellow band stuck round the cover, but I'd had them for
weeks. When I handed them in, the librarian clicked her
tongue and fined me 75p, so I had to fill in a form to say I'd
been unable to return them before due to serious illness. After
that I got some more books out, went down to the basement,
got a coffee from the vending machine, lit a cigarette along
with everyone else in there, and sat reading in the thick smoke.

I only had a day left on *Human, All Too Human* so I decided to finish it off and hand it back on the way out before I got any more fines. I flicked through it, looking at some of the passages I'd marked. There were a few I still didn't really understand but liked the sound of, so I copied them out on a sheet of paper. Then I folded the paper, put it in my bag, and went upstairs to give the book in at the counter.

When it was time to meet Rob, I walked over to the Falmer Bar. I arrived ten minutes late, just to make sure he was there first. Immediately I came in, I saw him, over at a table by the window. Sitting opposite him, her back towards me, was the dark-haired girl I'd seen at the John Martyn gig. She was leaning towards him, her hand on his arm, talking to him animatedly. Something in the way she touched him told me they were lovers, or had been, or were going to be, and a pang of jealousy ran through me, as it had done that morning when I'd seen her coming up the street and letting herself into Rob's house. I thought of turning round and walking straight out of the bar, or going up to the vending machine and getting some cigarettes and pretending I hadn't seen them, but as I stood there, Rob caught my eye. Before I could turn away, he waved at me, so I had to go over and say hello.

When I got to the table, I didn't sit down. Rob was looking flustered.

'Hi...' he said. 'Hi. I... umm...'

The girl turned round to look at me.

'Beth, this is... Susannah.'

There was a silence.

'Susannah, this is Beth.'

'Hi,' I said.

Beth didn't reply. She slowly looked me up and down, from my feet to my head, nodded coldly, and turned back round to talk to Rob, touching his arm once more.

I felt as though I'd been punched in the stomach. Rob turned bright red and looked down at the floor as Beth chatted on to him, ignoring me. He seemed rooted to the spot, unable to move, to get up, get me a drink, and explain what was going on. I felt an idiot standing there, waiting for him to do something, to take the situation in hand, and then I began to feel anger creeping through my embarrassment. Without a word, I turned on my heel and walked out.

I headed up to the European Common Room, my heart thumping in my chest. I didn't know why I felt so upset. After all, I'd just been thinking about two-timing Rob. Why shouldn't he do the same to me? And why should it matter to me how his scrubber of a girlfriend treated me? But as I walked along, I started to feel shaky, and tears started to well up in my eyes, so I put my head down so that my hair fell over my face, and quickened my pace.

Once I got to the common room, I got a coffee, sat down by myself in a corner, and lit a cigarette, hoping to regain my composure. But the coffee made my heart beat faster and the cigarette gave me a tight feeling in my chest. Waves of panic started to come over me. I wondered whether perhaps Jason had been right, and I should see a doctor. I felt nauseous and dizzy, and I could feel the hairs on my scalp prickling. To steady myself, I took out one of the new books I'd got out of the library and began to read.

We knowers are unknown to ourselves, and for a good reason: how can we ever hope to find what we have never looked for?

Reading Nietzsche always seemed to calm me down. Even though a lot of what he wrote was disturbing, it seemed to relieve me. Most of the time, in the back of my mind, I felt as though something awful was happening but none of us were talking about it; Nietzsche did talk about it, and although it didn't change anything, at least he wasn't ignoring the situation like the rest of us. As I read, Dennis came into my mind, and I wondered how he was getting on. I thought about the dream I'd had that morning, and I wondered what it meant. I thought about the hairs prickling on my scalp, and the strange feeling I had when I woke up in the mornings, after screaming myself awake, and wondered what was wrong with me.

The sad truth is that we remain necessarily strangers to ourselves, we don't understand our own substance, we must mistake ourselves; the axiom, 'Each man is farthest from himself' will hold for us to all eternity. Of ourselves we are not knowers.

I carried on reading for an hour or so. During that time, nobody I knew came into the common room, so eventually I decided to walk over to East Slope and make an appointment to see the doctor. I got up and gathered my belongings, feeling better for having taken the decision. But just as I was about to leave, Rob came in.

He practically ran over to me, grabbed me by the arm, and started babbling at me.

'I'm sorry,' he said. 'I'm so sorry... I couldn't... It wasn't my fault, she just came in while I was waiting for you and sat down and started talking to me, and then... there you were and I... I couldn't...'

His face was flushed and he stammered as he talked. I was irritated by his intensity.

'Oh, it doesn't matter, Rob.' I tried to sound unconcerned.

'Yes, it does. It does. Just let me explain.'

'Well, actually, I'm just leaving. I've got to go over to East Slope.'

'I'll walk with you.'

'No, it's OK. I'd rather go on my own.' I was determined to make him suffer.

'Please, Susannah. Just stay here a minute and talk to me. Please.'

I sighed. 'Oh, all right then. But I haven't got long.'

We stayed in the common room for the rest of the afternoon, drinking coffees and smoking cigarettes and talking. We began by discussing *The Genealogy of Morals*, and then got on to Kierkegaard's *Fear and Trembling*, which was the next topic for Modern European Mind after Husserl. Eventually, the conversation turned to Beth, and he explained that he had been going out with her since the first year, but that after all this time they still hadn't got it together, as he put it. She was very uptight and possessive and unreasonable. Apparently, she wouldn't sleep with him unless they got engaged. Obviously, that was completely out of the question, so he'd tried to make her see sense, told her that he wasn't into marriage and that whole scene, but she still wouldn't accept it. He ended by saying that he was getting completely fed up with her now, and he wanted to ditch her and go out with me instead, because I seemed to be a more together, mature person than she was.

While he was talking I started to feel uncomfortable. No wonder Beth had looked me up and down like that, as though I was something the cat had brought in. I felt confused. I knew it was uncool to be uptight and possessive like her, but when he started comparing the two of us, and trying to flatter me by calling me a together, mature person, which almost made me laugh out loud, I felt vaguely guilty. On top of that, even though I hadn't made up my mind whether I wanted to go out with him or not, I was starting to fancy him again. He was sitting very close to me, and flashes of the night we'd spent together, and the time we'd kissed in the Meeting House, kept coming back to me. I realised I wasn't really listening to what he was saying as he talked to me, I was watching his lips moving, noticing the way he ran his hand through his hair, and the way his shirt opened a little at the neck when he raised his arm. At one point, he pressed my arm, and my stomach seemed to flip over. Every time his eyes met mine, I felt as though I was sinking, and I had to look away. I had a desperate urge to reach over and touch him, but somehow I stopped myself. I wasn't going to give in. Not just yet, anyway.

'I've got to get going, Rob,' I said, at last. It was beginning to get dark outside, and I hadn't done anything I'd meant to do that afternoon. It was too late to go to the doctor now, but that didn't really matter. I was feeling more normal now, apart from the bouts of lust.

'Where are you off to?' he asked.

'I've got a few things to do on campus.'

'And after that?'

'I'm meeting up with some friends in town.'

Going to discos wasn't the sort of thing you talked about at Sussex, so I didn't go into details.

'Oh.' He looked disappointed. 'I was hoping you'd come along to this meeting with me.'

He took a crumpled flyer out of his pocket. It had a picture of a man with short hair and glasses on it with a banner underneath saying 'Venceremos'.

'It's tonight in the Student Union. Everyone I know is going. It's going to be a big event, really exciting. We're going to sign a petition and send it to the government in Chile, and then we're going to organise a lecture strike here on campus.'

'Oh I'm sorry, Rob,' I said. 'But I've got to meet my friends. It's all arranged.'

I wanted to support Allende, and I knew Pinochet was a bastard, but I wasn't prepared to change my plans at the last minute just to suit Rob. And anyway, I wanted to go out dancing that night.

Rob sighed and looked down at his shoes.

'… But I tell you what,' I said. 'Why don't you come into town afterwards and we'll meet up?'

I was taking a risk. Jason would probably be staying in London, but I wasn't certain about that. And Rob would have to come down to the Concorde to meet me. But all in all, I reckoned it was a safe enough bet. If Jason phoned and said he was coming back, I could just tell Rob I had to get home at the end of the evening. And if Rob thought the Concorde was a bit straight, it didn't really matter. Right now he seemed keen enough on me not to mind where we met. And I was beginning to feel the same way about him.

chapter 9

I WAS GETTING READY TO GO OUT. First of all, I plaited my hair into sections and wet them in the basin. Then I dried them with Jason's hairdryer and combed them out so that my hair stood out in a big, soft, crimped halo around my head. I didn't have a lot of choice about what to wear: it always came down to jeans, platforms, and my old blue velvet jacket, with a selection of about four different kinds of T-shirt. This evening I chose a tight, plum-coloured Biba one, with little buttons all the way down the front. I left a few of them open at the top. Then I got out my pot of Biba foundation, which was a smooth, pale brown colour, and some plum-coloured Biba lipstick, and applied them carefully. When I looked in the mirror, I smiled. My skin and lips were dark and gleaming, and the yellow and white of the amber and ivory necklace Jason had given me shone out against them.

Just as I was about to leave the flat, Jason called.

'Hello, sweetie pie,' he said. He sounded in a good mood.

'Hi, Jason.' I was glad he'd called before I went out. Now I would know the lie of the land. 'How did you get on with the milk-teeth box?'

'Good news, Susie, the guy at Sotheby's thinks it could well have been a gift to Princess Charlotte Augusta, although he couldn't say for sure whether the Prince Regent or her grandfather gave it to her.'

'Does it matter?'

'No, not really. I mean, if it is a Regency piece, we're made. I've got a dealer who'll snap it up tomorrow. If it's not, I'll just have to search about a bit for someone else to buy it. Shouldn't take long.'

'Great,' I said.

There was a pause.

'Look, I'm going to have to stay up here tonight. I'm seeing my dealer tomorrow. Why don't you catch the train up? I'll meet you at the station.'

'Jason,' I said. 'It's nearly nine o'clock already. I can't. Anyway, I've already arranged to go out.'

'Where to?' There was a note of suspicion in his voice.

'The Concorde. Girls' night out.'

Girls' night out. It sounded good when I said it over the phone. I'd never have used such an expression to Rob, but it was the kind of thing Jason could relate to.

Jason laughed. 'Oh, that old dive. The one on the seafront?'

'That's the one,' I said. 'What's it like?'

'Never been there, not my scene at all. Who are you going with?'

'A couple of girls in my year. Cassie and Fiona.'

Jason didn't know Fiona, but he had met Cassie once or twice. I got the impression he'd liked her. Most people did.

'Well, make sure you behave yourselves. Don't run off with any wide boys. Be good, Susie Q. I'll miss you. Call you in the morning.'

He seemed quite keen all of a sudden. Only a few days ago, he hadn't bothered phoning me at all to let me know what he was doing. Some sixth sense must have told him that things had changed and that now I genuinely didn't mind how long he stayed away in London.

'Don't worry,' I said. 'I'll be fine. I can take care of myself.'

There was a pause. It didn't sound like the sort of thing I normally said to Jason. So I added, 'I'll miss you too.'

We said goodbye and rang off.

I tied a woollen scarf of Jason's round my neck, let myself out of the flat, and walked down to the seafront. The walk down to the Concorde was a long one, and a cold wind was blowing off the sea, but I didn't hurry. It was a beautiful clear night and the sky was dotted with bright stars and a crescent moon. As I walked along, I picked out the constellations and stars I knew, naming them to myself: the plough pointing to Polaris, the north star; the W shape of Cassiopeia; the three stars of Orion's belt; and, following the curve of the plough's handle, the bright star Arcturus. My father had taught me their names and how to find them when I was a child. It seemed a long time ago now.

When I got down to the West Pier, I began to worry that I wouldn't be able to find the club. Then I saw a queue of people lining up, and knew that that must be the place. I quickened my pace, but as I drew near, I had a sudden urge to turn round and run home the way I had come. Now I was almost there, I didn't feel like going out dancing after all. Somehow being on my own with just the ruined East Pier, the cold wind, the sea and the stars for company had felt more comforting and familiar than the human world of cars and people and clubs down here in town.

I resisted the urge to turn back, and joined the queue, wishing that I had arranged to meet Cassie and Fiona somewhere else beforehand, so that we could all have gone in together. It wasn't very often that I went out somewhere by myself, and I didn't like it. I felt self-conscious, as though everyone was looking at me and wondering why I was there on my own. I hoped to God Cassie and Fiona were inside, otherwise I'd have to buy a drink and sit down at a table by myself, which would look as though I'd just gone there to get picked up. As the queue inched along, I put my head down so that my hair fell forward over my face, wishing now that I hadn't crimped it. I could feel my nose going red in the cold night air. I thought, what with that and the hair, I'd walk in looking like a circus clown.

Once I got nearer the door, I could hear the music thumping inside. I hadn't realised they played reggae on Fridays at the Concorde. When I got to the cash desk, there was an old black man with a leather cap on taking the money and giving out tickets. He called me darling and told me I didn't have to pay as it was ladies' night. I was relieved in a way, because I hadn't been sure how much the drinks would cost and whether I had quite enough money, but I also felt uncomfortable, as though I'd done something underhand, got in under false pretences; as though something was expected of me – being a lady perhaps – that I wasn't going to deliver.

Inside, the club was still half empty. I looked around, and thought, no wonder Jason had never come here. It was a dark, low-ceilinged room with a small dance floor in the middle and a rickety-looking light show at the front, where a DJ was standing behind a pair of turntables, making the odd remark into a microphone as he put on records. Around the dance floor there were some scuffed plastic tables and cheap wooden chairs, with a bar to one side. I scanned the scene, wondering what I would do if Cassie and Fiona weren't there – whether I'd go over to the bar and get myself a drink, or sit down without a drink in case I wanted to leave suddenly, or just leave straight away – when to my relief I saw the pair of them sitting over in the corner near the DJ.

Cassie saw me too, and waved me over. She looked good. She was wearing a glittery black and gold halter-neck top, and had combed her hair out into an Afro that made my crimps look conventional. Fiona looked just the same as usual, except that her long brown hair was loose over her shoulders instead of tied back in a ponytail. She hadn't dressed up at all, unless you counted wearing a long navy-blue cardigan with a tie belt over her T-shirt and jeans.

'Hey, you made it,' said Cassie as I sat down. 'I thought you'd blown us out.'

'I nearly did,' I said. 'It's freezing out there. Is my nose red?'

Cassie peered at me. 'Can't see in here,' she said. 'I like your hair, though.'

'Yours looks great,' I said. 'And your top. Amazing.'

Fiona shot me a frosty look. I turned to her.

'Hi. All right?' I tried to think of something nice to say about her cardigan but couldn't.

Fiona rolled her eyes. 'God, you two. Clothes and hairstyles. It'll be boyfriends and periods next.'

Cassie laughed. 'Sorry, Fiona. But we're women's libbers at heart, you know.' She tossed her head. 'We're not ugly, we're not beautiful, we're angry!'

Fiona gave a sigh of frustration. 'It's all very well taking the piss,' she said. 'But if it wasn't for the women's liberation movement you wouldn't even be here.'

I wasn't quite sure what she meant by that, and I had a feeling she wasn't either, but I wasn't going to start an argument.

'And anyway Cass,' she continued. 'They're not women's libbers, they're feminists. You should know that.'

I could see Cassie was getting irritated, but she was trying not to show it. I changed the subject. 'Where's Rick?' I asked. Rick was Cassie's official boyfriend, the one she lived with in town.

'God, he wouldn't be seen dead in here,' she replied. 'Anyway, it's my night off.'

'And Taylor?'

John Taylor was Cassie's tutor, the one she was having an affair with.

'Don't be ridiculous, he'd have a heart attack.'

Taylor was only in his forties, but Cassie always talked about him as if he were an old-age pensioner.

'Anyway,' she continued, 'what's happened to Jason?'

'Jason's up in London as usual. And he wouldn't have come down anyway. Says it's not his kind of place.'

'Good,' said Cassie. 'That's the whole point of coming here. Leave the men behind, that's what I say.'

'You mean, pick up a few more,' said Fiona. There was a silence, and then we all laughed.

The dance floor was filling up and the DJ was starting to talk in rhyme over the records. I could see that Cassie was itching to dance. She went off and got us some drinks, put them down on the table, but didn't sit down again. Instead, she hovered by the table, moving in time to the music.

After a while, to my surprise, Fiona got up and did the same. At first, I was too self-conscious to join them, so I sat there on my own, smoking a cigarette and looking down at the table. But as I listened to the music, I started wanting to dance too. I wasn't very familiar with reggae, but the records the DJ was playing were better than anything I'd heard before. The rhythm was deep and repetitive, but with a bounce in it that made it hard to keep still, and above it the singer's voice floated, light and high:

It's hard for a man to live without a woman
And a woman needs a man to cling to…

Fiona didn't seem to notice how chauvinist the words were, and was dancing with her eyes closed, moving her body in a slow, oddly graceful way. Beside her, Cassie was moving fast, her eyes wide open, looking around her and seeming to relish every detail of what was going on. When she caught my eye, she raised her hands in the air and wiggled her bottom.

'Come on, Susannah,' she said.

I couldn't resist the urge to join them, so I got up and the three of us went out on to the floor. It was easy music to dance to. The DJ was pacing the tracks so that each one connected to the last but was slightly different in rhythm or style; the pulse of it sometimes quickened, sometimes slowed, but each time eventually settled into a relaxed groove.

As we danced, I seem to lose my sense of time and space.

I began to feel very light, as though my body weighed nothing and was just moving of its own accord; and although the room was airless and dark, it seemed to me that there was a cool breeze running through my hair, and that a soft ray of light was shining down on me from somewhere up above. I felt comforted and relieved, the way I did when I listened to John Martyn or read Nietzsche, only this time it was more intense. The thought ran through my head that there was nothing for me to worry about; that everything, in the end, would be all right, whatever I decided to do; that, somehow, I was blessed.

The free spirit again approaches life, slowly of course, almost recalcitrantly, almost suspiciously. It grows warmer around him again, yellower, as it were; feeling and fellow-feeling gain depth; mild breezes of all kinds pass over him...

We stayed out there for what seemed like hours, only nipping over to our table occasionally to take a swig of our drinks. As the evening wore on, the DJ started moving from records I'd never heard to pop hits like 'I Shot the Sheriff' and 'The Harder They Come'. More and more dancers took to the floor, until it was so hot and sweaty that we gave up and sat down.

I went over to the bar and got us all some glasses of water. When I came back, a group of African students had joined Cassie and Fiona at our table. Cassie introduced me to the one sitting next to me.

'Susannah, this is Tunde,' she said.

We smiled politely at each other. I could see immediately that we had nothing in common. He was not my type at all, and I could see that I wasn't his. He was tall and good looking, with beautiful blue-black skin, but his clothes were all wrong. He was dressed up to the nines, wearing a multicoloured shirt and tight white trousers, and when I looked down at his feet under the table I could see that he was wearing patent leather shoes with tassels on them. He looked like the type of guy who lived in a boarding house in

Eastbourne and was studying engineering at tech.

We couldn't think of anything to say to each other, and it was hard to talk over the noise, so eventually he asked me to dance. I downed most of the glass of water and went back out on to the floor, relieved that he hadn't tried to engage me in conversation. But I realised when we started dancing that I'd made a mistake.

I'd always assumed that all black people, especially Africans, were good dancers, but Tunde was the exception. He had no sense of rhythm whatsoever. It had been easy dancing with Cassie and Fiona, but with Tunde I had to concentrate, and every time I looked at him, I lost the beat. He was very tall, and when he danced, his limbs flailed about all over the place. Instead of keeping a low profile and bobbing quietly to the music, as most people without a sense of timing would do, he twirled about all over the dance floor, almost knocking people over. Several times he trod on my toes, and as his feet were large and heavy, it hurt.

As we danced, I was praying that the song would come to an end and I'd have an excuse to sit down, but it was one of those long, hypnotic tracks that seemed to go on for ever. And I could see that Tunde was just getting into his stride. His movements became more and more acrobatic, until, to my amazement, he began to do back flips, throwing his body backwards on to the floor and bouncing himself up on his hands. Staying on the dance floor with him became positively dangerous, so most of the dancers moved away, hovering on the edge and watching the display, until I was the only person left out there.

At that moment, Rob walked in. My heart sank. I'd wanted to look good when he arrived. I'd imagined that I'd be sitting with Cassie and Fiona, smoking and drinking and laughing and talking with them, so that I could just turn round nonchalantly and say hello when I saw him, and casually ask him to join us. I hadn't told the others about him, and I wanted them to think we'd just happened to bump into each other. Instead, when he arrived I was standing in the most conspicuous place possible, cowering on a deserted dance floor with a lunatic doing back flips beside me.

I didn't know what to do, so I did as little as possible. I waved briefly to Rob, then hung my head down and edged over to the side of the dance floor, moving slightly to the beat in the least obtrusive way that I could. As I did, a cheer went up from the crowd and I looked up to see Tunde flip forward on his hands and then backwards again. By now, people were crowding round the dance floor to see what was happening, and nobody was taking the slightest notice of me – least of all Tunde – so I took the opportunity to scuttle over to Rob.

When I reached him, I caught a whiff of the cold, fresh outside air on his clothes and hair and remembered when we had kissed in the Meeting House. Before I could stop myself, I took his hand and squeezed it.

'Hi,' I said.

He had a bemused look on his face. 'This is quite a place, isn't it.'

'Well, we just come down here for a bit of a laugh,' I said. 'Shall we get a drink?'

We went over to the bar and ordered some beers. The barman poured them out from a party four into plastic cups, and they tasted soapy and gassy, but we gulped them down anyway. We stayed by the bar for a while to get away from the noise.

'Do you come here often?' asked Rob.

Then he realised what he'd said and we both laughed.

'How did your meeting go?' I said.

'Great... it took hours, though, and in the end it wasn't quorate, so we couldn't send a message. But we did start organising a lecture strike.'

I wasn't in the mood to discuss politics, so I didn't ask what quorate meant, or why anyone would care if students stayed away from their lectures. I just wanted to dance. By now, the dancers were crowding back on to the floor and the music was changing again, from reggae to soul. I couldn't see Cassie and Fiona or the African students, so I assumed they must all be out there on the floor along with Tunde.

Rob put his arm round me. 'It's great to see you,' he said. Then he kissed me.

I felt faint as his tongue slid into my mouth. I slid mine into his, and for a moment everything – the club, the dancers, the music – seemed very far away.

When we broke apart, I said, 'Do you want to dance?'

We put our beers down and walked over to the dance floor. As we did, I had a moment of panic. What if he was a terrible dancer? But as it turned out, I didn't need to worry. Rob wasn't a great dancer, but he wasn't terrible. He moved steadily in time to the music with a look of concentration on his face, watching me and copying the way I moved, trying to keep time with my steps. And as he got used to the music, he got better. I could see he had potential.

Woman, take me in your arms
Rock your baby…

The DJ started playing a romantic ballad with a light, high swing to it and the dancers pulled each other close. I drew Rob towards me, and soon I could feel his body next to mine, moving slowly beside me.

There's nothing to it
Just say you want to do it…

As the singer's voice began to soar above the music, I put my arms under his jacket, held him around the waist, moved in closer, and kissed him.

Open up your heart
And let the loving start…

As I did, I thought I felt the cool breeze in my hair again, and I seemed to see the stream of light shining down on me once more.

He kissed me back, and then I said: 'Let's go.'

*

When we came into Rob's room, we pulled off our clothes, got into bed, and turned out the lights. There were no preliminaries. He got on top of me straight away and we lay still, locked together.

'Don't move,' he said.

'OK,' I said.

But after a few moments he gripped me tighter and I felt his body harden and then, with a frightened cry, he came.

He held on to me without moving until finally I pushed him off gently and wriggled out from underneath him.

'Sorry,' he said.

'Don't worry, I don't mind,' I said. I didn't really, but I wondered what I was letting myself in for here. Rob seemed very young, and I didn't like feeling that he didn't know how to do the things men were supposed to do. For a moment I wondered if I was making a mistake. Jason had always been so confident about sex, and I missed that. On the other hand, it was a novelty to be in bed with a man who was nervous of me, who cared about what I thought and how I felt.

'I'm really sorry,' he repeated. 'It's just that...'

I put my hand out and pushed his long hair back from his face.

'Yes?' I said, as gently as I could.

'I'm not... I'm not used to this sort of thing.'

I smiled. 'Well, you seemed pretty used to it the other night.'

He turned on his side, leaning on one elbow, and began to stroke my hair.

'I know,' he said. 'Funny, isn't it.'

My eyes were getting used to the dark and I could just about make out his face. I moved my hand over and cupped his jaw.

'Not very,' I said. We both laughed.

'The thing is, I haven't had very much experience. You know, with Beth...'

I said nothing, so he carried on.

'Well, she didn't... well, as you know... she did let me do some things, of course, but all that time I never...'

'I know, you told me,' I said. I was trying to help. I could see he was getting flustered.

'And there wasn't anyone else,' he continued. 'So I never really... until the other night.'

For a moment what he was saying didn't sink in. Then I got it.

'Oh,' I said. 'So you were a...'

I stopped. I didn't like to say the word 'virgin'. It was one of the uncoolest things you could be at Sussex.

'So that was the first time for you, Rob.' I spoke quietly. I was feeling guilty now. I remembered that I'd got up early that morning and left, assuming that for him it was just a one-night stand.

'Yes,' he said.

I couldn't see his expression in the dark, but I felt his body tense up. I realised that I'd hurt him, and could do so again now if I wanted to. It wasn't a feeling I liked.

'Well.' I said. I didn't quite know what to say, so I made a joke of it. 'You did a pretty good job as I remember. For a novice, that is.'

His body relaxed and he gave me a playful punch. We both started laughing.

'Yes, I think you've got quite a natural talent there,' I added.

He nuzzled my ear. 'But I didn't do so well tonight,' he said. 'I don't know why. I think it's because... I think I'm really into you, Susannah. It's making me nervous.'

There was a pause. I wondered whether I ought to say I was really into him too, just to be polite, and to make him feel better. I knew I was happy here in bed with him, much happier than I was with Jason, and that I wanted to make love with him again, as soon as possible, but I wasn't sure that counted as really being into him. And I was worried that he was getting a bit too keen. So I said nothing. Instead, I leaned over and kissed him, twining my arms and legs round his and running my hands over his smooth skin, feeling the muscles underneath it. As I did, I felt him get a hard-on again.

I couldn't help bursting out laughing. 'Blimey,' I said. 'That was quick. A world record.'

We both hugged each other, shaking with laughter, but before long we grew serious again as lust overcame us once more.

'Well, you know what they say,' I said as he began to work his way down my body. 'Practice makes perfect.'

chapter 10

Wake up, little Susie, wake up...

I was lying on a bed of warm, dry leaves in a dark wood. I could hear the patter of rain in the trees up above, and I knew that soon I would start to get wet, but for the moment the rain wasn't coming down on me. In the distance, I could hear a man's voice singing. I wanted to get up and follow it, but I was too tired to move, so I snuggled deeper into the leaves and tried to ignore it, but it came nearer and nearer until it seemed to be right in my ear.

I opened my eyes. Jason was leaning over me, holding two cups of steaming tea.

'Come on, Susie, time to get up.'

The room was dimly lit by one of the nymphs holding a glass ball, and the curtains were half open. Outside it was pitch black and you could hear the gentle, rhythmic sucking noise of the sea.

'But it's the middle of the night,' I said, closing my eyes again.

'Bermondsey,' he said. 'Don't you remember?'

'Oh God,' I said, my eyes still closed. I hadn't been up to Bermondsey with Jason for a while, and he'd been nagging me to go with him again, until last night I'd finally agreed.

'You'll feel better once you're up. Here.' He put a mug of tea down on the bedside table and sat down beside me.

I propped myself up on my elbow and glanced at the

alarm clock. It was half-past four.

'Sorry, Jason,' I said. 'I really don't think I can. I feel awful.'

'Why, what's the matter with you?' He sounded irritated.

'I don't know, I think I must be getting flu or something. I don't think I can get up.'

I shut my eyes and lay back down again. 'I'll probably be all right if I get a bit more sleep.'

I began to drift off, but Jason shook me by the shoulder.

'Come on,' he said. 'Let's get going.'

I took no notice, but then his fingers tightened and began to dig into my flesh.

'Ow,' I said. 'Stop it. It's not my fault if I don't feel well.'

'Just get up, you've got five minutes.'

I heard him walk out of the room, slamming the door as he went. I lay back in the bed for a moment, savouring the warmth of the sheets and the softness of the pillows beneath my head. I would have given anything to stay in bed, but I knew Jason was in a mood now, and I'd have to get up.

The room was cold and I dressed as quickly as I could, then picked up my mug of tea and went into the bathroom to clean my teeth. When I looked in the mirror, I saw that my hair was tangled and messy, but I couldn't be bothered to brush it. I couldn't face putting any make-up on at this time of the morning either, so I just splashed my face with water and wiped the sleep out of my eyes. I looked at myself again, bleary-eyed in the mirror. My skin looked a sickly yellow and there were bags under my eyes, but I was reasonably clean at least, and that would have to do.

I went out into the hallway to get my jacket, wrapping Jason's big woollen scarf around my neck. He was busy packing up the stuff for the market. He was mostly dealing in silver now, so there were only a few cardboard boxes and carrier bags, but they were pretty heavy to carry around. I helped him take it all down to the car, wishing I was still in bed as he slammed the front door shut and the cold wind from the sea whistled up Brunswick Square, stinging our eyes.

We got into the Morgan, but when Jason switched on the ignition it wouldn't start. I was secretly hoping that the car would break down and we could go back to bed, but Jason kept trying, revving the engine until eventually it spluttered into life and we pulled out of the square. The streets were deserted so he put his foot down and we sped along Western Avenue, the windows and doors rattling, and out on to the London Road.

Conversation wasn't easy in the Morgan at the best of times, because it was so noisy and draughty in there, but that day we didn't speak a word to each other all the way up to Bermondsey. I looked out of the window as the dark shadows of trees and fields sped by, hoping the sky would lighten as we drove along, but it was too early for that. By the time we got to the market, it was still dark, and my feet and hands were numb with cold.

Jason parked the car and we carried the bags and boxes over to his stall to set up. On the way, he said hello to practically everyone we met, while I nodded vaguely in the background, hoping they'd get on with it so we could put down our gear. When we'd got everything over to the stall, Jason began to lay it all out, unrolling the felt that he kept the silver in, and getting out the little toothbrush and tin of silver polish that he carried with him. When he'd finished, he went off to find us some coffees, wandering through the stalls chatting to people, and picking through the piles of stuff dumped on the tables to find the best bargains before the crowds came in.

I'd always liked coming to Bermondsey up to now. It was cold and dark and damp at that time of the morning, but there was a friendly, conspiratorial air among the stall-holders at the beginning of the day, as if we were in on something special that ordinary people wouldn't understand. Only that morning I began to realise I wasn't in on anything at all, and never had been. I was just Jason's girlfriend, the one who nodded at people in the background when he talked to them, and minded the stall while he went off round the market wheeling and dealing; the one who never knew how much anything cost and had to run off and find him whenever someone asked.

'Ah, that's a nice piece.'

Vivienne from the next-door stall was peering over her glasses at me. She had her eye on a silver sugar shaker that was lying half-unwrapped in a cardboard box behind the stall. It was pretty but entirely pointless, like everything else on our stall.

'Is Jason around?'

'No, he's getting us some coffees.'

'All right, dear, I'll talk to him later.'

'OK.'

There was a pause. 'Cold today, isn't it.'

'Yes.'

Another pause. 'You all right? You look a bit peaky.'

'I'm fine. Just a bit chilly, that's all.'

'That man's not looking after you properly. You need feeding up.'

Vivienne was a middle-aged woman with bouffant blonde hair and a large bosom, on which rested a gold chain attached to a pair of pince-nez spectacles. She was always well wrapped up against the cold, and today she'd brought a thermos of tea and a bag of sausage rolls with her for internal sustenance.

'Here, have one of these,' she said.

'Thanks.' I took one and swallowed it down. It was warm and greasy and delicious. I realised I was starving. I hoped Jason would remember to bring me something to eat when he came back with the coffees.

I picked up the tin of polish and the toothbrush, unwrapped a tarnished silver butter knife, and began to clean it. Then I found a salt cellar, a tiny blue glass bowl set in a silver dish on legs, and cleaned that too. Next I polished up a ceremonial spoon with an enamel flag set into the handle at the top, and after that a curly art nouveau picture frame with a broken hinge at the back. After a while, I stopped because my fingers were raw with cold and the silver polish was beginning to bite into them. By now, it was getting light. An hour had gone by, and Jason still hadn't come back.

To cheer myself up, I decided to read some Nietzsche, and fished in my bag for *The Genealogy of Morals*, but I couldn't find it. In the rush to leave the house I'd left it behind. I realised I was stranded now, getting colder and colder, without even a book to read to pass the time.

I began to sift through the contents of my bag, just for something to do, and eventually came across the folded piece of paper with the *Human, All Too Human* quotes on it. My hands were getting stiff from the cold, but I unfolded it and began to read, finding it hard to concentrate because I was in such a filthy temper.

There is a middle point on the way, which a man having such a fate cannot remember later without being moved: a pale, fine light and sunny happiness are characteristic of it, a feeling of birdlike freedom, birdlike perspective, birdlike arrogance, some third thing in which curiosity and a tender contempt are united.

Nietzsche's words floated towards me like a warm breeze.

No longer chained by hatred and love, one lives without Yes, without No, voluntarily near, voluntarily far, most preferably slipping away, avoiding, fluttering on, gone again, flying upward again.

I stopped reading, closed my eyes and sighed. What was the matter with me? What was I doing, sitting here in the freezing cold like a fool, waiting for Jason to come back to me? What had become of me? I'd chained myself to him, allowed him to control my every move. But it didn't have to be like that. In reality, I was as free as a bird.

'Vivienne?' I said, getting up.

Vivienne was reading the newspaper, drinking milky tea from her thermos cap and munching her way through the last of the sausage rolls. She took off her pince-nez and looked over at me.

'Mmm?'

'Could you mind the stall for me for a minute?'

'Of course, dear.' She went back to her paper.

I set off through the market, thrusting my hands into my pockets to warm them up. As I walked along, my head down, I caught sight of a cardboard box sitting in a puddle on the ground, underneath a stall. It was full of bundles of letters in a neat hand, tied up with faded ribbon. All the ink had run where the paper had got wet. Next to it, lying open in the gutter, was a woman's purse, the leather cracked and stained, and inside it an old-fashioned powder compact and a lipstick. I looked away. I realised I hated this place. Here was the detritus of people's lives, on sale for a pittance. I couldn't stand the sight of all these private objects that had once been kept carefully on dressers and tucked away in drawers, now tipped out on tables and on pavements for scavengers to rummage through. I promised myself never to come up to Bermondsey with Jason again.

As I wandered through the stalls, I saw a van with an open-front hatch in the distance and walked towards it to see if it was serving coffees. As I came near, I saw that it was, and that a few people were clustered around it, leaning against the stalls and talking. One of them was Jason. He was deep in discussion with another antique dealer, a well-dressed man older than himself wearing a grey cashmere coat and a red scarf. Neither of them noticed me as I walked by. I joined the queue to get a coffee, ordering myself a bacon sandwich as well. While I was waiting, Jason caught sight of me and waved me over, but I turned away, ignoring him, and looked in the opposite direction, sipping my coffee. When the sandwich was ready, I picked it up, paid for it and walked on without giving him a backward glance.

I wandered aimlessly around the market for a bit longer, eating my sandwich and drinking my coffee. After a while, I began to feel better, so I headed back to the stall. When I got there, Jason was waiting.

'Where the hell have you been?' he asked.

Vivienne looked up from her paper.

'Just went to get something to eat,' I said, as evenly as I could.

A customer came up as I came round to the back of the stall. He talked to her for a bit and then, when she'd gone, turned to me.

'I thought I told you not to leave the stall.' He spoke in a low voice so Vivienne couldn't hear.

'I thought you said you were going to get some coffees.'

'I was, but...'

Vivienne looked up again.

'I'll talk to you later,' Jason said as another customer came up.

'Fine.'

We said nothing more to each other all morning. When the market was over we packed up our things in silence, said goodbye to Vivienne, and walked back to the car carrying the boxes and bags. It was only once we were sitting inside with the engine running that Jason spoke to me.

'Don't you ever do that again,' he said, staring straight ahead.

I looked out through the windscreen. It had two dirty arcs on it from the windscreen wipers.

'I'm sorry,' I said, 'but I was freezing. And you were gone for hours...'

'I don't mean leaving the stall,' he said. 'Though that was bad enough. I didn't want Vivienne to see that shaker.'

'Why not?'

'Never you mind. What I'm talking about is the way you cut me dead while I was talking to Dalton.'

'Who's Dalton?'

A gust of wind blew up outside, making a moaning noise around the car.

'He just happens to be the guy who's interested in the milk-teeth box, that's all.'

'Well, I'm sorry,' I said, 'but I didn't see you. Where were you standing?'

Jason leaned over and gripped my arm. 'Don't fucking lie to me,' he said. 'You saw me and I saw you. I told Dalton you were my girlfriend and then I waved at you to come over but you ignored me. I felt a bloody idiot.'

'Well, I don't see why it matters so much.' I pushed his hand away and gave him a light slap on the arm as I did.

The next thing I knew was that Jason's arm flew out, banging me hard across the shoulder. I gasped in shock, putting my hand up in front of my face and cowering behind it as he pulled back his arm, but then he lowered his hand into his lap.

The wind began to blow harder, rocking the car. We both stared out of the windscreen for a few moments before Jason leaned forward and switched on the ignition. I noticed his hands were shaking.

'I'm sorry,' he said. 'I shouldn't have done that.'

I didn't say anything.

'It's just that this deal is so important to me,' he went on. 'You don't seem to understand what's going on. This is my big break.'

There was a long silence and then he turned to me. His face looked pinched from the cold, or from worry.

'What's the matter, Susie? You don't seem to be interested in the business any more. What's going on?'

I felt like asking him whether he'd ever taken the slightest interest in my business, philosophy, or ever would, but I didn't dare.

'Nothing,' I said. 'I'm just tired, that's all. I've got a lot of work on at the moment.'

Jason turned his head and smiled at me. 'You're a funny

kid,' he said, revving up the engine and pulling out into the traffic.

'Lots of essays to write, eh?' he continued, as the car picked up speed. 'Never mind, you'll get them done. You're a brainy girl.'

He was trying to be nice, but there was an air of false bravado in the way he spoke. We slowed down as the traffic came to a halt.

'Where do you want to go?' he said.

'I've got to get back to Sussex,' I said. 'Can you drop me off at a station somewhere?'

He glanced nervously over at me as he drove along. 'OK,' he said. 'If you're sure you have to get back. I was thinking we could stay up here for a few days with Bear.'

'I can't,' I said. 'I've got a lecture today.'

We didn't say much else on the way to the station, but whenever he stopped at traffic lights, he put his hand on my shoulder and rubbed it, and once he put his arm round me and burrowed his head into my hair. The traffic was heavy and the journey seemed to go on for hours, but eventually we came to the station and he parked alongside it to let me out. Before I got out, he leaned over to me and kissed me.

'I'm sorry, baby,' he said. 'I really am.'

'When are you getting back to Brighton?' I said, ignoring his apology.

'Later tonight, probably,' he replied. 'If you're staying down.'

'Yes, but what time?'

He looked at me, his eyes narrowing.

'Why?'

'No reason. I just like to know when you're coming home, that's all.'

'Hmm.' He looked thoughtful. 'Well, I'm not sure yet. But it'll probably be pretty late. Don't wait up for me.'

'OK.' I leaned over and pecked him on the cheek. 'I won't. Bye.'

He caught me under the chin and kissed me again, this time on the lips. 'Bye, Susie Q. Be good. See you later.'

I got out of the car and stood in the wind, watching as Jason roared off into the traffic. I was shivering with cold, but I waited until the yellow Morgan disappeared out of sight. Then I turned and headed into the station to catch my train.

chapter 11

I'D ARRANGED TO MEET ROB in the lobby of the Student Union hall on campus, but by the time I got there the meeting was in full swing. Rob was standing by the door at the back of the hall, looking intently at the stage, holding a pile of leaflets, so I went over and stood beside him.

'Sorry I'm late.'

'Shh,' he said, without turning his head. 'We're about to take a vote.'

I looked around. The hall was packed, and people were moving about noisily at the front. On the platform was a trestle table with a row of blokes sitting at it, smoking and drinking beer and shuffling bits of paper around. They were all dressed identically, in donkey jackets, and all of them had Zapata moustaches and black-rimmed glasses. In the middle of the row, standing up, was the leader of the Student Union, Kit Kelly, a tall, imposing figure with long, wavy hair and broad shoulders, wearing a black leather jacket. I'd seen him many times before on campus, striding purposefully around in knee-high bikers' boots with buckles up the sides.

I couldn't make out exactly what was going on, but Kelly said something and there was a general booing, and then everyone put their hands up and said 'Aye' and there was a loud cheer. Immediately afterwards, the meeting broke up and everyone began to head for the door. Rob pushed some of the leaflets into my hand and started to give the rest out as the students passed by, so I did the same. They were roneod sheets covered in purple ink, and I noticed there was purple ink on Rob's fingers as well. Most of the students shoved past me pretending not to see me, but a few of them took the leaflets without looking at me, glanced at them, and then threw them on the floor in the lobby outside.

We stood there handing out leaflets until everyone had gone. A cleaning lady appeared in the lobby with a black plastic bag and began to pick up the leaflets that had been thrown on the floor, putting them into the bag. After that she walked round the hall, clearing away glasses of beer and plastic cups of coffee with cigarette ends swilling about in them, tipping the liquid into a bucket as she went. A few moments later, a man with a broom came in and began to sweep the hall, and they both started grumbling about the mess.

'OK, let's split,' said Rob, dumping the rest of his leaflets on the floor by the door.

I glanced over at the cleaners, who were glaring at us.

'Shouldn't we put them in a bin somewhere?'

Rob seemed not to hear me. 'I need a drink, let's get down to the bar.'

I ignored the cleaners, pretending not to notice Rob's leaflets on the floor, but I hung on to my pile as we went down the stairs and threw them in a bin outside the Falmer Bar. I kept one of them to have a look at when we went into the bar, and sat down to read it while Rob was getting the drinks. It was headed 'The Chile Solidarity Campaign' and was urging students to boycott lectures in an effort to hasten the downfall of Augusto Pinochet and the demise of US capitalism.

'So what do you think?' he said when he came back. 'Not a bad job, eh?'

'But how's it going to help?' I said.

'How do you mean?'

'Well, why should Pinochet or the Chilean people care if we go to lectures or not? Why should anybody care?'

'We can only do what we can.' He sounded offended. 'I should have thought that was obvious. We can withdraw our labour power, it's the only weapon we have.'

'But it's not as though we're driving trains, is it?' I was trying to be polite. I knew he had just spent hours copying the leaflets. 'Nobody's really going to suffer if we stay home, are they? The lecturers will still get paid if we don't go to lectures. The only people who will miss out will be us.'

Rob grimaced. I realised he hadn't kissed me hello yet, or put his arm around me as we walked along. He seemed to be holding himself at a distance from me, and not just because of my views on the Chile Solidarity Campaign.

'You're so bloody right wing,' he said. Then he added, 'Have you got any cigarettes?'

I'd run out, so we decided to pool our money to buy a pack of ten from the machine to share. As he walked over to get them, I watched him, mentally comparing him to Jason, and trying to find something about him that would put me off so that I could knock the relationship on the head and simplify my life. He was wearing a tatty brown jacket with his old unravelling jumper underneath, and a pair of jeans that had a crust of mud around the edge at the bottom. His hair was uncombed and his face was flushed from the heat in the bar, so that he looked younger than ever. But the set of his shoulders and the way he stood over the machine, resting his elbow on it as he put the money in the slot, made my stomach flip, and I realised there wasn't really anything I didn't like about the way he looked. He was completely different from Jason; so different that I couldn't see them as rivals, and in the end I gave up trying.

'Susannah?'

I looked up as someone tapped me on the shoulder. It was Fiona.

'Oh, hi,' I said.

She sat down on one of the stools next to me. 'Mind if I join you,' she said. It wasn't a question, so I didn't answer it.

She peered over at the leaflet. 'Oh, I didn't know you were into the campaign.' She sounded approving.

'Well, I'm just helping out a bit.'

'Good for you. It's time you got a bit more involved in campus life.'

I said nothing, wishing she would go away.

'Have you got shot of that creep you were living with in Brunswick Square yet?' she went on.

She was obviously in the mood for a chat and hadn't noticed that I wasn't.

Rob came back with the cigarettes, sat down, opened the packet, and offered them round. I dug out some matches and lit them. I was about to introduce Fiona to him, but it turned out that they already knew each other from the *Capital* Reading Group they'd both helped to set up on campus. They started arguing almost immediately about the theory of surplus value, and then Fiona began saying that state communism was just another form of male patriarchy, and Rob told her she was talking bollocks, and then three of Rob's friends came by and sat down and joined in the row, and soon there was a crowd around us, shouting and laughing and banging the table.

When Rob and his mates went off to get another round of drinks in, Fiona turned to me.

'So are you seeing Rob now?' she asked.

'Yes,' I said. 'Sort of.'

'What do you mean, sort of?'

'Well, it's early days.'

Fiona clicked her tongue. 'You mean you haven't got rid of the creep. I knew it.'

'Look,' I said. I didn't know why I felt I had to explain myself to her, but I did. 'It's just going to take me a while to sort out, that's all.'

'Well, I'd get on with it, if I were you. There are quite a

few people interested in Rob, you know. He's a great guy.'

At first I assumed that Fiona was referring to Beth, but when I looked at her, she looked quickly away, and I realised it was herself she was talking about.

'OK,' I said, trying not to sound irritated. 'I'll do my best. Thanks for the tip.'

We stayed in the Falmer Bar until closing time, and then six of us jammed ourselves into the A40 and Rob drove us back into Brighton, dropping Fiona and the others off at various points on the way. When we finally got back to the house in Hanover it was past midnight. We still hadn't eaten, but the kitchen was full of people, so we decided not to bother, and I headed straight up the stairs to Rob's room while he made us some tea. I took my boots off and lay down on the bed, resolving to stay awake, but soon I could feel myself drifting off. By the time he came up with the tea, I'd fallen fast asleep.

When I woke up again, I found myself in Rob's bed, with Rob asleep beside me. I realised that he must have tucked me into bed while I was asleep, then got in and fallen asleep himself. The hurricane lamp on the bedside table was flickering low. I looked at my watch: it was two o'clock in the morning.

'Rob,' I whispered.

There was no reply.

'Rob.' I shook him by the shoulder. 'I've got to go.'

Rob moved over towards me and put his arms round me. 'Mmm,' he said.

I sat up in bed. 'I said I'd get back tonight.'

Rob half opened his eyes. 'What?'

I swung my legs over the edge of the bed, picked up my jeans, pulled them on, and got out of bed to find my boots.

'What are you doing?' Rob was awake by now, looking confused.

'Sorry, I've got to get going.'

'But why? How are you going to get home?'

'I don't know,' I said. 'I'll walk, and if I see a taxi down on the Steine, I'll take it.'

'Have you got any money?'

'Well, not really, but I'll think of something.'

I found my socks, put them on and began to pull on my boots.

'Oh for God's sake.' Rob was waking up now, rubbing his hand over his forehead. 'If it's so bloody important, I'll drive you home. But you've got to sort this out. I've had enough.'

I came over and sat on the bed, relieved that he'd offered to give me a lift. I didn't have enough money for a taxi, and it would have taken me hours to walk all the way over to Brunswick Square from Hanover.

'Of course I will, Rob,' I said. I wasn't sure I meant it. I didn't really see why I had to decide just yet. I wanted to wait, as Cassie had told me to, and see how things panned out.

'But it's going to take time,' I went on. 'I can't just walk out on him like that. We've been together for, I don't know, ages now.'

Rob's face softened. 'OK, fair enough. But you've got to tell him... what's his name?'

'Jason.'

'Jason.' He said it slowly, as though trying to imagine what a person called Jason could possibly be like. 'You've got to tell him sooner or later.'

I knew I wasn't ready to tell Jason yet, but I wasn't sure why. There was a pause as I searched for something to say that would sound like an explanation. Eventually, I came up with a bit of philosophy.

'Have you read *Human, All Too Human*?'

I thought as it was Nietzsche, Rob might understand, but he just looked irritated.

'No,' he said. 'Not yet. What's that got to do with it?'

'Well, Nietzsche says that if you want to live as a free spirit, you can't be too attached to anyone or anything.

You've got to live your life as a wanderer. It's difficult, and lonely, but it's your task, your secret destiny. You can't be chained up to hatred and love like other people. You have to live like a bird, fluttering here and there, flying upward, without any certainties. You have to live without yes, without no...'

Rob gave an exasperated sigh. 'Stop talking bollocks, Susannah. You're just trying to wriggle out of making a decision.'

I felt my face flush.

'You're not being a free spirit,' he went on. 'You're just being a bloody coward.'

I knew there was something in what he said, but it wasn't the whole story. I was trying to find my freedom, in some way I couldn't explain, and I was hoping to find some kind of destiny for myself. I just hadn't been making a very good job of it so far.

'Oh really,' I said. 'Well if I'm such a coward, what about you, then? I suppose you've told Beth all about us?'

Rob looked away from me, towards the wall.

'Yes,' he said. 'Yes, as a matter of fact, I have.'

There was a pause as I took this in.

'She was really hurt,' he went on. 'I feel terrible about it.'

'Oh, Rob,' I said. 'I'm sorry...'

I moved up the bed towards him but he moved away from me, and got up quickly. He found his jeans and jumper and pulled them on, not looking at me. When he was dressed, he looked for his car keys, found them, and came over to sit beside me on the bed. The room was cold, and I was shivering. He took my hand.

'Look,' he said. His voice was quiet. 'I understand what you're getting at with Nietzsche, but you're wrong. He's wrong. We're human beings, not birds. We can't just fly about here and there as we please. We can't live between yes and no, or whatever it was you said. If we want to live as free spirits, we have to be completely honest with each other. So you've got to give me a straight answer, Susannah. I've done my bit. I've told Beth. And now you've got to tell Jason.'

I swallowed hard. 'OK,' I said. 'I'll try.'

He put his arm round me, squeezed my shoulder, and kissed me on the cheek.

'Come on,' he said. 'Let's get going.'

For a moment I thought of telling him I didn't want to go after all. I thought how nice it would be to get undressed, get back into bed with him, stay there until morning, and lie in bed together until lunchtime the next day, drinking tea and eating toast and listening to records and talking and making love. We'd never done that, and I wanted to. But I wasn't ready to make my decision, not quite yet. I wanted to live between yes and no for a little while longer.

'OK,' I said, burrowing my face into his hair. 'Take me home.'

chapter 12

SHE WAS A PRETTY CHILD of three, four, or so, with curly
blonde hair, round blue eyes and cupid's bow lips. She was
wearing a white dress with a blue sash round the middle and
a bit of lace at the neck. One of her chubby arms was raised,
and on her hand perched a day-old chick, which she was
gazing at adoringly.

Actually, when you looked at her closely, you could see
she wasn't pretty, exactly: her blue eyes were a little
bulbous, in fact, and beneath the rosebud overhang of her
upper lip her teeth stuck out slightly. But the overall impression was of a lively, bright child, full of energy and mischief,
a child who would have chattered a lot, and run around a
lot, and would have been hard to keep still for the portrait,
which I suppose must have been more about how the
painter thought of her than what he actually saw. I mean, it
would have been impossible to keep a kid that age sitting
there for hours like that, with her arm up in the air, perching
a chick on her hand, or even without the chick, which must
have been drawn in afterwards...

'Come on,' said Jason. 'I want to get up to the bedrooms.'

'OK,' I said. 'Sorry, I'm just...'

Jason came and stood beside me, putting his arm around
my waist. I was surprised. He hardly ever showed me any
affection in public. He'd brought me with him to the Royal
Pavilion that day, looking for something that would help

him find out who gave Princess Charlotte Augusta the milk-teeth box. Normally he wouldn't have thought of asking me along on this kind of trip, but now he seemed to want me with him all the time.

'Who's she?' he asked, looking at the painting.

'Princess Charlotte Augusta,' I said.

'Oh, right.' Jason didn't seem interested, which surprised me considering he had her teeth in a little box inside his jacket pocket. These days, he carried the milk-teeth box around with him wherever he went.

Some handwritten letters in a glass case beneath the portrait caught my eye.

'Oh, look...'

Jason sighed. 'Are you coming up with me or not?'

'Yes, of course,' I said, not turning my head. 'Just give me a minute... I'll see you up there, if you like.'

'No, it's OK, I'll wait with you.'

This wasn't the Jason I knew.

'I'll just be a sec, all right.' I still didn't turn my head. 'I just want to...'

I was already reading. For the moment, I'd forgotten about Jason.

My dear Hamy,
Only to tell you that the Prince Regent gives a magnificent ball on the 5th June. I have not been invited, nor do I know if I shall be or not. If I should not, it will make a great noise in the world, as the friends I have seen have repeated over and over again it is my duty to go there; it is proper that I should. Really, I do think it will be very hard if I am not asked...

'Look at this,' I said. 'It's a letter from Princess Charlotte to her governess. It's dated 1811, the year her father became Prince Regent. It must have been a celebration to mark the event, but he didn't invite her.'

Jason squeezed my shoulder.

'Come on,' he whispered.

'And here's another one, from her to the Prince.' I bent over to make out the words.

> My dearest father is always so kind and indulgent to me that
> I feel emboldened in troubling him with a few lines. It would
> be a very high gratification to me (if you should see no
> impropriety) to hear your Speech in the House of Lords, for
> it is a subject very interesting to all, particularly so to me, &
> therefore I feel extremely anxious to do so. If, however, you
> should, my dear father, find any objection to it or should
> disapprove, I shall give up all thoughts of it, perfectly
> satisfied that you have good reasons for denying me...

'She must have been about fifteen or sixteen when she wrote that, I suppose.' Jason was reading over my shoulder now, intrigued.

There were two other letters written by Princess Charlotte in the glass case, one to a friend saying her father had hardly spoken to her at the Eton Montem, whatever that was, 'and when he did his manner was so cold that it was very distressing'; and another to the same friend, upset at the departure of her mother, the Princess of Wales, who was leaving the country for good:

> I must say what goes most to my heart is the indifferent
> manner of taking leave of me... I feel so hurt at that being a
> leave-taking for God knows how long, or what events may
> occur before we meet again, or if ever she will return.

'Poor kid,' said Jason. 'What a bloody awful pair of parents.'

I raised my eyes to the portrait of the little girl. I felt sorry for her now, and yet you'd never have been able to tell from the painting that she was an unwanted child, conceived by a couple of people who had loathed each other, so much so that they couldn't bear the sight of her, and had locked her away with the servants since the day she was born. On the contrary, she seemed spirited, larger than life, rumbustious even, with her bold looks and chubby arms and flouncy white dress that you could see wouldn't have stayed clean for more than a minute. It may have been artist's licence that made the painter give her such an insouciant air, but I somehow felt that if she'd been mousy and miserable, he wouldn't have painted her like that – he would have made her good and sweet and well-behaved. He'd obviously taken to the child, you could tell that. He liked her. So there she was, bright, and blithe, and bouncing with life, despite the fact that her parents hadn't wanted her and that she was a complete embarrassment to them both.

Jason let out a laugh. 'Here's a bit about Ma and Pa's wedding night,' he said.

> After the ceremony, the bridegroom, though civil and gracious, was certainly unhappy; and as a proof of it, he manifestly had recourse to wine or spirits. This was borne out later by the bride, who declared that the Prince spent their wedding night on the floor, with his head in the grate. It was not till morning that sobriety returned sufficiently for him to perform the actions expected of him as a bridegroom.

I laughed too, and Jason put his arm round me. 'You were right, you know.'

'How do you mean?'

'Well, I should be looking at this kind of stuff as well. People, not just things. It all helps.'

Jason leaned over to kiss me on the cheek. I backed away a little, and as I did, I glanced over his shoulder and saw a group of people coming towards us. As they got closer, I realised that one of them was Rob.

My stomach turned over and the hairs began to prickle on my scalp.

'Come on,' I said, turning in the other direction. 'Let's go up to the bedrooms.'

'Wrong way,' said Jason. 'The stairs are over there.'

He pointed towards Rob. I hung back, not knowing what to do.

'Umm, I think I'll just nip off to the loo first...' I said. I bent my head down so that my hair fell forward, praying that somehow Rob wouldn't notice me as he walked past.

But it was too late. Rob had come face to face with us. There was no way I could pretend I hadn't seen him.

'Hi,' he said, stopping short. He looked tense. He had combed his hair and shaved, I noticed.

'Hi.' I could feel my face heating up. I hoped I wasn't blushing.

There was a pause, and then I said, 'Er, Jason, this is Rob.'

Jason nodded brusquely. Rob nodded back.

'Rob. Jason.' I swallowed hard.

A painful silence descended. Then the people who were with Rob came up and stopped too. We all stood around grinning politely at each other until Rob said, 'Susannah, my parents. My grandmother.'

He was mumbling now, looking down at his shoes.

His mother stepped forward and smiled at me. She was dark-haired, like Rob, but short and wide. His father hovered in the background, tall and thin and grey-haired, also intent on inspecting his shoes. The grandmother seemed uninterested in any of us, and instead looked up at the massive chandelier above our heads.

'Hi,' I said, addressing myself to his mother. 'I'm on Rob's course. Good to meet you.'

'Rose,' she said. 'I do have a name.' Then she smiled again. She had a sweet, warm smile.

I glanced at Rob, who was still looking down at his shoes. I tried to think of a way of wrapping the conversation up, but my mind seemed to have gone blank, so we stood there in silence again.

It was the grandmother who came to the rescue.

'Chinese,' she said.

'What?' said Rob. He sounded irritable.

'The chandelier. Chinese, dear. It must be. It's in the shape of a lotus blossom.'

'Actually, I don't think it is.' It was Jason who spoke. 'I think it was designed by an Englishman, Frederick Crace, in a Chinese style. It was a bit of a vogue at the time...'

Jason and the grandmother began to discuss the architecture of the Royal Pavilion, looking up and pointing at the chandelier as they did. Rob glanced at me. He didn't raise his eyebrows or roll his eyes, and neither did I, but there was something humorous and familiar and relieved in the look we gave each other, as if neither of us could believe that we were standing here listening to Jason and his grandmother deep in conversation about the shape of lotus blossoms. His mother must have noticed what passed between us, because when I looked at her again, she had a gentle, knowing expression on her face.

'Right, well we must be getting along now,' she said.

Rob's father immediately shuffled up beside her, eager to get away as soon as possible.

'Come on, Ma,' she continued, taking the grandmother's arm. 'We don't want to miss lunch, do we.' The grandmother looked confused for a minute, but let Rob's mother lead her away.

'Off we go. Nice to meet you, Susannah.' As she spoke, Rob's mother was already steering the family down the corridor.

Rob gave an audible sigh of relief as they walked away, and turned to me.

'See you, then.'

'See you.' I tried not to heave a sigh of relief too as he followed them.

As they disappeared round the corner, the grandmother turned and waved at Jason, who waved back at her.

'Nice old dear,' he said, as we made our way towards the

stairs. Then he stopped for a moment and looked at me, his head tilted to one side.

'Was that your little hippie boy, then?'

'Don't be ridiculous.'

I slowed down for a moment and then walked on. 'He's just a bloke on the course. I hardly know him.'

Jason fell into step beside me.

'Really?' There was a hint of sarcasm in his voice.

'Yes, really.' We began to climb the stairs.

'Well, he looked a bit gone on you.'

I decided that attack was the best form of defence.

'Well, maybe he is,' I said. 'Some people are, you know. There are probably loads of guys on campus who are madly in love with me. You're not the only pebble on the beach, matey.'

Jason laughed. We reached the top of the stairs and walked down the corridor towards the bedrooms.

Jason put his arm round me and squeezed my shoulder.

'OK, Susie. Point taken.' As he spoke, he was sliding his hand under my jacket, into the top of my jeans.

'Get off,' I said. 'For God's sake.' I giggled and pushed him away.

We stopped in front of one of the state bedrooms in Queen Victoria's apartments. It was cordoned off from the corridor by a red rope. The floor was covered in a richly decorated carpet and there was a beautiful, delicately patterned wallpaper on the walls, of birds with long beaks sitting on bamboo branches and flying between blossoming bushes. In the middle of the room was a huge four-poster bed, hung with opulent dark green silk curtains and a yellow silk bedcover, turned back to show striped green and white sheets. I wondered for a moment what it would be like if Jason pulled me onto the bed then and there, and we drew the curtains around us and made love in the dark, not making a sound, being careful not to disturb the draperies, with all the people filing past us and pointing at the decor of the room and Queen Victoria's bed in the middle of it.

'Wow,' said Jason, disturbing my reverie.

He let go of me and leaned over the rope. 'Just look at that wallpaper.'

He stepped forward as far as the rope would let him go, to take a closer look.

'It's hand-painted, you can tell.'

He had forgotten about me already.

'I just don't know if he fancies me any more, Cass.'

Cassie sighed, stubbed out her cigarette, and lit another one.

'Well, you've got Rob, haven't you? What does it matter? Just stay with Jason and get your kicks with Rob, or someone else, that's what I'd do.'

'Has this ever happened to you?' I asked.

Cass looked thoughtful. 'What, a bloke not fancying me? I can't remember, actually.'

She was lying, just to make me feel better.

'I bet it hasn't,' I said.

'Well, maybe not. But I don't see the problem. If a guy doesn't want to screw you, there are plenty of others who do. Just find someone you like and get on with it, Susannah.'

'The problem is, I kind of like Rob better, though.'

I could hear a whine creeping into my voice. 'But I can't seem to leave Jason, I don't know why.'

'Well, it's obvious, isn't it? Jason's a much better deal than Rob. You're doing the right thing. Just accept it and shut up about it.'

'Sorry. I'm sorry, I'll stop going on about it. But the thing is...'

Cassie interrupted me. 'Look, Faye Dunaway's just walked in. She's checking her pigeonhole.'

We were sitting by the window in the European Common Room, eating the cheese biscuits they sold at the coffee bar. I'd had about five packets already for lunch.

'D'you think she'll come over and say hello to us?' I asked.

'I doubt it. She'll probably get straight down to the library with her reading list.'

Faye Dunaway was the most beautiful girl on campus. She had a perfectly made-up face, long legs, and straight, shiny fair hair. She never spoke to anyone. She was rumoured to be a high-ranking diplomat's daughter, but no one really knew anything about her. She only came into campus to get her books and go to tutorials, and then disappeared again.

'Ooh look, there's Myron. He's just come in behind her.'

We started giggling like a couple of schoolgirls.

'Oh, he's seen her.'

'Look at him, he's gone all red in the face. He's probably wet himself.'

Cassie, Faye Dunaway and I had been in Maurice Myron's tutorial in our first year. I'd seen his name written up on the wall of the ladies' toilet the day I arrived at Sussex. He'd been top of a list headed 'Most sexist tutors on campus'. Naive as I was, I'd thought that sexist meant 'sexy', and when I was assigned to his tutorial, I'd been intrigued to meet him. But when he'd opened the door and ushered me in, I'd been taken aback. I'd spent the whole of the first tutorial looking at him and wondering how anyone could find this man in the slightest bit sexy. It wasn't that he was bad looking, although he was going bald and his skin was a bit leathery and his teeth were blackened from tobacco. It was just his manner: condescending, arrogant, yet somehow horribly unctuous, lecherous, and eager to please. After the tutorial, Cassie had invited me for coffee in the common room, and I'd told her about Myron's name on the list in the toilets, and she'd laughed and explained what sexist meant, and that was how we'd become friends.

'Turn round, Suse. Let's look as though we're talking

about periods. Otherwise he'll come over here.'

'OK.' I turned my back to them. 'What's happening now?'

'He's seen her. He's going over. She's pretending she hasn't seen him... He's asking her if she wants a coffee, I think. But she's not having any of it. Or is she... No. No, she's not going for it. He's slinking off now, back to the counter... God, he's looking our way, put your head down...'

Cassie and I bent our heads forward as if we were deep in discussion, holding our breath, and trying to suppress our laughter.

'Let me know when the coast is clear,' I said.

'He's getting his coffee... yup, he's on his way out. You can come up for air now.'

'That was a close one.' I turned my head round. 'I'm surprised he didn't come over here when he saw us. I thought he fancied the pants off you.'

'Well he doesn't any more,' said Cass, sitting back. 'Not since I broke his sink.'

'His sink?'

'Yes. I went to see him at the start of the first year because I wanted to change from Religious Studies to Philosophy. I'd only done Religious Studies to please my parents and get into Sussex, and the minute I got here, I was going to change. So I went and asked Myron about it, and he invited me round to his flat one evening to discuss it.'

'You must have been mad.'

'Well, I really wanted to get on the course. Anyway, I went round there, and he kept plying me with vodka. In the end I got so drunk I went into the bathroom and threw up in his sink, and then I tried to unblock it, and somehow while I was doing that it came unhinged from the wall, but I didn't tell him, I just went out and said I wasn't feeling well and could he get me a taxi home.'

'Did he try to jump on you or anything?'

'I don't think so, but I was so pissed I probably wouldn't have noticed. Anyway, he let me on the course after that, and nothing more was said.'

I was surprised she hadn't told me before. It was strange to think that when Cassie arrived at Sussex, only a year ago, she'd been as green as I was.

'D'you know what he put on my report at the end of the first term?' I said.

'What?'

'She is an elegant presence in the tutorial.'

'You're joking?'

'No, honestly.'

'You never mentioned it before.'

'Well, I was embarrassed about it,' I said. 'It made me feel stupid. As though I'd been sitting there batting my eyelashes all term instead of trying to get to grips with Schopenhauer's concept of the will.'

We munched on our cheese biscuits, going over the indignities of that first term in Myron's tutorial, until Cassie said she had to get going.

'I've got a rehearsal,' she said. 'I'm a backing singer in this new band this guy's formed on campus.'

'Oh really? What's it called?'

'Tripe Face Boogie.'

'Sounds awful. Can I join?'

'Yeah, course. Come down with me and we'll ask Paul.'

'Only joking, Cass. I'm not much of a singer. And I've got to meet Rob, anyway, in a minute.'

'Well, we'll be in the crypt if you change your mind.'

'OK. See you, then. Good luck.'

'*Ciao*, baby.'

Cassie stubbed her cigarette out, stood up, tossed her head, and walked off to join the band.

chapter 13

ROB AND I WERE LYING NAKED in Queen Victoria's bed, in the dark with the green silk curtains drawn all around us. Above us, golden tassels hung down from each of the corners of the four-poster bed. There was a quiet hum of voices outside us. We knew we couldn't make any noise or disturb the draperies. My heart was beating hard and I could feel that his was, too.

'Be quiet,' I said. 'Don't make a sound.'

The green and white striped linen sheets were damp and crumpled and our bodies against each other were slick with sweat. His hair was sticking to my face.

'Keep still,' I said. 'You'll make the bed creak. And don't kick the curtains.'

We started off slowly, moving gently, obeying my orders.

'No,' he whispered, his mouth close to my ear.

I was biting his earlobe to stop myself from crying out.

'Don't do that,' he said. He stopped moving. 'You'll make me come.'

'Sorry.'

'Think of something that will stop me.' There was a note of panic in his voice.

'Umm…' I couldn't think of anything.

'Get on with it. Quick.'

'Dennis?'

Rob let out a sigh of relief. 'OK. Keep going?'

'Harold Wilson.'

He started moving again. 'Go on.'

'How about... Angela Rippon.'

'Oh...' His face contorted in agony.

'For God's sake, you don't fancy Angela Rippon, do you?' I was hissing in his ear.

'Ahh... Don't move.'

I clicked my tongue in annoyance. That seemed to do the trick.

'Bad choice,' said Rob, calming down.

'But what about the way she rolls her "r"s when she says guerrillas?'

He wasn't listening. He was moving off again, slowly but surely. Before long, we were both clinging on to each other, trying not to cry out.

This time, the distraction came from outside.

'Hand-painted, you say?'

'Yes, every single bird, every single tree, every single blossom, in the whole room.'

'Gracious.'

'Incredible, isn't it?'

We stopped to listen. It was Jason and Rob's grandmother discussing the wallpaper.

'This is awful,' said Rob into my ear. 'I can't hold on any more.'

'Let me get on top of you, then.'

'You can't, you'll kick the curtain.'

'Just do as I say.'

I quietly manoeuvred us around until I was sitting on top of him. I braced one of my arms against the bedpost, and began to move slowly up and down. The golden tassel shook.

'Oh no, this is worse.' Rob was whimpering now.

'Shh. Listen,' I said. 'That'll help.'

Outside, we could hear Jason and the grandmother amid the hum of voices.

'Queen Victoria didn't really like it,' Jason was saying. 'She complained that she couldn't see the sea out of the bedroom window.'

'Some people are never satisfied,' Jason's grandmother replied.

We giggled. I went on moving, this time squeezing my eyes shut. I thought of Jason standing there outside the bed, cordoned off, and me in here with Rob, fucking in the darkness.

'Hold me tight round the waist. Quick,' I whispered.

I let myself fall forwards on to him.

'Harder. Much harder.'

He gripped me as tight as he could and I came, burrowing my head into his neck, my hair covering his face.

'I love you,' he said.

He turned to kiss me on the mouth, but I turned away.

'Have you come?' I asked.

'No.'

I said nothing, but manoeuvred myself back underneath him.

'OK,' I said when I was in position. 'Go.'

Rob launched himself at me, and suddenly he was in me, on me, all over me, biting my neck and grunting in my ear. I brought my legs up and locked them round his waist, willing him further into me, digging my fingers into his flesh as he moved faster and faster on top of me, until he cried out. This time I let him.

As he lay on top of me, I shut my eyes. Relief flooded my body. I remembered that night in the Concorde with him, when we were dancing and I thought I saw a light shining down on me, and felt a warm breeze running through my hair. Everything will be all right, I thought. It's going to be all right.

When I opened my eyes again, I was in Cassie's room on campus with Rob lying jammed up against me in the single bed. We had met up at the Falmer Bar, and then we'd gone to the Meeting House for a quiet chat, and then one thing had led to another, and I'd ended up bringing him here, to Cassie's room. I'd wanted it to be quick, but somehow we'd got carried away, and then I'd started fantasising about Queen Victoria's bed in the Royal Pavilion, and somehow the whole thing had taken up practically the whole afternoon. By now, it was getting dark.

'That was fantastic,' he said. 'The best fuck I've ever had.'

'Well, you haven't had that many,' I said.

Rob laughed.

'How was it for you?'

'Far out,' I said.

'No, seriously. How was it?'

'It was great. Really good. Honestly.'

'Was it the best orgasm you've ever had?'

'For God's sake, Rob, it's not a competition.'

'No, but was it?'

I thought about it. 'Yes, it probably was, I suppose.'

Rob looked disappointed. 'You don't sound very sure.'

'Well, I don't keep a league table, you know. Although if you want, I can start one.'

Rob laughed again, but then he grew serious. 'Was it better than…'

I knew what he was getting at. 'Yes, it was.'

'Really?'

'Yes, really.' There was a note of impatience in my voice.

'He didn't look like I thought he would.'

'Didn't he?'

'No, kind of older. Straighter. More of a man of the world.'

There was a silence.

'Your mother seemed nice,' I said, changing the subject.

'Is he better than me in bed, Susannah?' he said, changing it back.

I couldn't avoid the question.

'No,' I said. I was telling the truth, at least about my current sex life with Jason.

'He's more experienced, maybe... but I like it better with you.'

Rob smiled.

'I'm sorry,' he said. 'I don't mean to be nosey. It's just that when we... you know, you always seem... I don't know, far away. Not quite here, with me.'

'I was with you, Rob.' I didn't tell him I had been with him in Queen Victoria's bed, and that Jason and his grandmother had been within earshot, discussing the wallpaper. I didn't want him to think I was a pervert.

'I sometimes wonder if you're thinking about...'

'No. Really, I'm not.' It was true, I hadn't been in the bed with Jason. He had just been a bystander.

Rob sighed.

'You somehow seem, I don't know... miles away. Cut off from everything.'

I didn't reply.

'And it's not just when we're in bed,' he went on. 'It's all the time.'

'What do you mean, all the time?'

'I don't know. Whatever's going on, you always seem... sort of disconnected.'

Disconnected. The word made me think of a robot whose wiring had come loose. Was that how I seemed to him, to everyone? I'd tried to be normal, but people could see that I wasn't. They knew I was weird, that my brain was faulty. They knew about the dreams, about the screaming myself awake in the mornings. They knew I was like Dennis.

'Well, why do you want to go out with me then? If I'm so disconnected?'

Rob ignored my question. 'What's wrong, Susannah? Can't you tell me?'

'Oh not this again,' I said, my anger rising. 'I've told you, there's nothing...'

I stopped and then, to my surprise, I began to cry. Rob put his arms around me and held me close, stroking my hair as I sobbed into his chest.

'It's just... it's just...'

He said nothing, but carried on stroking my hair.

'Ever since my father died... I don't...'

I went on crying for what seemed like a long time, and then the tears began to subside. I wiped my face on his hair.

'I don't know,' I said. 'I can't explain it. I'm sorry, I just feel a bit distant from everything most of the time. It's really weird. I don't like it any more than you do.'

'You've lost your father, Suse. That's a big deal. It'll take you a while to get over it. Do you want to talk about it?'

'Not really,' I said. 'Not yet.'

'Well, you can, you know,' he said. 'Any time.'

'I know.'

'Is there anything I can do to help?'

The bed was tiny and I was lying beside him crammed up against the wall. I was getting a crick in my neck. I moved over so that I was lying on top of him.

'Well you could...'

I started kissing him, pressing up against him. He put his arms around my neck and pulled me down to him.

'Well, you could try and help me take my mind off it...'

'OK,' he said. 'I'll try.'

He pushed his tongue deep into my mouth, running his hands over my breasts. Then he moved his mouth down to them, pushing them together and biting and sucking each one in turn. I took his hand and guided it down so that he put his fingers inside me, first one, then two, and then three. Then he took me by the waist and pulled me up towards him, until his mouth was level with my fanny. I closed my eyes.

Just then, there was a knock at the door. We both froze.

The knock came again.

'Wait,' I whispered. 'They'll go away.'

I remembered that Cassie had a key to the room. As quietly as I could, I lay down on top of Rob and pulled the covers over us, in case she let herself in.

'Susie?'

It was Jason's voice.

We lay there in silence, listening. Rob still had a hard-on, I could feel it against my stomach. It didn't go down, even though I could see that his eyes were round with fear.

There was a sound of retreating footsteps and we both breathed a sigh of relief.

'Was that Jason?' he said.

'Yes,' I said. 'I don't know how he found out I was here. I didn't think he knew about Cassie's room.'

'D'you think he's gone?'

'Probably. But we'd better get our clothes on, just in case he comes back. Be as quiet as you can.'

We dressed in silence. I could see Rob trying to cram his penis into his underpants. His jeans were tight, and he had trouble getting them zipped up. I started giggling, and so did he. Then we heard the footsteps coming back, and held our breath.

Jason knocked again.

'Susie, are you in there?'

I tiptoed over to the window and opened it as quietly as I could. It was one of those big modern windows that opened with a handle from the bottom. We peered out. We were on the ground floor, and there was a grassy bank just underneath it. I nodded silently to Rob, who picked up his shoes and clambered through, making as little sound as he could. As I helped him climb out, I could feel his body trembling.

'Just coming,' I called. 'Hang on a minute.'

I closed the window and watched Rob running away over the grass in his bare feet, clutching his shoes. He looked silly, humiliated, like a character in a French farce. Even though I'd motioned to him to leave, there was something about him running off in that way that made me think less of him. I wished he'd stayed and confronted Jason. I wished they'd fought over me, and he'd won.

But he hadn't stayed, he didn't have the courage. He was too young, too green.

I walked over to the door and let Jason in.

MODULE 2

Martin Heidegger:
Being and Time

chapter 14

Father in heaven! When the thought of thee wakes in our hearts let it not awaken like a frightened bird that flies about in dismay, but like a child waking from its sleep with a heavenly smile...

I was sitting in the doctor's surgery reading for my next tutorial with Belham. Next on the list for Modern European Mind was Kierkegaard, so I'd got a book of his out of the library, but I couldn't seem to make any sense of it. It wasn't that the writing was difficult to understand, or boring; it was just that I couldn't concentrate. It was always the same these days. Every time I opened a book, I would feel so sleepy that I had to stop and either get up and do something like make a cup of tea, or lie down for a rest. It was the same with writing. I would begin to write a sentence, and then that feeling of torpor would wash over me, so that I couldn't collect my thoughts, and I would forget what it was that I had been trying to say. It had got so bad that I was falling behind with my essays, and in tutorials I couldn't seem to follow what was going on at all.

On top of that, the waking up in the morning business had got worse. I was screaming myself awake every morning now. Jason was really worried about it and had been on at me to go to the doctor for weeks, and Rob was convinced I was having some kind of mental breakdown. That was another thing: I still hadn't made my mind up about which one of them I was supposed to be going out with. I hadn't told Jason about Rob, though Rob knew all about Jason; and I'd told Rob that I was going to leave Jason any minute, though somehow I never did. My life had settled into a pattern now, whereby I spent a few nights a week over at Rob's house in Hanover, and the weekends with Jason at the flat in Brunswick Square or up in London at Bear's place. I felt as though I was living in two of Kuhn's incommensurable paradigms – two worlds that I travelled between, neither of them connected in any way to the other. Every time I was with Jason, my life with Rob seemed insignificant; and every time I was with Rob, Jason seemed unreal.

'Miss Jones,' said the receptionist, 'Doctor Morgan will see you now.'

I stuffed the Kierkegaard into my bag, got up and walked down the corridor. I still hadn't quite thought out what I was going to say. I knocked at the door with the doctor's name on it and he called out for me to come in.

Doctor Morgan was a short, middle-aged man with greying hair and glasses and a pleasant, fatherly look about him. He was sitting behind a desk with his name on a little nameplate in the middle of it. We said hello as I came in, and then I sat down and looked at my lap while he shuffled some notes about.

'So,' he said eventually, still looking at the notes, 'a Welsh Jones, is it?'

'Yes,' I said. I didn't volunteer anything else. I wasn't in the mood to talk about Wales, and which part of it I came from, and all that stuff that Welsh people always went in for whenever they met each other outside Wales, but I could see he was trying to be friendly.

'Cardiff, is it?' he said.

'No, Swansea,' I replied.

'Ah, I'm from Ammanford myself,' he said.

There didn't seem to be anything to add to that, beyond reiterating that I wasn't, so I said nothing.

'What seems to be the problem, then?' He looked up at me at last.

'Well, it's probably nothing much,' I said. 'It's just that I can't seem to wake up in the mornings.'

He laughed. 'That's a fairly common complaint among students. Anything else?'

'I can't seem to wake up properly unless I...' My sentence trailed off.

'Yes?'

'Well, unless I... kind of... scream, or something.'

There was a silence. I felt embarrassed. Then he said, in a matter-of-fact way, 'Well, let's have a look at you, shall we?'

He came round to my side of the desk, and started doing all the usual things like measuring my blood pressure and my pulse, and listening with a stethoscope to my chest and back. Then he sat down and asked me some more questions, with me replying that everything was normal, until we came to one and I stopped.

'Periods all right?' he said.

'Ah...' I couldn't remember when I'd had my last period, but I had a feeling that it was overdue.

'I think I might have missed one,' I said. 'But only by a few days. Or actually it could be...'

Now I came to think about it, I realised I'd lost track of that, as well as everything else, in the last few weeks.

'... a bit longer.'

'How much longer?'

'I'm not sure,' I said, feeling a bit of a fool. 'I'd have to check.'

'Do you have any reason to suppose that you might be pregnant?' He was choosing his words carefully.

'No, I'm on the pill.'

'And you've been taking it regularly?'

'Yes, of course. Although I might... I sometimes miss the odd one or two. Not very often.'

I was lying now. The truth was that I found it quite

difficult at the best of times to remember my pills, and recently I'd got worse. These days, I quite often looked at the pack at the end of the month and was amazed at how many were left in it.

'Right.' He looked at me quizzically. 'Well, I think we might do a test anyway. Just to be on the safe side.'

He gave me a bottle and asked me to go to the lavatory to do a urine sample, and then to bring it back in to him. I went out, found the loo, and did it, drying the outside of the bottle carefully with some loo paper afterwards. When I came back in and handed it to him, it was still warm, which embarrassed me, though I wasn't sure why. I could hardly be expected to pee cold just for the sake of politeness. He put a label on the bottle, and then sat me down and asked me some more questions.

'Are you under stress of any kind?' he said. 'Worried about exams?'

'No. Not really.'

'Anything else? Boyfriends?'

I looked down at my lap again. 'A bit.'

There was a silence while he waited for me to continue, but when it became clear that I wasn't going to say any more, he started shuffling his notes again.

'Well, Miss Jones, I think that's all for the moment. Try to relax. If the problem persists, we may have to put you on some tablets. And perhaps you'd like to pop back or ring us in a couple of hours to get your result.' He handed me a card with the surgery's number on it. 'We don't have to send the sample off to the lab these days, we can do the test here.'

'OK,' I said. 'Thanks. I will.'

I got up and said goodbye, and then, just as I got to the door, he said, 'Will you be going home for Christmas? Back to Wales? See the family?'

'Yes,' I said. I stood hovering by the door. 'I think so.'

'That's right,' he said, the way people did at home, as though satisfied to find you were playing your part to ensure that everything was carrying on as usual in the world.

'Bye, then,' I said, and before he had a chance to say anything more I turned, opened the door and went out.

As soon as I got outside the surgery, I started fumbling around in my shoulder bag to look for my packet of pills. I knew they were in there somewhere, lurking around at the bottom. I couldn't find them as I was walking along, so eventually I had to sit down on a step and sort through the contents of the bag. I took out the books and files and rummaged through all the rubbish at the bottom: broken pens and pencils, old tissues, a used-up lipstick, a tampon, an ancient mascara wand, a matchbox with burnt-out matches and a cigarette end inside it, and a packet of chewing gum I'd never opened. Then I came across something I'd completely forgotten about: the card that the Aleister Crowley freak had given me on the train. I turned it over and looked at the red-haired man with the bulging eyes for a moment, then put it back into the bag. I rummaged around some more, and finally found the pills.

They were small yellow ones in a silver packet with blue writing on it. There were several left in the pack, but that was normal, because I wasn't having my period. I turned the pack over and looked at the days listed on the back. The last day I'd taken one seemed to be Sunday. Today was Thursday I thought, but I wasn't quite sure, it could be Friday. Then I remembered that my Freud lecture was today, and my Hegel seminar had been yesterday, which meant that it must be Friday. I'd missed about four pills, which wasn't too bad. In the past, I'd sometimes missed as many as seven or eight, and I still hadn't got pregnant. In fact, I'd sometimes wondered if I was infertile, but I'd come to the conclusion that the real reason, despite what the doctors told you, was that the pills worked all right even if you didn't remember every single one. Either that, or I'd just been lucky. All the same, I thought, I really should try to be more organised in the future.

I took my pill for Friday as I sat on the step, then put everything back in my bag, got up, and walked on quickly into the centre of campus. I thought of going up to the European Common Room to see if Cassie and Fiona were there, but I decided not to. I wasn't in the mood to talk to them. I didn't want to tell them about the test, not because I was particularly worried that the result would be positive, but because I felt stupid that I'd missed so many pills. I knew that Cassie would be horrified, and that Fiona would lecture me, so I headed off to the library instead.

Once I got there, I pulled out Belham's reading list for Modern European Mind and scanned through it to see if there was anything on it that would distract me from thinking about my test during the next couple of hours. I already had Kierkegaard, but his writing seemed too clear for me at the moment; I couldn't bear it, it was too emotional and beautiful, like a prayer that you might hear in church. I wanted something more gristly to chew on, something ugly and dense, something hard and knotty and closed that would be a challenge to understand.

It was an easy enough choice. I'd heard Martin Heidegger's *Being and Time* was one of the most incomprehensible books ever written, and it was an optional text as well, which was another feature that attracted me: pointless as well as difficult. I went over to the short-loan shelf to see if I could find it, but it wasn't there, so I climbed up the spiral staircase to the philosophy section on the next floor. I didn't go up there very often, but when I did I always liked it and wondered why I didn't use it more. It was a quiet corner of the library where you could stand among the enormous leather-bound volumes and peer over the railings at the people below without being seen. Somehow being up there made me feel secure, as though I was observing the world from my stronghold of lofty ideas on high.

I found the book and took it down from the shelf. When I looked at the library stamp at the front, I noticed that hardly anyone had ever taken it out. As I flicked through the pages, I saw that the main text was full of German words, hyphenated phrases, and repetitive, apparently nonsensical sentences, and there were also passages in Latin and Greek. It looked completely impenetrable, which was just the kind of thing I'd been looking for, so I went over to a chair by the window and started to read.

I'd come across this sort of writing before, with Hegel, but Heidegger was farther out than that: so far out that he was almost just a dot on the horizon. Not only did his ideas go round in circles, like Hegel's, but there were also bizarre phrases like 'ready-to-hand', 'present-at-hand', 'towards-which', and 'for-the-sake-of' which jumbled ordinary words together in a way that seemed to make no sense. On top of that, every time he had something really important to say, he went into Greek or Latin, neither of which I understood, so I could only guess what he meant.

I mustered my concentration, but after an hour or so, I was none the wiser as to what *Being and Time* was about. Reading Heidegger was like listening to two people having a conversation in a foreign language: you occasionally thought you might have understood one or two words here and there, but you had absolutely no idea what they were talking about in general.

Even so, there was something about the text that fascinated me. Perhaps it was the idea that someone would set out to understand what it fundamentally means for us to be here, to 'be in the world' as he put it; and that they'd start by reviewing all philosophy hitherto, from Plato on, and pronounce that everyone else since the beginning of time had got it completely wrong; and that they'd go on to claim they'd finally found what it was that was missing from the history of human thought; and that they'd then dream up new combinations of words for their inexpressible ideas, and string them all together with hyphens, and expect people to take them seriously. It was such an impossible task, and so insanely ambitious to attempt it, that it almost brought tears to my eyes. And then there was the writing, which was so abstruse that I wondered at times if Heidegger was mad, or if this was a case of the emperor's new clothes and he was just taking the piss out of a load of academics, the way Nietzsche did a lot of the time; but whatever the case, you had to admire the guy's nerve.

After a while, the familiar torpor I'd been feeling every time I tried to study began to wash over me. The quiet of the library up there in the philosophy section moved in on me and began to wrap me up, while the bustle of people down below grew quiet and distant. I leaned back in my chair, closed my eyes, and rested my head against the rows of books behind it, feeling myself falling asleep, guarded by the dark red and green leather-bound volumes that stood like sentinels all around me.

When I woke up, it was beginning to get dark. I looked at my watch and realised I'd missed my Freud lecture, which was a pity because I liked the lecturer. She was an elderly woman named Maria Jakowska with a strong Viennese accent. She had apparently studied under Freud, and had escaped from the Nazis to England during World War Two. Her lectures were always packed: she made you feel that you were right there, in the thick of it all, horrifying the prim Viennese bourgeoisie with tales of the irrepressible libido; and when you listened to her steady, guttural voice you felt she was talking as Freud himself might have talked, and that you were listening to a piece of history.

Now that I'd missed the lecture, I realised that I'd been looking forward to it all week, hoping that it would take my mind off my trivial problems and make me feel I was part of something big. But instead, I'd fallen asleep after failing to understand a word of Heidegger, and missed the whole thing. What was more, I now had to make a telephone call and find out whether or not I'd been dumb enough to get pregnant.

I went downstairs, stood in line to take out *Being and Time*, had my book stamped, and then walked over to the Falmer Bar to make my call. There were two phones on the wall in the corridor outside it, and a dark-haired, good-looking guy was talking on one of them. I turned my back to him and dialled the number on my card. I could have gone back over to the surgery, but phoning seemed easier, more impersonal. When the receptionist answered, I gave her my name and asked for the result of the test.

'Jones... Jones,' she said, looking for it. 'Now what was it for?'

I lowered my voice. 'Pregnancy,' I said.

'Sorry?' she asked.

I hunched over the receiver. 'Pregnancy,' I said again, slightly louder.

'What was that?'

I was just summoning up the courage to bellow the word into the receiver when she found what she was looking for.

'Ah, right, Susannah Jones. Now let me see...'

I wondered whether this woman was trying to torture me.

'Yes, right, it's positive.'

Everything slowed down. I looked at the people passing by in the corridor and they were moving in slow motion. I felt the phone receiver in my hand, and it weighed a ton. There was a silence around me that stretched for miles.

'Miss Jones?'

I summoned my voice, which came slowly up from my chest.

'Miss Jones, are you there?'

'Yes,' I said, finally.

'Would you like to make an appointment to see the doctor?'

'No,' I said. 'Thank you.'

There was a silence. Then I said, 'I'm going to put the phone down now. Goodbye.'

I put the receiver back on the hook and stared at the wall. I noticed that the bricks were very pitted and a strange brownish-red, with mustard-coloured cement in between them. The phone was grey, not black, and made of shiny plastic. I looked down at my feet and saw that I was standing on some grey linoleum tiles with black streaks on them. It was hard to tell whether the streaks were dirt or part of the pattern. I looked at them for a long time and noticed that they were so regular that they must be part of the design. They were probably chosen to blend with the dirt.

I walked out of the Falmer Bar and out of campus to get the train. All the way home, I kept noticing the details of everything, and asking myself questions. The seats on the train: why did the fabric on them feel like the hairs of a brush? Were they made of some kind of carpet? Was this fabric especially made for train seats? The scratched bus windows: were they glass or were they plastic? Why were they so yellow? Was it nicotine, or was it just the way plastic went after a while? The tarmac on the road: were those blackened patches pieces of chewing gum covered in grime, or could they be something else? Knots of tar perhaps?

It was the same with human beings. When the man in the train office spoke to me, I found it hard to distinguish his voice from the voices of the people behind me in the ticket queue. On the bus, the conductor's voice seemed to merge with the voices of the passengers chatting to each other, and I didn't realise that he was speaking to me. It was as though every feature of the world around me, every sight and every sound, was screaming at me for attention and I had no way of telling which one mattered and which one didn't.

As I came up to the door of the flat, I found myself looking at it as though for the first time, noticing the big black door handle and the way the dark blue paint was chipped here and there with white showing through underneath. I wondered whether the door had been painted white before, or whether it was just the undercoat. I let myself in and climbed the stairs to our floor. When I got there, I saw that the light was on in the flat. It was shining through a small stained-glass window above the door, and I saw the way it threw patches of red and green on to the wall of the hallway, illuminating it brightly and changing the colour of the wallpaper. I looked up at the little window and noticed that it was Victorian, with a picture of a small brown singing bird etched in the middle of it, and on either side, pieces of coloured glass bordered with grey leading. It was pretty. I'd never noticed it before.

I got out my key to unlock the door and then I paused. I had forgotten that the light shining through the door meant something. It meant that Jason was in. I could hear his footsteps now, coming down the hall. As he came nearer, I reminded myself that he was my boyfriend, and I was going to have to tell him what had happened.

chapter 15

WHEN JASON OPENED the door, it was as though I was looking at him for the first time. I thought how tall and handsome he was, with his fair hair and his square shoulders and his sparkling blue eyes. When he hugged me and burrowed his head into my hair, kissing me on the neck, I thought how lucky I was to have such a good-looking, affectionate boyfriend; and when he helped me take off my jacket and scarf, hung them up, and led me down the corridor to the sitting room, I thought how warm and comfortable his flat was and what a nice place it would be to live in with him.

Cajun moon, where does your power lie
As you move across the southern sky

A record was playing as we came into the sitting room, and I listened to the words, even though Jason was talking to me.

'... It really all depends on whether it was from George III or the Prince Regent,' he was saying. 'There's no problem really, it's not that it's worth any less, it's just that you've got to find the right collector.'

The room was brightly lit. All around were statues of nymphs dancing, holding balls of light in their hands. In the middle, under a pool of light from a fringed standard lamp, was a coffee table with tools and wires piled up on it. Beside it was a battered leather armchair and a sofa. I sat down on the sofa. Jason sat down cross-legged on the floor by the coffee table with a screwdriver in one hand and a nymph in the other, and began to thread an electric cord through her body. As he worked, he carried on talking.

'We know it belonged to Princess Charlotte Augusta, but the question is, who gave it to her. I'm pretty sure it was from her father, the Prince Regent, but Dalton isn't convinced. And it's only the Prince Regent stuff that he collects.'

I had no idea what he was on about, so I kept quiet and listened.

'... He doesn't think the Prince would have given the baby a present like that. Apparently, the night of the marriage was practically the only time he ever had sex with his wife. He hated her. The baby's birth was seen as a disaster.'

What have you done, Cajun moon...

I began to feel queasy, but I said nothing.

'He thinks the box might have been a present from the baby's grandfather, George III,' Jason went on.

The box, I thought. The box. Then I remembered the box that Jason had shown me, the one he'd got from Bear's parents, the one that was supposed to make his – our – fortune.

He looked up at me. 'You know, King George, the mad, inbred one.'

Now I got it. He was talking about the milk-teeth box, and how it might not have been a present from the baby's father, the Prince Regent, but from her grandfather, George III, and how this somehow made a difference to something.

'You saw those letters the Princess wrote. She had a terrible childhood. Once she was born, neither of her parents wanted her around,' Jason continued, 'so the poor kid was stuck away somewhere, and the only person who bothered to visit her was Grandad. She used to clap her hands together when she saw him. Sad, isn't it?'

I tried to focus my mind on the tooth box. I thought of the portrait of the robust little girl I'd seen at the Pavilion, and her tiny blackened teeth lying on the frayed silk inside the box. I thought of how her selfish parents sent her away after she was born and never went to visit her. Yes, it was sad. But then I remembered the diamonds spelling out *dents de lait* on the lid of the box, and I thought, well, somebody must have loved her.

I hadn't answered Jason, and now I realised that he was looking at me.

'Are you all right, Susie?' he said. 'You look as though you've seen a ghost.'

'I'm fine,' I said. ' Just a bit... tired, I think.'

'Let me get you a drink, that'll perk you up. I'm on G & T.'

I noticed a tumbler sitting on the table beside the wires. You could see the bubbles of the tonic and the greasy slick of gin in it, with a slice of lemon and some ice cubes. I found myself wondering why the lemon stood upright in the glass, and how much juice came out of it into the drink, and whether it made any difference to the taste of it.

'No thanks,' I said. The thought of drinking a gin and tonic turned my stomach.

'Cigarette, then?'

'God, no.'

Jason lit one for himself. 'Well, let's have some wine later over dinner instead, I've got a really nice bottle for us tonight. Bear's coming down for the weekend. He should be arriving any minute. I'm doing coq au vin, it's all cooked and ready, waiting to go. I've just got to heat it up when he arrives. I hope you're hungry, Susie Q.'

Now that he mentioned it, I noticed that there was a faint smell of chicken in the flat. And I realised that if it got stronger, as it would do when he heated it up, I would feel very sick, and possibly even vomit.

I was going to have to tell him.

'Jason,' I said. ' I...' My voice trailed off. I couldn't finish the sentence.

Jason looked up at me, surprised. 'What is it?'

'It's just that...'

'Go on, spit it out.'

'I don't... I don't think I'll be able to eat the coq au vin, I'm not hungry at all. Sorry.'

Jason gave a short laugh. 'Well, don't get your knickers in a twist about it.'

He got up and came to sit on the sofa with me, still holding his screwdriver. He put his arm round me and tilted his head to look into my face.

'What's the matter? You don't look right at all. Did you go to the doctor this week about your screaming?' He'd been bullying me for weeks to go.

'Yes, I went today, actually.' I tried to sound smug, but failed.

'And what did he say?'

'Well, I had a test...'

'What kind of test?' There was a note of panic in his voice.

I raised my head and looked him in the eye. I heard my voice break the silence.

'Don't worry, there's nothing wrong with me, I'm perfectly normal.' I was trying to sound calm. 'But I'm pregnant.'

Jason dropped the screwdriver and it clattered against the leg of the coffee table. We listened to the sound of it. Then we both looked down at it lying on the floor.

Eventually, he spoke. 'You're not, are you?'

'Well, I wouldn't say I am if I wasn't, would I?' I sounded angry, even though I hadn't up until that moment, felt angry at all.

Jason took a deep breath, held it, and let out a sigh. Then, to my astonishment, his face broke into a broad grin. He put his arms around me and pulled me on to his knee, hugging me, murmuring my name and stroking my hair. I felt awkward. He was treating me like a baby.

'Pregnant!' he said. 'My little Susie, pregnant!'

A wave of fear came over me when I heard his words, and the hairs on my scalp prickled. This was all wrong. To Jason, I was a child, a pregnant child. He didn't seem to understand what was really going on here. But at the same time, his excitement was infectious, and for the first time since I had heard the news, I felt a tiny shaft of pleasure deep inside me.

Jason shook his head. 'I can't believe it,' he said. 'How on earth…? How did it happen?' He was smiling at me, bemused.

'The usual way,' I said. The anger was still there.

'OK, sorry, of course… but… I thought you were on the pill.'

'I was. But I forgot to take some of them.'

'I can't believe it,' he repeated, shaking his head again. 'Me, a father.'

I realised with a shock that Jason had taken it for granted that I was going to have the baby, and that it was his. It was all going too fast. I shouldn't have told him. I should have made my mind up first about what I wanted to do, and then told him my decision. As it was, I'd just blurted it out before I was ready and messed everything up.

'Actually, I'm not sure…' I began. 'I don't know…'

At that moment, the doorbell rang.

Jason got up to answer the door. I heard voices in the corridor, and then the voices went off to the kitchen. I looked around the sitting room again. It was exactly the same as it had been last time I came in here, yet I felt as though it was the first time I'd ever seen it. I wondered what it would be like if I had come here as a stranger, been introduced to Jason and the flat, and been asked to decide whether I liked them or not, whether I wanted this man to be my boyfriend and this flat to be my home. What would I have decided? I wasn't sure yet. They were both nice, but I hadn't quite made up my mind.

Bear came in with a gin and tonic in his hand, looking dapper in a forties' style pinstripe suit, his long, dark hair flopping over his forehead. He was wearing a pair of John Lennon specs with pale pink glass in the lenses. His clothes and hair were flamboyant, but there was something careful and neat about him all the same.

'Hello, old stick.' He bent over to peck me on the cheek, then sat down beside me on the sofa.

'How's it going?' I said.

'Sheer hell,' he said.

'Me too,' I said. We both laughed.

Underneath the suit, he was wearing a granddad shirt with the top buttons undone. His skin was smooth and olive-coloured, with one or two silky, dark hairs on his chest. I thought he looked a bit like Rob. I wondered, if I hadn't known he was Bear, whether I would have fancied him. I thought probably not, but I wasn't sure why. After all, he was good looking and well dressed, and I liked him. In fact, in many ways, I liked him better than Jason. I felt closer to him, he was more the same type of person as me. So why did I sense that he was somehow off limits? Was it just because he was Jason's best friend? I started thinking about it, asking myself questions in the same way that I'd done with the seats on the train and the windows in the bus and the undercoat on the front door and the lemon in the gin and tonic. Then I thought, I've got to stop doing this, it's weird behaviour.

Jason came in with a bottle of uncorked wine in one hand and three empty wine glasses in the other.

'Here we go,' he said. 'Hurry up and finish your drink, Bear. We're celebrating tonight. In style.' He waved the bottle of wine. 'Domaine de la Romanée-Conti.'

I didn't expect Bear to ask what we were celebrating, because with Jason we were always celebrating something, but this time he did.

'Wow,' he said. 'Must be something special. What year is it?'

'1966,' replied Jason. He put the bottle and the glasses down on the coffee table, clearing away the tools and the wire.

Bear watched him and grinned. 'Who'd a thought thirty year ago,' he said, adopting a ridiculous Yorkshire accent, 'that we'd a been sitting here drinking Chateau de Chasselet, eh Josiah?'

Jason laughed and sat down on the sofa between me and Bear.

'You're right there, Obadiah,' he replied. 'In them days we'd a been glad to have the price of a cup of tea.'

'A cup of cold tea,' said Bear. 'Without milk or sugar.'

'Or tea...'

They were off. They knew every line of the Monty Python sketch by heart, and by the time they got to the bit about living in a corridor they were holding on to each other in fits of laughter. I watched them, laughing as well, though I'd often heard them do the routine before.

'A corridor! We used to dream of living in a corridor!'

They carried on, doubling up with laughter and stopping to catch their breath every now and then. I waited for my favourite line about living in a brown paper bag in a septic tank, but when they came to it, I stopped laughing. I wasn't sure why at first, but then I realised it was because I felt excluded from the joke. It was about Bear and Jason, and what they had been through together at public school. It was to do with their past. And it had nothing to do with me.

They were hugging each other now, forced to give up speaking the lines because they were both in hysterics. They had forgotten me, and what it was we were supposed to be celebrating.

Then Jason recovered himself and sat forward to reach for the wine bottle on the coffee table.

'Sorry, Susie,' he said. 'Got a bit carried away there.'

Bear lay back on the sofa and sighed. There were tears of laughter rolling down his face.

'There's another one you might try,' I said. 'It's called the Philosophers' Football Match.'

'Really?' said Jason.

'Yes, I've only heard about it from some students on my course, I haven't seen it. The Greek philosophers are on one side, and the Germans are on the other. It's really funny.'

'Sounds hilarious,' said Jason. Then he leaned over and tousled my hair. 'If you're a philosophy student, that is.'

He said it affectionately. He wasn't being nasty, he was just making it clear that Bear was the person he did Monty Python sketches with. And I wasn't.

'OK, guys,' said Jason, straightening up his shirt and running his hands through his hair. 'Time for a spot of Romanée-Conti, I think.'

He picked up the bottle, poured out a glass, and held it up to the light. Then he tilted the glass, swirled it around, and sniffed it before taking a sip and sloshing it around his mouth as though he was cleaning his teeth. Finally, he swallowed it, gave a sigh of satisfaction, and sat back to think about it.

Normally I liked the glugging sound of wine being poured, and the idiotic rigmarole Jason went through when he tasted wine, but tonight it filled me with dread.

Jason poured out a glass each for me and Bear and handed them to us. I took mine without a word.

'Bear, we've got some wonderful news,' he said.

'Go on then, spill the beans,' said Bear, sitting forward, wiping his eyes.

I wanted Jason to stop, but there was nothing I could do. I felt like a paralysed rabbit in the headlights of a car.

'Susie's pregnant,' said Jason. 'I'm going to be a father.'

I looked at Bear. The colour seemed to have drained out of his face.

Jason held out his glass with a flourish and clinked it

against Bear's. 'Here's to us,' he said. Then he turned to me and clinked my glass against his. 'Here's to all of us.'

We each took a sip of the wine, and then Bear and I put our glasses back down on the table. I noticed that Bear's hand was shaking.

Jason held his glass up against the light to look at it again.

'Lovely, isn't it.' He seemed not to have noticed that neither of us had spoken.

'I can't believe it,' he went on. 'First the milk-teeth box, and now this. Just as I'm coming up to thirty. Everything's falling into place at last. I'm on a roll here.'

He looked at us both and laughed. 'You two are still in shock, aren't you,' he said. 'Well, so am I. We haven't had time to discuss it yet, have we, Susie' – he glanced at me – 'but we wanted you to be the first to know.'

Bear struggled to say something, but failed.

Jason laughed again, and went on chatting while we listened in silence, until eventually he got up and went into the kitchen to see to dinner.

It was an opportunity for Bear and me to talk to each other, but neither of us said anything. Bear finished his wine and poured himself another glass, his hands still shaking. He was drinking fast. I hadn't touched mine after the first sip.

After what seemed like an age, Jason called us into the kitchen and sat us down for the coq au vin. He had set out clean linen napkins, fresh glasses and another bottle of wine on the table, and there was a basket of French bread in the middle of it.

He brought the casserole over from the stove, holding it with an oven glove.

'Ta da,' he said.

As he lifted the lid of the casserole, the rich smell of the meat almost made me gag.

'Jason, I'm sorry,' I said. 'I'm not feeling very well. I think I'm going to go and have a lie down.'

I got up, thinking he would get up too and come to the bedroom with me so that we could at least have a quick chat before he went back to eat with Bear. But he didn't.

'You poor darling,' he said. 'You must be exhausted. All this excitement. Go to bed and snuggle down. I'll come in after supper.'

As I got up, he touched my arm. 'Goodnight, sweetie pie.'

I bent over and kissed him on the cheek. 'Goodnight. Don't stay up too late.'

Then I said, 'Goodnight, Bear.' I didn't dare look at him. He didn't say anything back.

As I turned, I saw Jason lean over, touch Bear's arm, and whisper something in his ear. He seemed to have forgotten about me already.

I turned the light off as soon as I got into the bedroom, opened the curtains, undressed in the dark, and got into bed. The cool sheets felt good against my skin, and the darkness of the room was deep and soft. It was a still, clear night and I could see the stars and a crescent moon outside. I took a deep breath and felt the tang of a thin current of salty air in my nose, coming in through the draughty window. In the distance, I could hear the rhythmic, sucking noise of the sea. I closed my eyes and ran my hands over my stomach and breasts. They were swelling already. This is all wrong, I thought. None of this should be happening.

Don't trouble your mind, whatever you do…

The roar of the sea grew nearer, and the darkness deeper and softer. I felt them coming towards me, and I tried to resist them. I needed to stay awake. I needed to think about what to do. But soon they began to wrap me up, and before long I surrendered and fell fast asleep.

chapter 16

NEXT MORNING I WOKE UP EARLY. There was a fine tracing of frost on the window pane, and through the open curtains I could see the sun shining in a clear blue sky. Somewhere outside, a bird was singing. When I heard it, I got straight out of bed. I wanted to be out there too.

Jason was snoring gently, and as I pushed off the sheets and blankets, he turned over, sighed, and went back to sleep. I put on his dressing gown and walked quietly through the sitting room to the bathroom, not wanting to wake anyone as I went. Bear was sleeping on the sofa, his dark head just visible on a pillow under the blankets. Beside him, on the coffee table, were the remains of the night before: a full ashtray, two dirty wine glasses, a bottle, a mirror, a razor blade, and a rolled-up pound note. I tiptoed past him but I needn't have bothered: like Jason, Bear was dead to the world.

In the bathroom, I went to the loo, washed my face, and cleaned my teeth. Then I opened the dressing gown and looked at my body in the mirror over the sink. I thought I could see that my nipples had darkened and that my breasts looked bigger than usual. I got up on a chair and looked at my belly in profile, and it seemed that there was a curve to it that hadn't been there before. I ran my hands over it, wondering if I was imagining that my stomach had already swelled into this womanly shape. As I looked at myself in the mirror, I felt curious and amused, as though I had tried on a new dress in a feminine style that I wouldn't normally wear: a dress that I could take off and never wear again if I decided it didn't suit me; a dress that – if I did decide I liked it – would make me look like a different kind of person altogether. I had a choice now: I could either carry on looking like a student girl with long hair and jeans and no bra under her T-shirt; or I could be a sexy, flouncy kind of woman who wore a dress, and proper underwear, and perhaps even stockings with seams up the back. I hadn't had that choice before. I knew that sooner or later, I was going to have to decide what I was going to do; but just for this morning I was going to take a walk outside, try out my new look, and see what the world made of it.

I brushed my hair, put on some lipstick, and went back into the bedroom to find some clothes. I felt like wearing a skirt, but I couldn't open the wardrobe in case I woke Jason, so I pulled on my knickers, jeans, T-shirt, socks and boots as usual. Then I went into the hall to look for the antique fur coat that Jason had given me. I'd never worn it. It was grey and cinched in at the waist, with a huge shawl collar and four big black buttons to do it up at the front. When I'd tried it on, I'd thought it made me look ridiculous, as though I was a little girl dressing up in my mother's clothes. He'd told me that it was made from lambs taken from their mothers' wombs before they were born and skinned, which had put me off it even more. But now I found it, buried under the other coats, and put it on. I went back into the bathroom to look at myself in the mirror, and saw that my hair looked wrong hanging down over my shoulders, so I pinned it up with some old-fashioned hairpins I sometimes used to put my hair up in a bun. I turned up the collar of the coat, put on some more lipstick, and let myself out of the flat.

Outside, a bitter wind was blowing off the sea, and I was glad to be bundled up in the fur coat. I walked down

Brunswick Square to the promenade. Although it was freezing cold, the sky was a piercing blue, and the sun was making the grey sea glint like silver. I sat down on one of the benches and looked out over the railings at the beach. In the far distance, a black tanker was moving slowly across the horizon. Nearby, on the wall of a flowerbed, a fat tabby cat was licking her paws and sunning herself. I breathed in the smell of the sea, rested my head on the back of the bench, closed my eyes, and put my face up to the sun.

I stayed there for a long time, occasionally opening my eyes to scan the sea and the sky. There didn't seem to be any particular reason to move. The shawl collar of my coat was shielding my ears from the wind; my face was warm in the sun; and the rhythmic suck and crash of the waves on the shore was making the noise of cars and people seem distant and insignificant. There was no one around that morning except me and the tabby cat and the tanker on the horizon; and like them, I didn't see any reason to hurry.

Eventually I began to feel hungry, so I walked along the promenade before cutting up to the shops on Western Avenue. I bought some warm bread rolls and a can of frozen orange juice as a treat for breakfast and headed back to the flat. Bear and Jason were still asleep when I got in, so I stayed in the kitchen, made some coffee in the percolator, buttered the rolls, laid a breakfast tray, and took it into the bedroom.

The smell of the coffee woke Jason as I came in. He sat up and stretched, his bare chest looking almost blue-white against the pillows.

'God, that smells good. Just what I need.'

I poured him a cup of coffee and put the tray on the bed. When he saw the rolls and the orange juice, he said, 'Susie, you are a darling,' and began to help himself.

'Jason, we've got to talk,' I said. I noticed that his eyes were bloodshot and there were bags under them.

'I know, we've hardly had a minute to ourselves, have

we.' He began licking the frozen orange juice off a spoon.

'I don't think you've really taken in what's going on here.' There was an angry edge to my voice.

He stopped licking and looked at me. 'What do you mean? Obviously it's come as a complete shock, but I'm quite pleased about it really. I think it might work out rather well. I think it's time I – we – did something like this.'

'Well, if you're so pleased about it, why didn't you come to bed with me last night?' I tried to keep my tone even, but I could hear my voice rising.

Jason picked up a roll and bit into it, saying something indistinguishable as he did, and finishing '... with Bear here.'

He didn't seem altogether capable of holding a conversation, but I carried on regardless.

'Well, you could have come in and talked to me when I went to bed, couldn't you?' I said. 'You haven't asked me how I feel, whether I want the baby, what I want to do about my course, what I want to do about... us. You haven't asked me anything.'

Jason frowned, as though he was having trouble understanding my words. He kept sniffing, as though he had a cold coming on.

'Sorry, Susie, I've only just woken up.' He paused. 'So what you're saying is that I haven't asked you anything. How you feel. Whether you want the baby. Of course you want the baby, don't you?'

'There's no of course about it, Jason. I might, and I might not.'

'But why wouldn't you?'

I couldn't believe he could be so obtuse. 'Because it's a bloody accident, isn't it,' I said. 'Because this isn't what I planned. Because I'm a twenty-year-old student with no money and a boyfriend who lives in bloody cloud cuckoo land.'

Jason blinked and rubbed his eyes. 'But you know I'll

look after you. We're going to have plenty of money after I sell the milk-teeth box. It couldn't be a better time for this to happen. What's the problem?'

I sighed. It was hopeless trying to talk to him.

'You've just got no idea, have you,' I said. 'You haven't got the faintest clue what it means for me to be pregnant.'

Jason was still frowning, and then he tutted and shook his head.

'God, I'm an idiot,' he said. '*Haven't asked you anything.* How could I be such a fool.'

He got up out of bed naked, went over to a chest of drawers, opened one of them, and rummaged about in it. He took out something, came over with it and put out his hand. In his palm was a gold ring with a greenish blue stone set in the middle of it.

'There you are,' he said. 'It's an aquamarine. The colour of the sea. I was saving it to give you for your birthday, but we can use it as an engagement ring. You'll want us to get married, won't you?'

He looked up at me. His blue eyes seemed to have darkened and softened. I looked down at him, at his broad chest and his fair-skinned body, and my eyes filled with tears.

'Do you like it?'

'Yes,' I said. 'It's lovely. Thank you.'

'It's beautifully set, probably late nineteenth century. I got it up at Bermondsey. Of course, I can get you something else if you'd rather…'

'No, it's fine. It's lovely.'

'Try it on.'

I slipped it on the fourth finger of my left hand, just to please him.

He held my hand and looked at it. 'It fits fine. It looks nice on you.'

'Actually, I think it's a bit tight.' I took it off and put it on the bedside table.

He seemed to have forgotten that he'd just asked me to marry him, and that I hadn't answered yet.

He got up and went over to put his dressing gown on. Then he came back and sat next to me on the bed and kissed me on the cheek.

'The amazing thing is,' he said, 'that Flick and Toby are getting engaged. She told me about it last week when I was in London. They're going to throw a big party for the engagement and then have a huge wedding. They're planning it already, or rather Flick is.'

I said nothing.

He put his arm round me. 'I'm going to phone her and tell her the news right now. And my parents. Who knows, maybe we could make it a double wedding.'

A wave of nausea came over me. I pushed him away from me and put my head forward over my knees. I felt faint.

'Please, Jason,' I said. 'Stop it. For God's sake.'

'What is it?' he said. 'What's wrong? Morning sickness? Shall I get a bowl?'

'Yes.' For a moment I thought I was going to throw up, and then the sensation passed. 'I mean, no. I don't know.'

Jason was about to go off for the bowl, but as he got up I gripped him by the shoulder.

'Stay here a minute,' I said. 'Just sit down and listen to me for once. Forget about Bear, Flick, your family, and whoever else for now. This is between you and me. I don't want anyone else involved. OK?'

My voice came out in a rush, but there was a calm quality to it that took him by surprise.

'OK then,' he said. 'Fine. Fire away.'

'There are some things you don't know about this,' I began. There was a pause.

'Go on.'

'Well...' I didn't want to tell him, but then I thought of the ring and Flick and Toby and his parents and the double wedding and realised that I had to.

'The thing is, I might want an abortion.'

Jason said nothing.

'Or I might not. I haven't decided yet.'

'OK,' he said. 'Fair enough. You need time to think about this. But you know how I feel. I want you – us, I mean – to have this baby.'

'And there's something else.'

Jason waited.

'It might not… there's a possibility that it might not be yours.'

I looked at him. He pursed his lips together, bowed his head, and began to rock very slightly back and forth beside me on the bed.

'Sorry,' I added. 'Sorry.'

I put out my hand to touch his shoulder but he pushed it away.

'I'm sorry,' I repeated. 'It was just something that happened.'

He stopped rocking and looked at me, his eyes glittering. 'Just something that happened? What the hell are you talking about?'

It was rare for Jason to lose his temper, but I knew he was capable of it. We'd only fought once or twice before. I thought of that time in Bermondsey when I'd given him a light slap and his arm had flown up against my shoulder and face with his full force behind it.

'It all started when you went away and didn't phone me for days. I got fed up and…'

'Who was it?' he interrupted.

'Someone on my course. No one in particular,' I said.

'I knew it,' he said. 'That stupid little hippie boy. Are you still seeing him? Or fucking him, should I say?'

'No, of course not.'

There was a long silence. Jason stood up, picked up the ring on the bedside table, and put it in his dressing gown pocket. Then he looked down at me, still sitting on the bed.

'How could you?' he said. 'You scrubber.' I looked away from him. 'You dirty little scrubber. Get out of my house.'

I stood up and faced him. I was trembling and my heart was beating fast.

'OK,' I said. 'I'll be glad to. Leave you here with your boyfriend. He'll look after you, won't he.'

Up until that moment, I'd never let the thought that Jason and Bear were lovers come into my mind. But as I spoke, I knew that they were, and that they had been all along, and that somehow I had always known it.

Jason seemed to take a step back, stagger, and then recover himself.

'What did you say?'

'Nothing.' I turned away from him, conscious that I didn't want him to hit me, not anywhere near my stomach, anyway. But when he spoke, his voice was quiet and cold.

'How dare you,' he said. 'Now, I'm going to go into the bathroom, and when I come back I want you out of here. Take your things and get out. For good. I never want to see you again.'

'Fine.' I went over to the wardrobe and began to look through my clothes, turning my back to him. As I did, I heard the door slam behind me.

chapter 17

'CASSIE?'

I was standing in a phone box on Western Road. It stank of urine and stale fags, and I was trying to wedge the heavy door open with my foot to let out some of the smell. As I did I noticed that the bottoms of my flares were trailing in the yellow puddles on the concrete floor, so I stood on tiptoe and tried to push the door with the side of my leg and my elbow instead.

'Who is it?' asked a male voice.

'Susannah,' I said, and then I remembered that I should have made up a name. Cassie often told her boyfriend that she was with me when she was with the tutor or off on one of her other flings, and now I realised I might have blown things for her. After all, it was only eleven o'clock on a Saturday morning. If she wasn't in Rick's bed, she'd be in somebody else's.

'Oh, right,' said the voice. I recognised it as Rick's. 'Hi, Susannah. I'll just go and get her.'

I breathed a sigh of relief.

'Sorry to phone so early,' I said, but Rick had already left the phone.

While I was waiting, I breathed into the sleeve of my jacket to try and stop myself gagging on the smell in the phone box. I hoped she wouldn't be too long or I'd have to find another one and ring back.

'Bloody hell, Suse.' Cassie's voice came on the line. 'Bit early, isn't it?'

'Sorry,' I said.

She lowered her voice. 'Good job I was here, too,' she said in an accusing tone.

'I'm really sorry, Cass. But it's kind of an emergency. I'm in a bit of a heavy situation.'

'What's happened?'

'I've split up with Jason. Just now, actually.' My voice started to quaver slightly, but I kept it as steady as I could. 'I'll explain it all when I see you. But for now, I just wondered if I could use your room on campus. I've got the key.'

'Of course you can.' Cassie's tone had changed to one of concern. 'But why don't you come round to mine? You sound upset.'

'No, honestly, I'm fine.' I couldn't face the prospect of telling Cassie I was pregnant just yet, and anyway, we probably wouldn't have a chance to talk with Rick hovering in the background.

'Will you be all right on your own over there? Shall I come and see you? I'm worried about you.'

The more kindness she showed the worse I felt. Tears started streaming down my face. I covered the receiver with my hand in case I started sobbing.

'Susannah?'

'Sorry, Cass.' I spoke as normally as I could but my voice came out oddly strangulated. 'I've got to go now. This phone box stinks so much I think I'm going to throw up. We'll talk later. Thanks a million. Bye.'

I put the phone down before she could reply.

I heaved open the door of the phone box and took a deep breath of fresh air, which smelt of car exhausts. After the reek of the phone box, it was delicious. I picked up my suitcase, which I'd left outside to avoid the puddles, and headed up to the station to catch the Falmer train.

As I walked up the road, a bus to Hanover came past. By the time I got to the bus stop it was still there, with a queue of people waiting to get on. For a moment, I had an impulse to join it, get on the bus, and go over to Rob's. I pictured the scene in my mind. He'd open the door and I'd be there with my suitcase, and I'd tell him I'd made my decision, that I'd split up with Jason at last, and now I'd come to be with him. He'd be thrilled, of course, and we'd go up to his room, and he'd tell me how much he loved me and we'd lie on the bed and he'd stroke my hair and make me feel secure, and then … and then I'd have to say, but there's just one thing… I thought of how he'd described his relationship with Beth, about how he'd said he wasn't into that whole marriage and family thing, and I realised he'd be horrified when I told him I was pregnant. He'd probably be quite nice about it on the surface, but I'd be able to see that underneath, he'd want to get rid of me at the first opportunity. Pregnancy and babies and stuff just didn't come into Rob's world: they weren't his scene at all. He wouldn't know how to deal with the situation, he'd just be scared and disgusted and embarrassed and think I was an idiot. I couldn't face the rejection of that at the moment, not after what had just happened with Jason. There was no way I could go over to his house and see him now; in fact, it would be better to steer clear of him completely until I'd got out of this mess.

I walked past the bus queue without slowing down, and made my way up Western Avenue towards the clock tower. The streets were busy with Saturday shoppers. I passed a couple of girls standing looking into a shop window. They were about my age but neatly dressed, with long shiny hair and pink lipstick, wearing identical, spotless off-white jackets. They were trying to decide which shoes to buy, and discussing which disco to go out to that night. They were the kind of girls I normally thought of as stupid and straight, shop girls probably, who lived with their parents and got engaged and saved up for years, and only got married when they'd bought every last teaspoon for their new house. But just for a moment I wished I was like them, part of the old pattern of life where everything was set up for you in advance and all you had to do as you went along was to decide between this pair of shoes, this boyfriend, this disco, or that. I wanted to have a life like theirs, where trivial decisions were the only ones you had to make. Then I realised that, up until yesterday, I had.

As I passed the clock tower, I noticed that a new record shop had opened there. I glanced in the window as I went by, and saw that inside, it had cut-outs of clouds hanging down from the ceiling, and brown curvy shelves everywhere that looked like mounds of earth, with records poking out of them. There was even a small cardboard tree in one corner, with LPs hanging off it. I hung about pretending to look at the albums in the window display and peering into the shop to see what was going on. Everyone in there was male, and everyone had long hair; there were no straight guys at all. Then, in the corner, I spotted two men with shorter, curly hair, talking to each other. With a shock, I recognised both of them. One of them was Belham, and the other was John Martyn.

John Martyn had his back to me, and Belham was showing him a record he'd pulled out of a mound of earth beside him. They moved over to the window to look at the sleeve in the light, and as they did, Belham saw me peering in. He took a moment to register who I was, then smiled at me and gave me a little wave. I smiled back and raised my hand but didn't wave it, in a gesture I hoped looked reasonably cool. I prayed that, at that distance, he wouldn't be able to see that I'd been blubbing, and that my nose hadn't gone red and shiny, which it normally did when I cried.

Before they got any nearer, I turned and scurried off up the hill to the train station, hoping Belham wouldn't notice me carrying the suitcase. For some reason, carrying suitcases in public always made me feel bad. Whenever I had to take one anywhere, even on holiday, I felt as though it showed that I had no proper life at all: nowhere to live, no friends, no one to help me, nothing in the world except my pathetic, unnecessary belongings weighing me down and making my life impossible. For that reason, I usually travelled light. But this time, there'd been no alternative.

Once I got to the station, I hopped on to the Falmer train, which was pretty busy. The passengers were all shoppers, and I was the only person travelling with a suitcase. It wasn't a very big one, but wherever I put it, it was in the way. People began to look at me and tut as they tripped over it. It seemed to draw attention to the fact that something odd was going on in my life, and I began to hate it. When I got off the train, I felt like leaving it behind, but that would have seemed even odder, and anyway I didn't want to get arrested for freaking out everyone on the train thinking that there was an IRA bomb in there.

Because of the suitcase, I had to go down the underpass to cross the dual carriageway, instead of nipping through the hole in the hedge like I usually did. I was dreading walking through campus with the bloody thing, but luckily there was no one around. I hadn't realised how deserted the place was at weekends. I stopped at the campus shop and bought some teabags, milk, bread, butter, baked beans and oranges to keep me going for the weekend, still feeling conspicuous, but there was no one in the shop except the cashier. In fact, there were no signs of life anywhere until I got to Cassie's student hall, and even then I only saw a few foreign students making homesick telephone calls in the lobby.

I got up to Cassie's room, feeling relieved that I'd made the whole journey through campus without anyone seeing me. I fished out her key and unlocked the door. Inside, everything was very neat and tidy, probably because Cassie hardly ever came here. There wasn't much to mess up, anyway: a single bed in the corner, a chair, a desk with an anglepoise lamp and some shelves above it, and on the other side of the room a washbasin with some built-in cupboards around it. On the floor were some petrol blue and black carpet squares and there was a matching petrol blue and black curtain in the window with a sixties' design of circles on it. Outside the window was a bank of grass.

It was all very plain and unfashionable, not my taste at all. In fact, I'd never noticed any of it when I'd been in here before, but as I looked around now I thought, this is just what I want. I knew I didn't like art deco lamps and old leather sofas and all that stuff that Jason was so keen on; but now I realised I didn't like Rob's Indian scarves and pictures of Che Guevara that much either. I began to wonder what my taste actually was. It wasn't this, but it was something like it. All I wanted in a room was a bit of peace and quiet: white walls with nothing on them; a bed to lie down on; a desk to sit at; a lamp to read by; a window with a patch of grass outside. And maybe something beautiful to look at, but I hadn't worked out yet what that could be.

I dumped my suitcase on the floor and hung my jacket up on the hook on the back of the door. I went over to the basin and washed my face and hands, then looked for a towel in the cupboard. I found some towels and sheets neatly piled up in there, just the way they would have been in my mother's linen cupboard at home, which surprised me. I pulled out a towel and dried myself, and as I did I noticed it was embroidered in one corner with the name 'Keziah' and a cross. For a moment I wondered what it meant, and then I realised it was Cassie's name, and that it must have been hand-sewn for her by her mother.

I went over to the bed and noticed that there were fresh sheets on it. It was still only lunchtime, but as I looked at it, the temptation to get in to it, go to sleep, and forget about the world, overwhelmed me. I opened my suitcase, and took out an old viyella nightdress that my mother had given me years ago. It was pale blue with pale pink flowers on it. I only wore it if I was sleeping by myself and no one could see me.

I drew the curtain over the window, took off my clothes, and put on the nightdress. I got the Heidegger out of my bag and got into bed, relishing the feel of the clean sheets against my skin. I began to read in the darkened room, but I was too tired to concentrate. I put the book down, pulled up the covers, and turned to the wall. As soon as my head hit the pillow, I fell fast asleep.

By the time I woke up, it was dark outside. I got out of bed, dressed quickly, and went down the corridor to find a loo. Then I went back to the room, picked up my food, and took it into the kitchen. I was dying for a cup of tea.

Fortunately there was no one in the kitchen. I made the tea, drank it, and then realised I was ravenously hungry. I heated up some beans, toasted some bread, buttered it, and scoffed the lot. Then I sliced some more bread and ate it with cheese, finishing off with an orange. I was still hungry. I wished I'd bought some cake or something. Tomorrow was Sunday and the shops would be shut.

Just as I was contemplating another round of beans on toast, a girl walked into the kitchen. Damn, I thought. This was exactly the kind of situation I'd dreaded, hanging out with first-year students in the kitchens on campus. She was a good-looking girl, tall and slim with long legs and long blonde hair, but there was something about her that told you she hadn't realised it. She looked lonely and apologetic, somehow. I wondered if she was a Christian with stuffed animals on the bed.

I was about to make a move towards the door when she spoke.

'Umm... Hhh...' she said.

Oh no, I thought. A spastic.

'Umm... Hhhh...'

She was obviously making a tremendous effort to say something. I couldn't go now. Fuck, I thought. If only I'd taken the food back to my room and eaten it there.

'Umm... Hhh... hhh... hello.' She finally got it out.

'Hi,' I said, as briefly as I could. The last thing I wanted was to get stuck here with her. If she took that long to say hello, I could be here all night waiting for 'how are you'.

'I'm Clare,' she continued. She sounded surprisingly normal all of a sudden. Perhaps she wasn't a spastic after all.

'I'm just making some ummm... hh... hh... hot chocolate. D'you want some?'

I realised what it was now. She had a terrible stutter. It only seemed to come out on some words, and not on others.

She looked up and smiled at me. When she did, I realised that she was actually a stunning looking girl. She had very blue eyes almost the colour of her jeans, and her skin was tanned, with a sprinkling of freckles over her nose.

Hot chocolate, I thought. This is what it's come to. It'll be pillow fights and apple-pie beds next. But I had to admit that in fact, just at the moment, a cup of hot chocolate was exactly what I wanted. And, despite her speech impediment, Clare seemed OK. She was very pretty, anyway, too pretty to be a Christian.

'Thanks. That would be great. I'm Susannah, by the way.'

I offered her some of my milk for the hot chocolate and we said nothing more as we made it. Not surprisingly, Clare seemed to like keeping small talk down to a minimum. When the hot chocolate was poured out, we stood and talked for a bit, blowing on our drinks. Most of the time, she was able to speak normally, but there were certain words she couldn't say, often ones that began with vowels. When that happened, she'd put an 'Umm' in front of the word and keep going at it, again and again, until it came out. I sensed that the best thing to do was just to wait while she did it, rather than to supply the word, which was usually pretty obvious.

After a while, I got used to the way she spoke, and she

began to talk more easily. It turned out that her parents lived in Kenya, and that she was studying zoology. She was going to go back there when she'd finished her degree to become a scientist of some sort. She was particularly interested in elephants. I couldn't imagine someone whose interests were more different from mine, but I quite liked her. Maybe living on campus for a while wasn't going to be so bad after all, I thought. At least it made a change from Jason and art deco lamps and quadraphonic stereos and Chateau de Chasselet.

When the conversation came round to me, I wasn't very keen to supply details. I just said I'd split up with my boyfriend and was staying in my friend's room here for a while, till I got something else sorted out. Then we finished our drinks, washed up our cups, and went back to our rooms. Just before we did, she told me her room number and said I could drop round some time if I wanted, and I did the same.

I spent the rest of the afternoon unpacking. I didn't have much stuff, but I enjoyed deciding where to put everything. The cupboards were all empty: apart from the sheets and towels, Cassie didn't seem to keep any of her belongings in the room. When I'd finished, I sat down at the desk, fixed the anglepoise lamp in the right position, and got stuck into Heidegger.

I spent the rest of the evening reading and making notes, studying at my desk in the way you were supposed to, instead of lounging about on a cushion on the floor like I usually did. I stopped thinking about Jason, about being pregnant, about what I was going to do. I just acted like a student, a second-year student studying conscientiously for a degree in Philosophy. It was a situation I'd always avoided like the plague, living like an ordinary student on campus, but now that it was happening to me it seemed to be a blessed relief.

At around one in the morning, I got up from my desk,

yawned, and went to bed. It was very quiet as I lay there in my viyella nightdress in Cassie's clean white sheets. Just as I was falling asleep, I heard an owl hoot and a mouse squeak somewhere outside my window, but it didn't disturb me. In here, tucked up in my single bed, it all seemed very safe and ordered.

I slept a dreamless sleep until morning.

chapter 18

I WOKE UP EARLY ON SUNDAY MORNING. It was still dark outside, but I got up and went out to the kitchen to make myself a cup of tea. I took it back to bed with me, drew the curtain, and watched the sky lighten over my patch of grass as the dawn became the day. It seemed to happen very gradually yet very fast, in a way that had always mystified me as a child, and still did. I realised I hadn't seen the dawn come up for a long time.

While I watched, I thought about philosophy. Tomorrow was my last tutorial with Belham before the end of term. I was supposed to have handed in a title for my Modern European Mind dissertation, but I hadn't had time to think about it. I'd been planning to do something about Nietzsche and the way he ranted on in *The Birth of Tragedy* about philosophy having become a dry, decadent, soulless activity in the West instead of a Dionysian celebration of life and its carnal pleasures, but that seemed a bit abstruse now that I had more pressing questions to tackle – such as what I was going to do about being pregnant.

I started to wonder whether there was anything in *Human, All Too Human* that would help me. I cast my mind back and tried to remember the words from the preface. What was it now, something about the task, the secret destiny, commanding us like...

I reached over quickly and picked up my bag, which was

lying on top of a pile of clothes on the floor by the bed. I scrabbled about in it looking for the sheet of paper with the *Human, All Too Human* quotes on it, and finally found it tucked away in a corner. It was covered in grease stains from a packet of cheese biscuits that I'd put in and forgotten about. I brushed off the crumbs, unfolded the paper, smoothed it out, and read:

The secret power and necessity of this task will hold sway within and among our various destinies like an unsuspected pregnancy, long before we have looked the task itself in the eye or know its name…

Incredible, he'd used those very words. For Nietzsche, the task, the secret destiny was *like an unsuspected pregnancy*. He'd seen it as a metaphor, not a reality – because he was a man. But my task, my secret destiny, as a woman, wasn't a possibility among many others, *like* an unsuspected pregnancy: it *was* an unsuspected pregnancy. I couldn't change direction, or wander off and leave it behind. Maybe the male philosopher could be a free spirit and a wanderer, but a female one couldn't. I was attached, held down to life, by sheer virtue of my biology; even without knowing it, I'd become joined to the foetus growing inside me. So I couldn't fly about, like a bird, living between yes and no. It wasn't an option for me. Unlike the male free spirit, the wanderer and philosopher, I had to make a decision.

I crumpled the greasy paper into a ball and chucked it over to the bin by my desk. Then I picked up my mug of tea and took another sip. Rob had been right about Nietzsche. He wasn't much good when it got down to the nitty gritty of the human social world. He wasn't going to be any help to me, not in my present condition anyway. He was a man, and a philosopher, and he just didn't deal with questions like what to do about being pregnant. Neither did any of the philosophers I'd come across so far, of course – they were all of them men – but I sensed for some reason, I wasn't sure why, that this new one, Heidegger, might possibly be able to help.

I hadn't understood much of what I'd read in *Being and Time*, but I had the feeling that what Heidegger was on about was pretty mind-blowing, and could change the way I thought about everything. As far as I could fathom, he was saying that up to now, Western philosophers had put forward the incredibly stupid idea that human beings are essentially minds trapped inside bodies, somehow peering out at the world as though through a plate-glass window, and wondering what's really out there, if anything. But the reality is that we human beings find ourselves in the world, are 'thrown' into it, as he put it, and have to sink or swim as best we can. We have to do things, make things, to survive: find food, shelter, and so on. We do all this without thinking: we only need to think, in fact, when some problem arises. It's like driving: you just do it automatically, and it's only when you notice you're about to crash that you have to start paying attention.

So thinking, Heidegger seemed to be saying, is a kind of aberration. Before we start thinking, things just carry on, and we kind of merge into life without being conscious of ourselves as subjects separate from the world of objects and other people. Instead of being trapped inside the plate-glass window, and looking out, and wishing we could connect, here we are, 'being in the world', right in the cut and thrust of life all the time, if we only knew it.

I didn't know how all this was going to help me, but I sensed I was going to have to think about this pregnancy differently from how I'd thought about things before. Whatever happened, I was going to have to be in the world in a new way in future, maybe start thinking about not thinking...

I finished my tea, pleased that I was beginning to make some kind of sense of *Being and Time* at last. Then I got out of bed, put my jacket on over my nightdress, and went into the kitchen to get something to eat. There was no one in there so I made myself beans on toast and tea, and took it back to my room. After breakfast I got back into bed and drifted off to sleep again, relishing the sensation of the food in my full, warm belly.

When I woke up, there was someone knocking at the door. I thought it must be Clare, so I got out of bed and opened it. But standing outside were Cassie and Fiona.

'Hi,' I was still half asleep. 'What are you doing here?'

I didn't mean to sound rude. I was just surprised.

'Can we come in?' said Cassie.

'Yeah, of course, what time is it?'

'About two,' said Fiona. I wondered if she sounded disapproving, or if I'd imagined it.

They came in. Cassie went over to the mirror and started inspecting her make-up, while Fiona picked my plate and mug off the floor and put them on the desk, tidying the papers to one side as she did. Then they both sat down, Cassie on the end of the bed, and Fiona on the chair by the desk. I got back into bed, partly because there was nowhere else for me to sit, and partly to draw attention away from the flowery nightdress.

'D'you want some coffee or something?' Then I remembered I didn't have any. 'Or tea?'

'In a minute,' said Fiona. 'We've come to see if you're all right.'

'Thanks for the room, Cass,' I said, ignoring Fiona. 'I've been sleeping like a log in here. It's really cosy.'

'Yeah, it's nice, isn't it,' said Cassie. 'I mean, for a change. You wouldn't want to live here, obviously.'

'No, obviously,' I agreed.

Fiona butted in. 'Well, are you?'

'Am I what?' Fiona's hectoring tone was irritating me.

'Leave her alone, Fee,' said Cassie. Nobody called Fiona Fee except Cassie.

'Are you all right?' repeated Fiona. She spoke slowly, as though she was talking to someone very stupid.

I could feel my irritation rising.

'No, Fiona.' I spoke slowly, mimicking her tone. 'No, I'm not all right, since you ask. I'm not all right at all.'

The anger in my voice was unmistakable. Fiona was about to respond, but Cassie gave her a look and she checked herself. There was a long silence.

Then I said, 'As it happens, I'm pregnant. I got the results of the test on Friday.'

There was a gasp from the end of the bed. I looked at Cassie. Under her brown skin, her face had gone an odd shade of yellow.

Fiona grimaced, got up, walked over to the bed, sat down between me and Cassie, and put her arm round me.

'Don't worry, Suse,' she said. 'It'll be all right.'

I felt uncomfortable with Fiona's arm around me, so I put my head forward until my hair fell over my face, looked at the floor, and said nothing.

Cassie began to cry at the end of the bed.

'Oh, for God's sake,' said Fiona.

'Sorry,' said Cassie, but she went on crying.

'Get a grip on yourself, you bloody idiot.'

At that point, I started laughing.

'Sorry, Fiona,' I said, giggling as she patted my arm soothingly.

'Never mind,' Fiona said. 'You're just hysterical.'

Then Cassie began giggling as well, much to Fiona's annoyance.

'Look,' said Fiona. 'Stop mucking about. You're behaving like a couple of schoolgirls, both of you. This is a serious situation. We've got to discuss it properly. I'm going to go and make some tea, and by the time I come back, I want you both to have calmed yourselves down.'

Fiona picked up my plate and mug and marched off to the kitchen.

As soon as she went out, Cassie and I stopped laughing and looked at each other.

'Jesus, Susannah.' Her eyes seemed bigger and rounder

than usual. 'What are you going to do?'

'I don't know, I haven't decided yet.'

'Yet?' she echoed. 'What do you mean, yet?' There was a note of panic in her voice.

'I just want to think about it, that's all.'

'Is it Jason's?' she asked.

'Well, actually… I don't know. It could be. Or it could be Rob's.'

Cassie's face seemed to drain itself of colour again, and she covered her eyes with her hand. She didn't ask me any more questions. She seemed lost in her own thoughts.

We sat in silence until Fiona came back with the tea and started fussing around with milk and teaspoons and some lumps of sugar she'd nicked from somebody else's store in the kitchen. When she'd handed out our teas she sat back down in the chair by the desk.

'Right,' she said, stirring her tea and taking a sip. 'How far gone are you?'

'I don't know,' I said, feeling stupid. 'I've missed a couple of periods.'

'Well, I'm sure that's no problem.' She spoke as though she knew what she was talking about, but I had a feeling she didn't. 'The first thing you'll need to do is make an appointment at the health centre tomorrow.'

'Fiona,' I said, 'thanks, but I need time to think.'

'There's nothing to think about,' Fiona said. 'You've got to get on with it. You shouldn't have a problem with the doctors at Sussex, they're pretty good about this sort of thing. And if you do, we'll get my women's group to pressurise them.'

'But Fiona, I haven't even decided whether I want an abortion.'

Fiona glanced at Cassie. 'OK,' she said. She was trying to be patient. 'So what do you want?'

'I don't know. I just need to think about the options.'

Fiona took a deep breath, held it, and let it out slowly.

Cassie bit her lip, looked away, and said nothing.

'What options?' said Fiona, finally. She spoke quietly, but the hectoring tone had come back into her voice.

'Well, you know. A woman's right to choose, and all that,' I said.

'Don't be stupid,' she said. I could see I'd annoyed her. 'It doesn't mean a woman's right to choose a baby. It means a woman's right to choose to have an abortion.'

'I don't think it does,' piped up Cassie. 'It means you can choose to have an abortion or have a baby, doesn't it?'

Fiona shot Cassie a look of contempt. 'Of course it doesn't.'

She gulped down her tea and went on, speaking faster as she warmed to her subject.

'It means you don't have to fulfil your biological function as though you were some kind of milk cow. You can choose to be free of all that now. You can have some control over your destiny. Bloody hell, you two, which planet have you been living on? This is the 1970s, not the Dark Ages.'

'OK, OK,' said Cassie. She was glaring back at Fiona. 'Cool down, Fee. Can't you see Susannah's upset? She doesn't want a lecture about feminism right now, if you don't mind.'

'Look, this isn't just an abstract argument about politics,' said Fiona. Her voice was rising. 'This is about control over our lives. Haven't you read *Our Bodies Ourselves*?'

'No, I bloody haven't,' said Cassie. 'And I'm not going to. It's all about getting the clap and looking up your fanny with a wing mirror and a bike torch, isn't it?'

I tried to suppress the urge to laugh, but an exploding sound escaped me.

Fiona ignored me. 'No, it isn't, as it happens. It's about having some respect for yourself as a woman. It's about looking after your body and being careful who you sleep with. It's about how to avoid getting sexually transmitted diseases, or getting pregnant... It's about all sorts of things you don't seem to have thought about for a second, either of you...'

She stopped suddenly and her face went red. She turned to me.

'I'm sorry, Susannah. I didn't mean...'

'It's OK,' I said. 'You've got a point. I know I should have been more together about all this.'

'Well, what the hell,' interrupted Cassie. 'It's done now. It doesn't matter whose fault it is. The question is, what do we – I mean, you – do now?'

I sighed. 'I know this sounds stupid...'

Cassie and Fiona were both looking at me intently.

'... But I just thought it would be quite nice...' My voice trailed off.

'Go on,' said Cassie.

'Well, you know...' I stopped again.

This time, no one said anything.

'... to have it.'

I felt like an idiot. I was talking about having a child as though I was choosing a pair of shoes or deciding where to go out for the evening.

There was a long silence and then Fiona leaned over from her chair and touched my hand.

'You can't, Susannah,' she said. 'Honestly, you just can't. It wouldn't be fair to bring a child into the world in such circumstances.'

Fiona didn't even know the full circumstances. She didn't know that the baby's father might be Jason, or it might be Rob. She didn't know that Jason had just chucked me out of the flat and called me a scrubber. Or that he was a poof. Or that Rob was probably only sleeping with me because Beth wouldn't. She knew nothing about what had gone on. She was in no position to judge what I should do, but all the same, I knew that she was right.

'OK,' I said. 'Fair enough. I'll go and make the appointment tomorrow.'

'Oh shit,' said Cassie, and started crying again.

★

When Cassie and Fiona left, I spent the rest of the afternoon studying Heidegger, making notes for my dissertation. It was a relief to get back into a world of hyphenated abstractions, but now I felt slightly guilty about it. I didn't know what had made me think that *Being and Time* could have any bearing on what I should do about my situation. Now, I was conscious that I was simply using it as a convenient way of escaping from reality.

In the early evening I went downstairs to the lobby to phone my mother. It wasn't that I thought I could discuss anything with her. That had never been the case. It was just that I wanted to hear the sound of her voice.

'Mam?' I said, as she answered the phone.

There was a long pause. 'Hello?'

'Mami, it's me. Just thought I'd give you a ring.'

Another long pause.

'Hello, Susannah,' she said. 'And how are you?'

My heart sank. I wondered why I'd wanted to speak to her. I'd forgotten that she talked like this now, using formal words in a slow, flat tone, as though she was reading from a script. From time to time she'd try to inflect her voice, to bring some brightness into it, which made it worse.

'I'm fine,' I said. 'Looking forward to coming home for Christmas.'

'Yes,' she said. 'That'll be nice. Very nice.'

She'd been like this ever since my father's death. She'd been hysterical at the time, which was understandable – he'd just dropped down dead from a heart attack as he was eating breakfast one Sunday morning – but then the doctor had put her on some tablets and she'd gone to the other extreme. She was doped up to the nines the whole time, and having a conversation with her was like wading through mud. Over a year later she was still acting like a robot. I felt sorry for her, but it pissed me off as well. And the funny thing was, I always forgot she was like that now, and only remembered when it was too late.

'It'll be next week, Mam.' I spoke slowly as well. 'Do you think you could meet the train?'

'Of course, love.' The forced brightness came in again.

'Bring Auntie with you.' At least my aunt, her sister, still had all her marbles.

'Of course.' She paused, looking for a topic of conversation. 'How are the exams going?'

'No exams this term, Mam. But I'm working hard on my dissertation.'

'That's right. Good girl.'

'And I'm pregnant,' I wanted to add. But I didn't.

The conversation ground painfully on until we came to saying goodbye. Then, just as she put the phone down, she said something that made me feel better.

'*Dal ati!*'

'*Dal ati,*' I replied.

It was a Welsh thing my father used to say. It didn't mean much, just 'keep up the good work' or some such nonsense, but saying it seemed to comfort us both. At any rate, it showed she was still alive, somewhere in there.

I walked upstairs again, thinking about the phone call. It hadn't helped much, but at least it had made clear what I already knew: that my mother couldn't help me, and that I was going to have to deal with this on my own.

chapter 19

I WAS UP EARLY ON MONDAY MORNING. I had a lot on that day. I had my Modern European Mind tutorial with Belham, and I was going to have to tell him the subject of my dissertation. Rob would be in the tutorial, and I was going to have to think of a way of avoiding seeing him afterwards. Then I was going to have to get down to the health centre and book my appointment for the abortion.

I still hadn't phoned Rob, though I'd thought about it every time I went past the phones in the lobby. I wanted to see him, to talk to him, to explain everything, but I knew I couldn't. He wouldn't understand, and I'd blow the whole thing. I thought of getting back with him and not telling him I was pregnant, just carrying on as normal, and arranging the abortion on my own in secret, but I knew I wasn't up to that. I'd crack sooner or later and let on what had happened, and then he'd dump me and I'd feel terrible. In the circumstances, it seemed best to get on and have the abortion as soon as I could, and then get in touch with him afterwards, once the decks were cleared. I missed him, and I knew it was going to be difficult to keep making excuses not to see him – he was probably furious with me already for not contacting him in the last few days – but for the time being there was no other alternative.

As it grew light outside the window, I started wondering why I hadn't been waking up screaming in the mornings lately. You'd have thought that being pregnant, and splitting up with Jason, and not having anywhere to live, and now having to go through with an abortion, would have made me worse than ever. But here I was, sleeping like a log every night, and waking up in the mornings feeling refreshed – happy, even. It was curious. I felt as though my life was moving very fast and very gradually at the same time, in some preordained, mysterious way that I didn't understand but was actually very ordinary, like the sun coming up in the morning. Perhaps I just hadn't faced up to the reality of my situation. Or maybe it was the Heidegger that was frying my brains.

'Rob? Susannah?'

Belham was looking at each of us in turn. 'Any ideas?'

I hoped Rob would say something.

'The leap of faith,' Belham reminded us. 'Any thoughts?'

I had no thoughts on the leap of faith. Neither did Rob, by the look of things.

Belham sighed. 'Have either of you read the set text for this week?'

I kept quiet.

'Sort of,' said Rob.

Belham sighed again.

I searched about for something to say. I'd only read about two sentences of Kierkegaard when I was in the doctor's surgery, but now they came back to me: something about a frightened bird flying about in dismay, and God, and waking up from sleep with a heavenly smile.

'I suppose it's kind of...' I said.

'Yes?' said Belham. He tilted his head to one side encouragingly.

'Well, say you have to make a decision,' I went on. 'Say you're frightened and you don't know what to do.'

Rob had been sitting with his head bent down, his hair

falling forward over his face, doodling on his notepad, but now he looked up. I was aware of his eyes on me.

'Say you try to think all the arguments through, but there comes a point where they're not enough. Where reasoning doesn't help you. Then you have to take a leap, based on...'

I stopped.

'On... what?' Belham spoke quietly.

'I don't know,' I said. 'I don't know what. That's the point, though.'

'What's the point?' said Rob. There was an aggressive edge to his voice.

'Well, it wouldn't be a leap of faith if you knew what, would it?' I tried to keep my tone level, but I could hear that I sounded impatient.

'You're just talking about faith in God,' said Rob, equally impatient.

'Not necessarily.' Belham put his oar in. 'Go on, Susannah.'

'Well, perhaps what Kierkegaard is saying...' I paused, remembering that I knew absolutely nothing about him, which was a leap of faith in itself. 'Maybe what he means is that when you make the leap, you're not doing it because you know God will help you. You're doing it in the absence of any knowledge at all. But actually making the leap stops you flying about all over the place like a bird in dismay.'

I paused again. Coming out with the quote made me sound as though I knew what I was talking about, so I went on.

'It gives you a purpose,' I went on. 'It gives you faith, in a way. That's what God is, perhaps. The courage to make the leap. Kind of thing.'

'That's still religious thinking,' said Rob with a pedantic air.

'I don't think so,' said Belham. 'I think Susannah's got a point here.'

Rob clicked his tongue quietly under his breath and

began doodling again. I knew he was irritated because he'd read the text and I hadn't, but it wasn't my fault he was being uptight and refusing to discuss it in the tutorial. I wasn't trying to get one up on him, I'd only pitched in because I thought Belham deserved something better than a couple of lazy, monosyllabic students to teach, especially now he'd lost Dennis.

Belham started talking about Kierkegaard's attack on Christendom, drawing Rob into the discussion, and by the end of the tutorial everyone seemed to be in a better mood. As we got up to go, Belham wished us both a good break over the Christmas holidays, and then, as we were packing up our stuff and I was wondering how I was going to get out of going for coffee with Rob in the common room, Belham asked me to stay behind.

Rob walked out of the room and gave the door a bit of a slam, which made Belham look up with a puzzled expression on his face.

'What's the matter with Rob today?' Belham asked as I sat down again.

'No idea,' I said. 'Just a bit touchy, I think.'

'Really?' He gave me a searching look.

I changed the subject. 'Is it... did you want to ask me about my dissertation?'

'Well, yes, I suppose so. But there's no real hurry about that. It's more...' He paused. 'I just wondered if you were all right, Susannah.'

'How do you mean, all right?'

'You seem to have been a little... distracted lately.'

'Do I?' I felt alarmed. I'd hoped he hadn't noticed. 'Sorry. I'm just a bit tired, that's all, what with the end of term and everything.'

'Is there anything wrong?'

'No,' I said. 'I'm fine. Absolutely fine.'

'Good.' He didn't sound convinced. 'It's just that after Dennis... I, well, you know...' His voice trailed off.

'How is Dennis?' I said, changing the subject again.

'I don't know,' he said. 'I wrote to him, but I've heard nothing back. I think he's still living with his parents.'

There was a silence, and then Belham added, 'He was a talented philosopher.'

'Mmm,' I said.

Silence descended again and Belham started scratching his ear. Then he said, with what seemed like an effort, 'And I think you could be, too, Susannah.'

'Oh. Thanks,' I said.

Even though Dennis was obviously one of Belham's favourite students, I wasn't altogether thrilled to be compared with him.

'You seemed to be enjoying the course earlier in the term,' he went on. 'I don't know what happened. And now Rob...' He looked down at the floor dejectedly.

I realised that Belham was blaming himself for the fact that all his students seemed to be screwing up lately.

'Oh no,' I said. 'It's not you... it's not the course,' I said. 'The course is great.'

'Well, what is it then?' He looked up at me. I noticed the bluish shadows under his eyes, and how the trace of stubble on his face made him look worn out, but in a sexy kind of way.

It was then that I started crying. It seemed to happen at the drop of a hat these days.

Belham got up from his desk and came over to where I was sitting. He sat down on the chair next to me and gingerly patted my shoulder. He didn't seem to want to get too close.

I put my head in my hands and began to sob violently. Once I started, I felt as if I'd never stop again. I hung my head so that my hair fell forward, to hide the tears and mucus and dribble running down my face.

Belham fished in his pocket and brought out a handkerchief that didn't look all that clean, but I took it and blew my nose.

'Sorry,' I said, not looking at him. The sobs were coming more quietly now, in shuddering aftershocks, as though I was a child.

'Don't be sorry,' he said. 'These things happen to all of us.' I noticed the sadness in his voice as he spoke.

'No,' I said. 'They don't. They just happen to me.'

Then I told him that I was pregnant, and that in a minute I was going to have to go down to the health centre and book myself an abortion. I wasn't sure why I did it, because I'd always quite fancied him, and even though I never really thought that he'd fancy me, I'd always kind of hoped that one day he might look up and notice me as a woman, rather than as just another student like Dennis. But he never had, and now that I'd been crying like a baby in front of him, with my nose all red and snot running down my face, I realised he probably never would.

This time, he put his arm round me and squeezed my shoulder briefly, then sat back away from me again. He seemed uncomfortable whenever he came anywhere near me.

'Does the father know?' he said.

'Well, that's the thing,' I said. 'I don't know who... I mean, I'm not sure...'

'Ah, right,' he said, a little too quickly. I didn't look at him, but I could sense his discomfort.

I didn't say anything more for a while, and neither did he.

Then he said, 'Susannah, what would you choose if you were free to do anything you wanted to?'

I looked up at him. Up close, I could see crinkles of skin around the edges of his eyes, and there were some grey bits of stubble around his chin. He couldn't have been more than thirty, yet there was something almost haggard about him. I thought, he looks old, really old. But I fancied him, there was no doubt about it.

'I'm not sure,' I said.

'Well, think about it,' he said. 'Think about it carefully. Aim high. You can do anything you want to, you know. It's not either or.'

When I left Belham's room, I found Rob waiting for me in the corridor.

'Hi.' I put my head down so that my hair fell over my face. I didn't want him to see that I'd been crying.

'What the fuck was all that about?'

I started walking down the corridor towards the stairs, and he fell in beside me. 'All what?' I said.

'You know what, Susannah.' He sounded angry.

'No I don't. What?'

'First of all you disappear for days, then you ignore me in the tutorial and suck up to Belham, then you stay behind and chat to him for hours to try and avoid me afterwards. What's going on?'

As we walked down the stairs, he seemed to be much too close, leaning in on me. I tried moving away but he kept moving with me.

'Nothing's going on,' I said. 'We were just talking about my dissertation, that's all.'

We reached the door to the outside world, and I stopped to open it. It seemed heavier than usual and I struggled with it.

'OK, but at least you could explain where you've been hiding all this time. D'you want to go for coffee?' It sounded more like a demand than an invitation.

'I can't, Rob, I've got to get down to the health centre.'

He gave the door a bad-tempered shove and we walked through.

'You're always going to the health centre,' he said. 'What the bloody hell's wrong with you?'

It was my turn to feel angry now. 'None of your business.'

I quickened my pace, leaving him behind, but he started shouting my name as I did. People were turning round to look.

He caught up with me, his face flushed, and gripped me by the arm. 'You've got to tell me what's going on. You owe it to me.'

I stood there with his hand closing around my upper arm, squeezing my flesh until it hurt. He dug his fingers harder and harder into my skin, but still I said nothing. I was enjoying the pain. It was making me angry, to the point where I felt I really didn't owe him anything, except perhaps a kick in the balls.

Then I saw that there were tears in his eyes and I snapped. 'I don't want to go out with you, Rob,' I said, looking past him. 'That's what's going on.'

He let go of my arm and doubled up as though I'd punched him in the stomach. Then he straightened up, took a deep breath, and closed in on me again, gripping me by the shoulder. 'But why? Why?'

A feeling of triumph came over me as I saw the bewilderment on his face. But then, seeing his look of shame as he raised his head to stop the tears falling down his cheeks, I suddenly felt ashamed too. I knew I was purposely trying to hurt him, but I didn't know why.

'I'm sorry, Rob.' My voice was shaking, and I could feel that he was shaking too. 'I'll explain all this to you one day, but I can't now.'

'Well, when can you?' There was an urgency in his voice that excited me. He really wanted me. Having told him that it was all over, I began to want him again.

'I need time to think,' I said, still looking past him. 'Let's meet after the holidays…'

But Rob wasn't listening. He'd seen something in my face that told him I wanted him again, and he was moving in fast, while it lasted.

He started kissing me, biting my lip as he did and

running his hands through my hair, pulling it hard so that it hurt. I began to feel dizzy and for a moment I lost consciousness.

When I came to, I saw that I was standing outside, looking up at a grey sky. Rob was holding me in his arms.

'God, are you all right?' he said.

'I think so.'

'What happened?'

'I just felt a bit faint,' I said. 'I'm OK now, I think.'

'Jesus,' he said. 'I'm really sorry. I didn't realise... I didn't mean to hassle you. It's just that...'

'I know,' I said. 'But I can't talk about it now. I promise I will, though. When we come back...'

'... After the holidays,' he said. 'But just tell me now. Is it that there's someone else?'

'No.' This time I wasn't lying. 'It's not that.'

'You're not...' He paused. 'You're not terminally ill or anything, are you?'

I laughed. 'Not as far as I know.'

I started walking again, and Rob fell in beside me. He walked me down to the health centre, and when he left, he took off his silver bangle and put it on my wrist. 'Christmas present,' he said.

'Thanks.' I felt like crying, but I stopped myself. 'I haven't got anything to give you. Sorry.'

'Happy Christmas,' he said, drawing me close and kissing me.

'Happy Christmas,' I replied, kissing him back.

'Shall I come in and wait with you?'

'No, it's OK.'

'Give me your phone number, then. I'll call you later.'

'I haven't got one. Not at the moment, anyway.'

He pulled a piece of paper out of his pocket and handed it to me.

'Well, here's my parents' number. I'll be there for most of the holidays.'

'Thanks,' I said, folding the paper and putting it in my jacket pocket. 'I've got to split now. Bye.'

I turned and walked up the steps of the health centre.

'Bye,' he called, but I didn't look back.

chapter 20

INSIDE THE HEALTH CENTRE, I walked up to the reception desk and asked if I could make an appointment. I didn't ask for Doctor Morgan by name. I couldn't face trying to explain myself to someone who looked like one of my father's friends, and I was hoping they'd give me someone else. But when the receptionist asked who I was and I told her, she immediately got on the phone. The next moment, she was saying, 'Doctor Morgan will see you now,' so I had no choice but to walk up the corridor and knock on his door again.

'Come in,' he called.

I opened the door and went in to find him sitting behind his desk, shuffling his papers as he'd done before.

'Ah, Miss Jones,' he said. 'Do take a seat.'

I sat down and said nothing while he shuffled on. Then he stopped, took off his specs, and peered at me shortsightedly.

'Well,' he said. 'We've had a positive result for your test. Now, where does that leave us?'

I bowed my head. I couldn't think of anything to say.

There was a silence.

'I expect this has come as a bit of a shock to you,' he said, fiddling with his glasses.

I nodded silently, still looking at my lap.

'Miss Jones,' he said. 'May I call you Susannah?'

I nodded again. I couldn't give a shit what he called me to be honest, but I didn't say so.

'You must understand, there's nothing for you to be ashamed of,' he went on. 'You've made a mistake, that's all. You're not the first and you won't be the last.'

I looked up, surprised. I'd been expecting him to give me a lecture.

'The question is, what do you want to do about this?'

For a moment I thought of telling him everything: about Jason, about Rob, about my father dying and my mother being a zombie now, about Fiona's advice, and about what Belham had said. For a moment I imagined I could talk it all over with him and come to some kind of decision. But then I remembered he was a doctor, an Ammanford man my father's age: someone who had been in the war, and worked hard, and paid his way, and slept in a twin bed beside his wife for the last thirty years.

'I want to have an abortion, of course,' I said.

The way it came out, it sounded coarse and harsh, as though I didn't give a damn about my unborn child. And as though I was rebuffing his attempts to be sympathetic as well.

Doctor Morgan shifted in his chair. I could tell he was offended. He coughed, and then said, 'Have you discussed this with the father?'

'No,' I said. 'And anyway, I don't know who the father is. I'm going to have an abortion, and that's that.'

I wondered why I was being so rude to him. Perhaps it was a way of hiding my embarrassment. All I knew was, I couldn't stand his concern. It was cloying, and worse, it made me wonder if I had any idea what I was doing.

'Well, if that's really the case...' He looked at me quizzically, but I said nothing.

'Have you discussed this with your parents?' he asked, changing the subject.

'No,' I said. 'My father's dead, anyway.'

'I'm sorry to hear that.' His tone was gentle but even. I got the impression he was beginning to realise that I didn't want his sympathy. 'Recently?'

'A year and three months ago.' I was surprised how quickly it came out. I never thought about exactly how long it was since my father had died, but whenever anyone asked me I seemed to be able to tell them straight away.

'Ah,' he said. 'I see.'

I hated the way he said that, as though he understood something about me that I didn't.

'And your mother?'

'I can't talk about this with her. She suffers with her nerves.'

'Nerves' was a well-known condition back home, one that, once raised in conversation, was never discussed any further.

'Oh. I see,' he said again. I wanted to slap him.

'And this question of the father...' he went on.

I sighed. 'Look, Doctor Morgan, there are two possibilities. One of them is my ex-boyfriend. I've told him and he doesn't want to know. We've split up now. The other...'

'Yes?'

'I'm sure he wouldn't want to know either.'

Now that I said it out loud, I wasn't so sure. In fact, I began to wonder why I hadn't told Rob. Maybe it wasn't because I thought he'd reject me like Jason had. Maybe he hadn't just been sleeping with me because he was dying for a screw after years of going out with Beth and getting nowhere. Maybe I'd kept it from him because I was scared he'd want the baby, and me, and then I'd be stuck with him for the rest of my life.

'I think you owe it to him to tell him though, Su... Miss Jones.'

Rob's words came back to me: *You've got to tell me what's going on. You owe it to me.*

'OK,' I said. 'Maybe I will. But it won't make any difference. I'm still going through with this, whatever happens.'

*

By the time I left the health centre, I'd signed the papers for the abortion. Doctor Morgan had gone through all the forms with me, asking me if there was a grave risk to my physical or mental health if I continued with the pregnancy, to which I'd answered yes, even though I couldn't see why I had to pretend I was going to die or go off my head just because I didn't want to have a baby. Once we'd filled out the forms, he'd told me that he'd have to get another doctor to sign them, and that my application would then go through to the hospital, and that the whole process might take weeks. He'd given me an information booklet, which listed some private clinics in Brighton where I could obtain a 'speedy termination', as he called it, in the meantime. He'd explained that, up to thirteen weeks of pregnancy, the procedure was fairly simple: they just sucked the foetus out of the womb with a type of Hoover. After that, he said, it got more messy and complicated, but he didn't go into details. He'd told me that I could change my mind at any time, and asked me to come back and see him after the break, and I'd said I would, although I didn't see any reason to. When I got up to go, he wished me a good break, but he didn't say Happy Christmas, and neither did I.

I stuffed the booklet into my bag to hide it as I walked through campus. I couldn't face reading it right away, but I knew I'd have to force myself to do it before long. I didn't know much about abortions, but I'd heard that if you left it too late, you had to give birth to a dead baby, and there were horror stories about it coming out alive, or deformed, or screaming in agony, and having to be murdered on the spot. Sucking a few cells out with a Hoover sounded altogether different. I'd heard of women having operations like that for period pains; in fact my mother had gone into hospital overnight for something like that a few months ago, but she hadn't told me exactly what it was. 'Women's problems', like 'nerves', were not something you discussed back home, even with your daughter.

On the way up to Cassie's room, I stopped at the European Common Room to look in my pigeonhole. Thankfully, there was no one there I knew. I picked up some reading lists for the holidays, and a few Christmas cards that other students had sent me, the straight ones on the course who still hadn't realised that you didn't do things like that at Sussex. Most of the mail was internal, but there was also a letter addressed to me care of the university. With a shock, I recognised Jason's writing on it. I wanted to tear it open and read it right then and there, but instead I picked it up with my other papers and walked quickly down the corridor to the loo. Then I locked myself in, sat down on the seat, and opened it.

Dear Susanna, it began.

Not darling, or Susie. And he'd spelt my name wrong, as he always did.

I hope you are well.

I knew Jason wasn't much of a writer, but this was pathetic.

I'm sorry about what happened. Can we meet up and talk? I miss you.

So he really was sorry. He wanted me back.

XXX Love Jason.

P.S. I still want to marry you if the baby is mine.

When I read the postscript, I couldn't help bursting out laughing. As I did, tears began to prick my eyes, but I didn't cry. What a bloody idiot Jason was. Why had I ever taken him seriously? He might have been ten years older than me, but he had the mentality of a child. It would be useless trying to explain to him that if you loved someone, you didn't carry on like this: you took on their problems, their life, their mistakes, lock, stock and barrel. Fair enough, I'd been unfaithful, I'd hurt him. But if it was really me he wanted, he'd meet me on my own terms, and we'd talk the whole thing through. As it was, all he could do was to make another of his dramatic, childish gestures that ignored everything and everybody except his own needs.

I heard someone come into the toilets, so I put the letter in the bin for sanitary towels next to the loo, pulled the chain, unlocked the door, and walked out to wash my hands. As I did, I looked at my face in the mirror. I couldn't be sure, but it seemed to have got rounder. My cheeks seemed to have puffed out, and the flesh around my chin and on my neck was plumper than usual. I looked younger somehow.

Six weeks pregnant, and already it was showing, even on my face. I had to get this abortion over and done with as soon as possible.

That afternoon, I rang one of the numbers on the information booklet Doctor Morgan had given me. I gave the receptionist my details and told her that I wanted to book an appointment for an abortion as soon as possible after Christmas. I had to speak quietly because I was ringing from a phone box on campus. The receptionist told me that there was nothing available in the week between Christmas and New Year because that was a very busy time at the clinic. She sounded disapproving every time I said 'abortion' and corrected it to 'termination', so in the end I followed suit, even though the word sounded euphemistic and petty bourgeois to me. She said she couldn't fit me in until two weeks after, so in the end I rang another clinic, and another, but they were all full. Apparently, I'd picked a bad time, as most of the clinics were booked out over the Christmas holiday with Catholics coming in from Ireland. Finally, I found a clinic that could take me, so I put my name down and agreed to post them the fee in advance, which was seventy pounds, payable by cheque. The money had to be cleared by the time I came in for my examination, and after that I'd have the operation under general anaesthetic and stay overnight in the clinic.

I hadn't realised I'd have to get hold of the money so quickly, or that it would be so much. But I knew immediately what to do. I had a savings account at the bank with a hundred pounds in it, which my father had set up for me when I'd first gone to university. I'd managed to keep it all this time. Even when I'd been completely broke, I hadn't touched it, but now I needed it. It wasn't exactly what he'd envisaged the money would be spent on, I knew, but this was an emergency. I didn't feel guilty, just relieved that I wouldn't have to phone my mother and lie about why I needed seventy pounds all of a sudden.

Once I'd made the calls, I went straight down to my bank on campus and moved the money over into my current account. Then I wrote a cheque and posted it off to the clinic, which was called 'The Arbours' and was in a part of town up by Preston Park full of neat, low-rise blocks of flats and retirement homes. After that, I phoned Cassie to tell her what I'd done, and asked her to pass the message on to Fiona. Cassie sounded bewildered and upset, and asked me if I wanted to come over, but I said I was leaving the next day and had to pack. Then she said that Fiona was with her and wanted to talk to me, so she put her on the line.

'When's the date fixed for?' said Fiona, who had obviously been listening to the conversation.

'Hi,' I said. 'How are you?'

'Do you want me to come with you?' she carried on, ignoring my attempt at a normal conversation.

'Thanks,' I said, 'but it'll be in the holidays before you come back. Anyway, I don't know if you're allowed.'

'Of course I'm allowed. Remember, Susannah, you're calling the shots here. You're paying. You can do whatever you want. I'll come back early and take you in if you like.'

'There's no need.' I really didn't want Fiona breathing down my neck and bossing me around while I was having an abortion. 'But thanks anyway.'

Once I'd declined her offer, I wondered if I'd made a mistake. Fiona could be a pain in the arse, but I knew she'd stand up for me if anything went wrong. And I had to admit that, if I thought about it too closely, the prospect of the operation frightened me quite a bit.

'Is this a reputable clinic that you've booked yourself into?' asked Fiona.

'Well, it was on the list that the health centre doctor gave me,' I said.

'Hmm,' she said. 'I suppose that's all right. You'd better let the doctor there know where you're going, though.'

I hadn't thought of that. 'OK.'

'And if you change your mind, phone me at my parents',' she said, giving me the number. 'I'll come straight down.'

'Thanks, Fiona.' I was touched by her kindness.

'And don't worry, you're doing the right thing. You know that, don't you?'

'Yes,' I said.

'You're taking control of your life.'

'Yes,' I said.

Then I asked to be put back on to Cassie to say goodbye before the conversation went any further.

On my way back through campus, I passed by the health centre and gave the receptionist a note for Doctor Morgan, with the name and address of the clinic on it, and the date of my operation. Then I headed up to my room to pack. I didn't have much to take, as I was only going to be at home for a week. I'd have to think up an excuse for my mother as to why I had to come back so soon, but that wouldn't be difficult. I could say that I had some studying to do. She'd be happy with that.

While I was packing, Clare stopped by to see me. I asked her what she was doing for Christmas, and she told me she was going to stay with her aunt, who lived in a flat in Bournemouth, and that she'd be coming back to campus before term started as it was always so boring there. I had a sudden urge to ask her to come home and spend Christmas with me, but then I pictured my mother trying to make polite conversation through a fog of tranquillisers, and I thought better of it. I told Clare that I'd be coming back before term started as well. She seemed surprised, but pleased that I'd be around. I was pleased she'd be around too, but I didn't tell her why.

By the time I went to bed, the room was neat and tidy, and my suitcase was packed. Before I turned off the light, I looked around, wondering if there was anything else I still had to do. I knew you were supposed to clear all your stuff away in the holidays, so that the cleaners could come in, so I'd put all my books and files away in the cupboard, and left some clothes in there too, carefully folded beside the sheets and towels. I'd done a good job. Apart from the suitcase on the floor and my toothbrush and toothpaste in a mug by the sink, there was nothing in the room to show that I'd ever been there.

I turned off the light and listened for the owl I'd heard outside the window the first night I'd been here. For a long time there was nothing, and then, in the distance, came its cry. First a short wail, and then a long hoot, like an eerie laugh. It was too far away this time for me to hear its prey squeak. I was glad of that. I was about to run my hands over my belly to see if it was any more swollen, but something stopped me. I closed my eyes and began to fall asleep, wishing I could hear the sea and feel the sting of salt in my nose, as I had just a few nights before in Brunswick Square. It seemed a lifetime ago now.

MODULE 3

Søren Kierkegaard:
Fear and Trembling

chapter 21

When you can snatch the pebble from my hand, grasshopper, then it will be time for you to leave...

It was Saturday afternoon and I was watching TV in the student common room at Sussex. David Carradine snatched the pebble and then began his eternal walk into the sunset while an oriental flute played the *Kung Fu* theme tune. I smiled to myself. Rob had once mentioned to me that he loved this programme. I could see why. Corny eastern philosophy and kung fu, spaghetti western-style. I wondered if he was watching it now.

The episode started well, with the pebble and the sunset and the theme tune, but after that there was just a lot of fighting with a fatuous story line hung on. The only saving grace was Carradine, whose expression of sorrowful boredom never altered throughout, even when he was delivering his killer kung fu chop to the many enemies that crossed his path. Carradine was pretty cool, I thought. He was definitely a Knight of Infinite Resignation. He had made the first movement from the world of the finite. But I doubted whether he was a Knight of Faith. If he had been, he wouldn't have come over as so distant and superior.

Over the Christmas break, I'd started reading Kierkegaard's *Fear and Trembling* and it had blown my mind, even more than Heidegger. In some ways, I wished I hadn't. It was too close to the bone. It was all about the biblical story of Abraham sacrificing his son Isaac to God; about what it means to kill your own child; about how you can justify that to yourself or anyone else. I kept thinking, this guy's a Christian, and I'm not: this doesn't apply to me. But I knew it did, because Kierkegaard's God wasn't a father who told you what to do; his God was a conscience that tormented you day and night until you were forced to choose your fate for yourself.

While I'd been at home, I'd tried not to think too much about the abortion. It was all fixed up, and there was no point in dwelling on it. It hadn't been all that hard to put it out of my mind, because going back to Swansea was like going back in time, to when I was a child in my parents' house. My room was much the same as when I'd left it, even though now it had the feel of a spare room, like a lot of the rooms in the house did since my father's death. In the run-up to Christmas, I'd gone shopping and seen some of my old schoolfriends, who were mostly working by now. Only one of them, Eleri, was at college like me, training to be a librarian. We'd gone out for coffee as we usually did in the holidays, to catch up on each other's news. We'd been close when we were at school, and I'd thought I might tell her about the abortion, but when she sat down and announced that she'd got engaged to someone she'd met on her course, I couldn't face raising the subject, so I'd just made small talk instead, trying to ignore the fact that she looked hurt by my polite answers to her questions about what was going on in my life.

On Christmas Day I'd gone to chapel with my mother in the morning, and then to Auntie Luned and Uncle Ifan's for lunch. They were my father's brother and sister who lived together, both strict teetotallers and chapelgoers. Meals at their house took about twenty minutes maximum. In the old days, when my father was around, we'd have had lunch at home and invited them over, and there would have been wine with the meal, because Dad had been interested in wine and had a collection of French wines in the cellar. We'd have taken our time over eating, and Luned and Ifan would have pretended not to notice the booze but stayed anyway and enjoyed themselves. Nowadays, with my father gone, my mother never entertained any more. There was still wine in the cellar, but nobody drank it. After lunch, we'd watched the Queen's speech on TV and then gone home and watched *Morecambe and Wise*. Mam had laughed a bit then, and so had I. I'd wondered if she was getting better. On Boxing Day we'd visited more relations, and the next day I'd gone back to Sussex. I'd told her that I had to work on my dissertation. She hadn't seemed too upset. She was still in her own world, after all this time.

As the *Kung Fu* credits went up on the screen and the flute played the programme out, I got up to go. Nobody else moved. There were a lot of chairs in the room, but only a few students, slumped about in corners, each one far away from the others. They looked as though they were there for the duration, and would watch whatever came on next, until the little dot showed and the bleep sounded. Before the Christmas break, I'd never have come in here, even if I'd been bored out of my mind. I'd have stayed in my room and read. But now, Kierkegaard had driven me down here. By coming in here this afternoon, I'd finally surrendered and joined the ranks of institutionalised student inmates; but I wasn't planning to stay long.

As I climbed the stairs back up to my room on the second floor, I noticed that my body felt sluggish and I was panting a little. The thought crossed my mind that there were only a few days to go until my operation. As I reached the top step, I stopped to catch my breath, feeling slightly dizzy. At that moment, I realised that there was nothing else for it now: I was going to have to put my mind to the question of whether to have an abortion or not. Granted, it was all fixed up, and I wasn't about to cancel my appointment. But it wasn't a foregone conclusion, much as I wanted to make it so. It was something I had to think about carefully. Something I had to agonise about, probably. A torment. A test of faith. Kierkegaard had won, the bastard.

There wasn't much time. I had three days, not counting the rest of today, to make up my mind. Three days, like Abraham's journey to the mountains of Moriah.

On the way to my room, I knocked on Clare's door to see if she was back from her aunt's yet. She was, and she seemed pleased to see me, inviting me in. She'd been listening to Emperor Rosko on Radio Luxembourg and working at her desk, but now she went over and sat on the bed, offering me the chair. The bed was covered in a brightly coloured African textile, and there were matching cushions on it. Above it, on the plain white wall, she'd fixed a couple of carved wooden masks that looked slightly menacing. They kept catching my eye as she talked to me, and I wished I was sitting on the bed instead of her so that I couldn't see them.

We talked about the Christmas break. Hers seemed to have been as boring as mine. I asked her what she'd been doing since she got back and she came over to the desk and showed me the application she'd been making. It was to help out at a project for orphan elephants in Kenya over the summer. Their mothers had been killed by ivory hunters, she said.

Orphan elephant babies, I thought. First *Fear and Trembling*, and now this. It seemed that everything was conspiring to remind me of my pregnancy, of the fact that I was planning to have an abortion in a few days' time without really having thought about what I was doing. I hoped Clare would change the subject, but she was in full flow now. She started talking about how hard it was for humans to imitate the elephant mothers, and how labour intensive it was to replicate the herd's way of raising the babies, showing me pictures of Africans playing with them and trying to feed them with bottles. Few of the orphans survived, she said, but the more research that was done on elephant behaviour, the better the prospects of saving their lives.

'If I'm lucky I'll be assigned an orphan to look after,' she said. 'I'll have to sleep next to it at night to feed it and keep it warm, and stay close to it all day, sheltering it from the sun the way its mother would have done.'

I said nothing.

'... It's pretty hard work,' she went on. 'I'll have to play with the other babies as well. The research shows that it's not healthy for a baby elephant to get too attached to its mother. In the wild, other adult elephants would play with it and help to bring it up. It would be cherished by the entire herd.'

A lump came to my throat. 'Oh really?' I said.

'Yes. Elephant society is matriarchal, you know. There's a female elephant in charge of a close-knit family herd. She knows where to find food and water, and how to protect the herd from danger. When the mothers in the herd give birth, she or one of the other older female elephants acts as a midwife. It's amazing, isn't it?'

Clare looked up at me, smiling.

'Yeah, great.' I swallowed, trying to get rid of the lump.

Clare turned away, embarrassed. 'Sorry, I tend to get carried away about umm...'

I waited.

'Umm...'

I knew what she wanted to say, but I didn't want to supply the word for her.

'Umm e...'

She'd have to get it out on her own.

'Elephants.'

Now that she'd started stuttering again, I realised that she hadn't done it once up until now. It was obviously being made to feel that no one was listening that set her off.

'No, it's really interesting,' I said. It was. In fact, I envied her. She seemed to know exactly what she wanted to do in life, and was setting about doing it, unlike me. 'It's just that I'm a bit freaked out at the moment...'

Emperor Rosko was babbling away in the background so I went over and turned him off. Then I told Clare I was pregnant, and that I'd fixed up an abortion in three days' time, but that I was now having second thoughts about it. I wondered how someone who was going to devote her life to orphaned animals would take the idea of a woman purposely aborting a baby, but Clare was pretty matter-of-fact about it. I suppose it came from being a zoologist.

We talked for a while, and I told her about Jason and Rob, and what a mess it all was. She listened carefully, but didn't offer any advice. I got the impression that human society was something she didn't understand or feel she could comment on. So after a while, I changed the subject.

'How do female elephants choose their mates?' I asked.

Clare looked thoughtful. 'I don't know. That's something I haven't studied. I'll find out for you, if you like.'

'And once they're pregnant, do they stay in a pair with the father?'

'Yes and no. As I said, the baby is brought up by the whole herd, and it's a matriarchal clan, so the fathers don't take a major role. The baby feeds on its mother's milk for about four years, so it stays close to her during that time, but all the adult elephants in the herd look after it and play with it as well.'

'Like in a commune,' I said.

'I suppose so,' said Clare, looking baffled by this remark.

I got up to go. 'Well, I'd better be off. I still haven't started my dissertation. Good luck with the application.'

'Thanks. Good luck with the umm...'

I waited.

'The umm... ab...'

This time I didn't wait.

'See you around,' I said.

*

I didn't want to admit it, but Cassie's room was starting to feel like home. I hadn't put anything up on the walls, but there were books stacked neatly on the shelves and files laid out on the desk, with pads of squared paper for making notes, and lined ones for writing essays. Beside them were biros and felt-tip pens in black, red and blue, and thick 6B pencils that I used for marking passages in books, rubbing the lines out with a putty rubber when they had to go back to the library. There was even a fountain pen I wrote my essays with, and a bottle of blue-black Quink beside it. My father had given me the pen, and although it was messy and old-fashioned, I enjoyed the rigmarole of filling it up. And when I started writing, I liked the scratch of the pen as it crawled along the paper, and the way, when you'd finished a page, you had to stop and press blotting paper over it to stop it smudging, and the way the ink came out like mirror writing on the blotting paper. The whole process was all so deliberate, and painstaking, and unhurried. It reminded me of my father. And it helped me to think.

I sat down at the desk and got into the pen routine, unscrewing it, sticking the nib into the bottle of Quink, squeezing the little rubber tube inside it until it sucked up the ink, wiping the sides of the pen with a tissue, and then shaking it over a piece of blotting paper to check the ink was running through properly. While I was doing it, I was thinking about my dissertation. It was going to be something about Heidegger and Kierkegaard, about 'being in the world', about the 'knight of faith'. It was going to be something about this abortion too, but I couldn't say that.

I started with a quote from Kierkegaard:

For my own part I don't lack the courage to think a thought whole. No thought has frightened me so far. Should I ever come across one I hope I will at least have the honesty to say: 'This thought scares me, it stirs up something else in me so that I don't want to think it.' If that is wrong of me I'll no doubt get my punishment.

Three days from now, I was going to go to the clinic and have the foetus inside me sucked out. The foetus my breasts and belly had been swelling for. The foetus who was growing, day by day, into a baby. My firstborn child. My father's grandchild, who might somehow follow his trail and bring him back to me, to us. I wasn't as brave as Kierkegaard. The thought scared the shit out of me. But I knew that, if I didn't want to punish myself, I was going to have to think it.

I wrote down the title of the essay. 'The Knight of Faith: a critique of Kierkegaard's concept of faith on the strength of the absurd in *Fear and Trembling*, with reference to Heidegger's notion of Dasein in *Being and Time*'.

It wasn't very snappy. Dennis wrote essays for Belham with titles like 'Does Prayer Work?' and 'What Is Time?' but I wasn't up to that level. And I couldn't very well call it 'Should I Have an Abortion?', which was really what it was about. The title would just have to do for now. I could cut it down later.

I put the pen down and looked out of the window to think.

Right. OK. Come on, Susannah. You've arrived at the clinic. You've had the examination. They're going to put you under for the abortion. What are you going to do?

Get up and leave.

Why? Because you're scared of operations?

Maybe.

That's a bit pathetic, isn't it? You're going to bring an unwanted child into the world just because you're scared of having an abortion?

But maybe I want the child. Maybe that's why I'm scared. Because I know I'm doing something that's not right for me.

OK, so you want the child.

Yes. I think I do.

Can you imagine being a mother?
No.
Do you think you'd be any good at it?
No.
Do you know any children?
No.
Are you married?
No.
Do you know who the father is?
No.
Do you have a place to live, or an income?
No.
So what makes you think you want the child?
Well, from my reading of Heidegger and Kierkegaard...
I picked up the pen and began to write.

chapter 22

BY FOUR O'CLOCK THE NEXT MORNING I had finished my dissertation. And I had decided I was probably going to have the baby.

It had started quite gradually, with Heidegger. I'd been writing about his notion of Dasein, being in the world, when I'd realised that being pregnant wasn't actually a problem as such. It was just part of being in the world, part of what happens, part of what people – women – do, like getting up in the morning or going to bed at night. It wasn't exactly 'natural' – that was a loaded term and I wasn't going to get into all that stuff about women's biology and the nature/nurture debate – and it wasn't exactly 'normal', which was another can of worms. It was simply part of the day-to-day business of living in the world. It was a state of being that did not, in itself, require thought. As such, it was not a problem.

It only became a problem when you started thinking, when you began to imagine the future: what you were going to do, how you were going to live, how it was all going to work out. But that, essentially, was a challenge created by the conditions of the outside world, something you were going to have to tackle: finding food and shelter for yourself and your child. Women had done that for centuries, either with men, or on their own. It was not an impossible task; in fact, it was probably easier now, at least in the world I lived in, than at any other time in human history.

What I had to keep in mind was that there was nothing actually wrong with me. I was just doing what people – women – do. But I was living at an odd time, in an odd place, where for a young woman to conceive and bear a child was seen as an aberration, a piece of bad luck, like getting struck by lightning or falling down a manhole in the street: an interruption to the business of living, instead of part of the business of living itself.

The other thing Heidegger was saying, which I still couldn't quite grasp, but which hovered above me like a religious vision, was that there wasn't really a difference between subject and object. As long as you drove your car along the road with no obstacles in view, you weren't aware of yourself driving and the car being driven. Only when a car loomed up at you, coming the wrong way, did you start thinking in those terms and taking evasive action. In the same way, I was moving along with the baby inside me, and it was hard to say in the end who was doing the driving. Obviously, if I looked ahead one day and saw that we were about to crash I would need to take control. But I wasn't at all sure that we were about to crash. In fact, we seemed to be running along quite smoothly.

Now that I came to think about it, ever since I'd become pregnant, I'd stopped dreaming about cars and roads and crashes. I'd been sleeping soundly, and waking refreshed. For the first time since my father had died I'd felt a sense that everything was going to be all right: that the way up ahead was clear and that we were moving along at a slow, sensible pace, for the moment at least.

At around six o'clock in the evening, just as I was coming to the realisation that there was nothing really to stop me having the baby, Cassie had phoned. She knew the number of the hall of residence, which had been her number, and had persuaded one of the inmates to come up to my room and tell me I had a call.

When I got down to the lobby, I found the receiver of the phone hanging suspended from the booth, so I assumed the person on the other end had been cut off or given up waiting. But when I picked it up, she was still there, hanging on.

'Hi Suse,' she said. 'How's it going?'

'Oh Cass, it's you,' I said. 'Thanks for calling.'

I was aware that I was struggling to understand what was going on down here in the real world. I'd been in the realms of Heidegger for several hours by now.

'Are you all right? You sound a bit odd.'

'Sorry. I've just been writing my dissertation. I've had a bit of a breakthrough, as it happens.'

'How are you feeling about the... you know,' said Cassie, ignoring my news.

'Oh, right. Yes. Well, I'm not sure... I don't know if I'm going to go ahead with it.'

'Oh.' Cassie sounded confused. 'Why's that? Have you made it up with Jason?'

'Jason?' I felt as though I could hardly remember who Jason was. 'No, of course not.'

'Oh,' she said. 'Rob, then?'

'No,' I said. I thought, I should phone Rob sometime soon. I still had his numbers on a scrap of paper in my purse. He'd be expecting to hear from me now that Christmas was over. But as yet, I didn't know what to tell him. I'd phone him just as soon as I'd made up my mind.

'So what's changed?' asked Cassie.

'Oh, nothing really. Nothing like that, anyway. It's more... well, it's to do with the subject and the object, Cass. It's a bit hard to explain.'

There was a pause.

'Are you sure you're all right?' Cassie asked again.

'Yes, I'm fine,' I said.

'You haven't cancelled it, have you?' There was a note of panic in Cassie's voice.

'Not yet. I've still got some reading... some thinking to do. I haven't quite made up my mind. But I'm having second thoughts.'

I heard someone come into the room at Cassie's end. Then she said, almost whispering, 'I'm sorry, I can't talk now. I'll phone you again as soon as I can. Don't do anything silly, will you?'

'No, I won't,' I said. 'Of course I won't. I've never felt less silly in my life.'

On the way back up the stairs, I forgot our conversation and started thinking about Heidegger again. There was something he'd got wrong. By the time I'd sat down at my desk again, I'd worked out what it was, and I started writing. Belham is going to like this, I thought. The tutors at Sussex always appreciated you giving the big names like Plato and Descartes and Kant a good kicking, as long as you wrote 'it can be argued that' before you started saying what a load of bollocks they were spouting. Heidegger was more of a challenge, because his writing style was so insane, and it was almost impossible to work out what he was on about in the first place, but I decided to wade through the hyphens and have a go anyway.

According to Heidegger, human beings are 'thrown into the world' and have to sink or swim wherever they land. A picture came into my mind of babies flying through the air and landing in their cots, ready for action. It was ridiculous. Only a man could have come up with such an idiotic idea. As I saw it, what actually happens is that babies are part of the world from the beginning, merged with their mothers inside the womb. In a quite literal way, from the off we are never separate subjects. We are part of another person, another body, from the moment we are conceived. It's nothing to do with being thrown anywhere.

I worked slowly and methodically, stopping to look up quotes, and thinking out my sentences before I wrote them down. Round about midnight the hall of residence quietened down. There were no voices in the corridor or thumps on the ceiling, and outside it was pitch black. I listened for the owl, but I couldn't hear it. As it got later, I thought of all the philosophers who had scratched away in candlelight with their quill pens, far into the night. I thought of the way my father used to work in his study at home, and how musty the room smelt now that no one went in there any more. I'd sometimes had the impression that he'd wanted me to follow him into medicine – after all, I was his only child – but he'd never pushed it. I wondered, for a brief moment, whether I should have, whether I could have; whether he would have died happier if I had.

At around four o'clock in the morning, I stopped writing. The dissertation was almost finished. Although it was still too short, I knew I had enough material there for the whole thing. All I had to do was witter on a bit longer and drag out a few more quotes, possibly even start talking about 'the metaphysics of gestation' or something pretentious like that. But I still wanted to get on to Kierkegaard. Heidegger had helped me work out why I felt OK about being pregnant, why I wasn't tearing out my hair and contemplating throwing myself off a bridge. But that wasn't enough. If I really was going to cancel the abortion and go through with having a baby, I was going to need more than just feeling OK. I was going to need faith. And I didn't know yet if I had it; or if I didn't, how to get it.

chapter 23

FIONA AND I WERE WALKING along Brighton pier. She'd turned up at my room that morning and dragged me out, 'to get some fresh air', she said. Cassie had rung her to tell her I was having second thoughts about the abortion, and she'd taken a train straight down from London, where her parents lived, to come and see me. I was touched that she'd bothered, but I wished she hadn't.

There was plenty of fresh air on Brighton pier. As we walked into the bitter wind, our eyes stung and watered so much we had to take shelter in one of the booths that lined the centre of the walkway. We sat on the wooden seat under the scratched plastic cover and looked out to sea. There wasn't much of a view, just grey fog and brown water. Even though it was Sunday, there were no other people on the pier. You could see why.

'You're just nervous,' Fiona was saying. 'Anybody would be.'

I looked up at the sky. It was a purple, yellowish grey, like a bruise.

'But you're only eight weeks,' she went on. 'So it's really nothing. You'd hardly call it an operation. It's just like having a tooth out at the dentist's.'

I wondered if it would rain.

'Susannah, are you listening to me?'

I thought it might.

'For God's sake,' she said. 'Say something.'

I gave a sigh. Fiona had been giving me a pep talk ever since she'd arrived. I'd let her go on, but I wasn't listening. I'd really been getting somewhere with Heidegger and Kierkegaard and the abortion, and I didn't want her to interrupt my train of thought. But now, sitting on the pier with the wind lashing the booth, I realised I'd have to respond.

'The thing is, Fiona,' I said. 'I've been doing some thinking about this. It's not as though I'm going into it with my eyes closed. But I need time...'

'You haven't got any time.' Fiona sounded irritated.

'Don't interrupt.' My tone was sharp. 'Who's having this abortion, you or me?'

Fiona looked taken aback. I didn't normally talk to her so abruptly.

'Sorry,' she said. 'Go on.'

'Yes, well, as I was saying...' I paused. I'd explained this to myself but not to anyone else. 'I seem to be feeling happy to be pregnant. I'm not having nightmares any more. I'm waking up fine. And that makes me think that this is kind of... the right thing to do. It's an everyday, ordinary process that it makes sense for me to go through. Part of the business of living, if you know what I mean.'

Fiona looked nonplussed.

'If I stop thinking about the future,' I went on, 'I like the way I feel. I like being pregnant. I feel sort of...' I searched for the words. I hadn't explained this to myself before. 'Sort of womanly. As though I've become an adult at last.'

I thought of the day I'd got up early, put on the fur coat and sat watching the sun on the sea with the tabby cat. 'It's quite sexy, actually.'

The moment I said that, I wished I hadn't. It sounded frivolous, the sort of thing Cassie would come out with.

Fiona frowned, but said nothing. Drops of rain began to fall on the plastic cover, the wind splatting them down hard like gobs of spit.

'I can imagine,' she said. 'It must be nice.'

Her reaction surprised me.

'I feel like somebody now,' I went on, encouraged. 'Somebody with a task to do. I feel as though I have a future. I haven't felt like that since my father died.' I stopped.

'Go on,' she said.

I looked out to sea. 'Having babies is just a normal part of living, Fiona,' I said. 'It's what people do, you know. What they've always done. We're no different. It kind of takes the sting out of... I don't know. Life. Death.'

I hadn't explained any of this to myself before. It was all new to me.

Fiona said nothing. When I turned to look at her, there were tears in her eyes.

'I know,' she said. She spoke quietly. 'I completely understand. If the circumstances were right... but they're not. However happy it makes you feel to be pregnant now, Susannah, it's not going to go on for ever.'

I looked back out to sea.

'The reality is that in nine months' time you're going to have a baby on your hands,' she went on. 'You'll probably get through it somehow, but it's going to be bloody tough for you. The child won't have a proper father. You'll either have to look after it yourself and have no money, or go out to work in some shit job and never see it. You'll have to leave Sussex. You won't get your degree. You won't have a career. And however much you love the child, it'll all be a bit of a mess.'

She was right, I knew. It would all be a terrible mess. But it might be one that I had to make.

'The thing is, Fiona,' I said, after a long silence. 'This has happened now.' I touched my belly through my layers of clothing. 'I think I'm going to have to go through with it.'

'But that's the whole point,' Fiona said, turning back to me in exasperation. 'You don't have to go through with it. Don't be so bloody passive. For the first time in history, women are in control of their fertility. We've got the pill, and legalised abortion now, everything we've fought for. We're the first generation of women who can take advantage of that. Our mothers, and our grandmothers, didn't have that choice. They didn't have careers, they were tied to domestic drudgery, dependent on men, all their lives. They never got a chance to find out who they were, what they could do in the world, and look how frustrated and miserable they all are. We don't have to be like that. We're not determined by our biology any more. We can choose to have children when we want to, or not to have children at all. We can do anything we want to. We're free. Don't you see?'

Fiona had given me this lecture many times before, but I'd never listened up till now.

'Yes, of course I do,' I said. 'But I don't think it's as simple as that. We can't just shrug off our femininity, our bodies, in that way. Germaine Greer's got it wrong.'

I pictured the cover of *The Female Eunuch*. It was a woman's body shaped like a swimming costume, with handles on the hips, hanging up on a line. The image had impressed me more than the book, which seemed more like tabloid journalism than serious writing to me. She'd announced at one point that if you hadn't tasted your menstrual blood you weren't a proper woman, so I'd tried it, just to show willing. I'd somehow expected it to be a significant experience, but it wasn't; the blood had tasted a bit metallic, like blood from a cut on your finger or anywhere else on your body. The whole book seemed to be like that: designed to shock but a bit of a let-down in the end.

'The thing is,' I said, 'we can take the pill and have abortions as much as we like. But we're still women. We're still going to want to have babies.'

'Yes, but we're no longer just baby-making machines. That's the difference. That's what Greer is saying.'

The rain was beginning to pelt down now, and the wind was blowing it off the sea into the shelter. I started to shiver, but I still didn't move.

'And the other thing is,' I said, raising my voice to make myself heard above the wind, 'I think you're wrong about this abortion. It's not just like having a tooth out. It's not just a bunch of cells. It's a potential human being.'

'Yes, but it's still very undeveloped,' Fiona shouted back.

'Maybe. But it's a living being. I don't know if I can kill it.'

The wind started howling round the shelter. We were yelling at each other now.

'You can. You must.'

'Why must I?'

'Because you're not in a position to look after it properly, Susannah. You know that.'

She had a point.

'It's not fair to bring a child into the world under these circumstances.'

Now I wasn't so sure. She'd said that before, when I'd first told her I was pregnant, and it didn't ring true, then or now. I couldn't say why, but it sounded wrong. I needed to get home, on my own, and read Kierkegaard, and think about it.

The wind got so loud we couldn't hear ourselves, so we got up and walked back down the pier in the pouring rain, heads down into the wind, holding on to each other to stop ourselves being blown away. When we got to the end, we were soaking wet. We took a bus up to the station, the windows so fogged with steam that you couldn't see out. Then we waited for Fiona's train on the London platform. She didn't mention the abortion again, and neither did I.

'Thanks,' I said, when the train came in. 'It was nice.'

She smiled. Her dark hair was all wet and her face was flushed. She looked pretty.

'Yes, it was,' she said. 'I'm glad I came down.'

'Lovely fresh air,' I said.

She laughed.

'I'll phone you,' I said.

'OK,' she said. 'Make sure you do.'

'Bye, then.'

'Bye. And good luck.'

She turned and got on to the train. I didn't wait for it to pull out of the station. I had a train to catch too, on a different platform.

When I got back to the hall of residence, I found someone waiting outside the door of my room. I saw him from the end of the corridor. He was wearing a black fedora and a long black coat. It was Bear. It couldn't have been anyone else.

My heart started beating fast and for a moment I felt like turning round and running away. But I made myself walk up to him.

'Bloody hell,' I said when I got there. 'What are you doing here?'

I hadn't meant to sound rude, but it came out a bit blunt.

Bear laughed. 'Hello, old girl,' he said, pecking me on the cheek. 'How's it going?'

I fumbled for my key and opened the door of the room. 'Fine,' I said. My voice sounded nervous.

'Gosh,' he said when we got into the room. 'You've been busy.'

There were piles of books all over the floor with little bits of squared paper sticking out of them, that I'd used as markers, and the desk was covered with neatly handwritten sheets of lined paper.

I moved some of the books and cleared some of the papers away so that he could sit down. I offered him the only chair in the room, at the desk, and sat down on the bed myself.

Bear took off his hat and coat, hung them carefully on

the back of the door, and went over to the desk to sit down. Under the coat, he was wearing a sort of brocade jacket with wide shoulders and lapels, and underneath that a black shirt unbuttoned at the neck, and baggy, high-waisted 1940s-style black trousers. He looked so completely out of place sitting at my desk in my student room that I almost burst out laughing.

'Susannah, you're soaking,' he said. 'What on earth have you been up to?'

'Oh, just getting some fresh air on Brighton pier,' I said.

'Hadn't you better get out of those wet clothes?' he said.

'Yes, I suppose so. Are you planning to stay long?'

Bear laughed again. 'No, not really, but listen, why don't I go and make us some tea or something while you change?'

'OK.' In the past, I'd have worried about what he might think of the kitchen, or what the other students might think of him, but right now, I couldn't care less. I wanted some tea, and I wanted to get warm and dry. 'It's just down the corridor. My cupboard's the one on the left by the sink. You'll find everything you need in there.'

'Right oh. I'll be back in a jiffy.'

While he was out, I peeled off my wet boots and socks, changed into my other pair of jeans, and put on a clean T-shirt. The only warm jumper I could find was one that Auntie Luned had knitted me for Christmas, in a pretty but old-fashioned shade of china blue. I didn't have time to look for anything else, so I put it on. I towelled my hair dry quickly and then combed it out in front of the mirror.

Not long after, there was a knock on the door and Bear came back in with the tea. He handed me one of the mugs. He'd remembered how I liked it, white with two and a half sugars.

He sat down at the desk, blowing on his tea, and I sat on the bed, blowing on mine.

'Nice jumper, Susannah,' he said.

'Thanks,' I said. 'Auntie's Christmas present.'

'Well, it suits you. English rose, I mean, Welsh rose, and all that.'

'Thanks. You're looking pretty cool yourself. Kind of man about town.'

'Oh yeah, that's me, all right.'

We both laughed.

'So how have you been?' I asked. 'How's... things?'

'Well, not great. But not terrible. What about you?'

I thought about it. 'Everything's still a bit up in the air,' I said eventually.

'Are you still...?' Bear's voice trailed off.

'Yes, I am. But I'm booked in for... I'm going to have an...'

I couldn't say it.

Bear tried to help me along. 'Oh, so you're going to have an... you've decided not to have the baby.'

'Well, I'm booked in for the... But I'm not sure. I haven't cancelled it.'

'Right.' Bear looked confused.

'To be honest, I still haven't made up my mind. And it's the day after tomorrow.'

There was an uncomfortable silence while Bear tried to think of something to say.

Then I broke the silence. 'Why are you here, Bear?'

Bear took a deep breath, held it, and then let it out. 'Well, under the circumstances... I don't know, Susannah, I don't want to put my foot in it...'

'Oh, go on,' I said. 'Put your foot in it. You can't make things any worse than they are.'

Bear grinned wryly. 'OK,' he said. 'I will.'

He reached into the pocket of the brocade jacket and brought out a small black bag.

'Here we are,' he said, loosening the strings at the top and pulling out a small ebony box with some white stones set into the top of it.

I recognised it immediately. It was the milk-teeth box.

He held it out in the palm of his hand and I saw the curly writing on the lid: *dents de lait*.

'This is for you,' he said, passing it over to me. 'For the... the baby. If you have it.'

I took it and looked at it.

'Oh fucking hell, Bear,' I said, and began to cry.

Bear came over and sat by me on the bed. 'I'm sorry,' he said. 'I didn't mean to... I told you...'

He put his arm round me.

I snivelled into his brocade jacket for a bit and then pulled myself together.

'I don't want it,' I said, wiping my eyes. 'You can tell Jason I'm not interested.'

Bear went over to the sink and found a towel. He handed it over to me and sat down at the desk again.

'This is nothing to do with Jason,' he said. 'It's a present from me.'

'But I thought it was Jason's,' I said, wiping my face with the towel. I blew my nose on it too, which I normally wouldn't have done, but I couldn't be bothered to find a tissue. 'I thought...'

'Jason virtually nicked it from my parents,' Bear said. 'He thought it was worth a fortune and he paid them a pittance for it. I was livid when I found out, so I took it back from him. I returned it to my mother and she said I could have it if I liked it. For my children.' He paused. 'And as I'm not likely to have any, I'm giving it to you.'

'But does Jason know?'

'No. And I'm not going to tell him. It's mine to do what I like with. It's nothing to do with him.'

'But it's worth a lot of money, isn't it?'

'Well, not really, as it turns out. Theoretically, it should be, but Jason's dealer, Dalton, wasn't prepared to buy it in the end. He said he couldn't be sure if it was given to Princess Charlotte Augusta by King George or the Prince Regent, and that if it wasn't the Prince Regent he didn't want to know. Jason kept trying to find a specialist who would persuade Dalton that it was a Regency piece, but he couldn't, and in the end Dalton decided not to take the risk. Without a buyer, it's worth about five hundred quid at the most.'

'Well, you should keep it then, shouldn't you?'

'No, I want you to have it. I feel pretty bad about the way Jason treated you, slinging you out of the house like that. When you were... are... you know. This is the least I can do to make up for it.'

'Thanks, Bear,' I said. 'But I still can't take it. I might not have the baby. As I told you, I might be having an... abortion.'

I'd said it.

Bear wasn't fazed. 'Makes no difference. If you need the cash, you'll always have it to sell. Or if you want, you can keep it for the next one.'

'What do you mean, the next one?'

'Well, you're bound to have a baby at some time in the future, aren't you? Most women do.'

The thought had never occurred to me. But now that he pointed it out, I realised that this wasn't the only baby I'd ever be able to have. This wasn't my last chance. At a better time, in a better place, I could do this again. Properly.

There was a pause, and then I said, 'So you really want me to have this? No strings attached?'

'Absolutely none. Though if you do ever have children, you'll have to make me a godfather.'

I laughed. 'OK then. Thanks. You've got the outfit for it, anyway.'

'I'm making you an offer you can't refuse,' Bear said, muttering through his teeth like Marlon Brando, and we both laughed.

Then I changed the subject.

'Are you and Jason still... friends?' I said.

'Yes,' Bear hesitated.

'Are you...?'

'Well, yes. Yes, we are. We always have been. But he won't admit it.'

'Why not?' I said.

'Well, you know what he's like. He doesn't want to admit he's gay.'

I'd heard the term 'gay' before. It was the new word for homosexual. Bear said it lightly, and I resolved to do the same in the future. Gay. Not poof. Or queer.

'He doesn't see our relationship as the real thing,' Bear went on. 'To him, it's just a hangover from adolescence, from boarding school, when there were no women around. He keeps thinking he'll grow out of it. But I know he won't.'

I thought back over my time with Jason. So that was what it had all been about. No wonder I hadn't been able to get close to him. All that time, he'd been sleeping with Bear as well as me. I suppose he'd been trying to find a way to escape from what he was, and I'd been looking for someone to take control of my life. No wonder it hadn't worked in the end.

'So what are you going to do, then?' I said.

'Stick it out, I suppose,' Bear replied. 'I love him, you know.'

'Yes, I know,' I said.

We looked at each other, and I remembered the way we'd sat in the Madagascar that evening just a couple of months ago, watching Jason and his sister holding court. We'd both been in love with him then, I realised. That had been the unspoken bond between us. Everything was so different now, for me, anyway. Jason hadn't crossed my mind for weeks. Now I came to think of it, the way he'd chucked me out had actually been a liberation for me. He'd done me a favour. I was free of him at last. Then I remembered I might be carrying his child, and I realised I wasn't, and possibly never would be.

'Well, I'd better get going,' Bear said, finishing his tea and getting up.

He went over to get his coat.

'Let me know what happens,' he said, putting it on. 'I'm at Jason's now. You know the number.'

'Oh, you're living down here now, are you?' I said.

'For the moment,' he said.

'OK,' I said. 'I'll give you a ring.'

Bear paused. 'And Jason will want to know too if... well, he'll want to know, obviously.'

'Don't worry,' I said. But the thought of what Jason would do if I had the baby and it was his did worry me. And I could see it worried Bear as well. 'I'll be in touch.'

'Good luck, old stick,' said Bear. He gave mc a kiss on the cheek. 'Whatever happens.'

'Thanks,' I said. 'I'll need it.'

He put on his fedora. I opened the door and stood there watching him as he walked off down the corridor, his black coat flying out behind him. Something about his demeanour seemed to have changed since I'd last seen him, I thought. He seemed older, more confident than I'd remembered him. Although we'd laughed about it, I realised he did look like a man about town now. From a distance, anyway.

chapter 24

He knows it is beautiful to be born as the particular with the universal as his home, his friendly abode, which receives him straight away with open arms when he wishes to stay there. But he also knows that higher up there winds a lonely path, narrow and steep; he knows it is terrible to be born in solitude outside the universal, to walk without meeting a single traveller.

I was walking on the hills with Søren Kierkegaard. It was summer, and around us were rolling green hills. Far below us were meadows full of flowers and cows with clanking bells. As we walked, the mooing of the cows and the clanking of the bells grew more and more distant. Up ahead of us towered a snow-capped mountain. Our path was taking us towards it. I could just make out the shape of the path as it wound up the craggy sides of the mountain. It looked dizzying and dangerous. I hoped I wouldn't have to go up there, that I could turn back when we got to the bottom of the mountain; or that if I did have to press on, Søren would come with me.

'So what do you think of Fiona's argument?' I asked him.

Søren was a slight man, not much taller than me, with a peculiar limp that made him walk in a jerky way, but other than that he was quite attractive. He was dressed in a tight black suit, with a flowing white shirt underneath. He had a lot of wavy brown hair and a pale, scholar's face with large, intelligent eyes. He looked a bit like Belham, though not as swarthy.

'Have you read Hegel?' he said.

'Sort of,' I said. I had, but most of it had gone above my head.

'For Hegel, there is a hierarchy of thought, of spirit,' he said. 'At the top is the universal: philosophy. Below that is religion. And below that is the ethical realm. That is what Fiona is talking about.'

'So do you think her ethics add up?' I asked.

'If you take the Hegelian view, that everything is subsumed under the universal, perhaps,' he said. 'If you take my view, that beyond the universal is the particular, then no.'

'Right,' I said. There was a silence as we both tramped on. The path was becoming steeper and we were both beginning to breathe harder.

'I don't quite see what you mean, actually,' I added.

'Well,' Søren continued, 'for Hegel, everything in the world is beautifully ordered: the lowly individual – the particular – through the study of ethics and religion, can develop a higher and higher consciousness, travelling towards universal mind or spirit. In my world, that is not so. My world is one of conflict: in it, the individual travels through the universal, the social realm, where actions can be explained in terms of ethics, until he reaches the realm of the particular. At that point he must leave the social realm behind and travel on alone. At that point he becomes a knight of faith.'

'Or she,' I said.

'Of course,' he said.

I quoted his words back to him. I remembered them, because they'd impressed me. *'She will then introduce herself into that order of knighthood which proves its immortality by making no distinction between man and woman.'*

'Exactly. Now let's take Fiona's first point. She told you that having an abortion is like having a tooth out. In the realm of the ethical, this is a point that can be debated: the extent to which a foetus is a person, the rights of the foetus as against the rights of the woman, and so on. But beyond that, in the realm of the particular which is above the universal, the answer is unknown. The knight of faith must find the answer alone; he – or she – must make the movement of faith, on the strength of the absurd.'

'But how?' I said. 'How do you know what is the right thing to do?'

'You don't,' he said. 'You can only struggle with it. As you have done. As you are doing, Susannah.'

We stopped to catch our breath.

'And what about "it's not fair to bring a child into the world under these circumstances"?' I said.

'Well, what do you think?'

'I think – if I understand what you're saying – that one could have that discussion in the social realm and come to some conclusion, based on some moral idea of what is "fair" and so on. But beyond that, the pregnant woman is on her own. She somehow has to weigh up whether her child would be better off having a difficult life or not being born. She has to judge what the value of life is. And she can't really. But she has to try.'

'Yes. Like Abraham, she must make that journey on her own. At the end of it, she may be judged as a murderer or as a saint, depending on the outcome. But her true greatness will not lie in her actions, which will be judged by the social realm; it will lie in the extent to which she has struggled in private, has kept her faith with herself.'

We started walking again, side by side, although the path was beginning to become narrower.

'And what about, "you'll be throwing your life away"?' I said.

'You will only throw your life away if you sit out the dance,' Søren said.

His cryptic pronouncements were beginning to get on my nerves.

'You sound like David Carradine,' I said.

He laughed, his eyes lighting up. 'When you can snatch the pebble from my hand, grasshopper...'

By now the path was only wide enough for a single walker. The grassy hillside around us had given way to rocks and boulders. Up ahead, the terrain on either side of the path seemed to be falling away. I had an urge to turn round and go back the way I came, but I knew I couldn't.

'This is where I must leave you, Susannah.' Søren's voice was gentle.

'Don't,' I said, clutching his arm. 'Please don't.'

He removed my arm from his, and pointed at the narrowing path up ahead.

'Look,' he said. 'There's only space for one of us.'

'Well, why can't it be you?'

'I've been up there already. It's your turn now.'

I suddenly felt very tired. I sat down on a hillock beside the path and started crying.

'I can't,' I said. 'I can't, not by myself. I'm scared of heights.'

'Well go back down, then,' he said. 'Go back to the meadows with the flowers and the clanking cows. Go back to "it's just like having a tooth out".'

I knew that I couldn't now.

'Come with me,' I said. 'Please.'

'No.' His tone was stern.

I covered my face with my hands. 'It's not fair,' I sobbed, sounding like a child. 'I'm not as brave as you. I'm not as clever. I won't know how to...'

'Faith is a marvel,' he said, bending over me to take my hand.

I pushed his hand away angrily.

'And yet no human being is excluded from it,' he went on. 'For that in which all human life is united is passion, and faith is a passion.'

I felt like telling him to fuck off with his faith and his

passion, but when I looked up at him, I noticed that he looked tired too. I realised it must have been difficult for him walking even as far as this with his limp.

'I must go now,' he said, straightening up from bending over me. 'Goodbye, Susannah.'

I stood up in front of him. He grasped me firmly by the shoulders and looked into my eyes. 'Good luck. Remember, faith is an end, not a beginning.'

Then he turned round and walked off down the hillside.

After he left, I sat back down on the hillock for a while, and wondered whether to carry on or to follow him down. Eventually, I decided to press on. I was terrified of climbing up the steep mountain path, but knew I'd feel ashamed of myself if I turned back. So I got up and started walking.

Further up, the sides of the path were beginning to fall away, until it was left jutting out on a ridge. It became narrower and narrower, until I had to put one foot right in front of the other to walk along it, holding out my arms to balance myself as though I was on a tightrope. I tried sitting down and pulling myself along with my arms, because it was safer that way, but my progress was so slow that I stood up again and inched my way along.

After what seemed like hours but was probably only minutes, the path petered out altogether, and I found myself standing at the edge of a deep ravine. A rope bridge with wooden slats was slung over it. The rope was old and worn, and some of the slats in the middle were missing. I didn't dare look down into the ravine, but I sensed that if I did, I wouldn't be able to see the bottom.

I edged my way on to the bridge, holding tight to the ropes on each side, not looking down except to check whether the slats for my feet were in place. I moved along carefully, but then a wind started to blow up from the ravine and the bridge began to sway from side to side. I clung on, praying that the wind would die down and that I'd get to the other side. Then it happened. The rope behind me snapped.

I was left swinging from side to side over the ravine. At that moment, I lost my fear. I had to; it was my only chance of survival. I began to clamber up the rope, using my arms and legs, until I got near to the other side of the ravine, where the rope was hanging from. Once I got there, I realised, I'd have no way of getting back down to the path. I'd be stranded on the mountain. But I pressed on: at least I'd be safe up there, on solid ground again.

I woke up with my head on my desk. There was a crick in my neck, and my cheek was sore where it had pressed against the edge of the pad of paper I'd been writing on. When I looked up, the anglepoise lamp was shining into my eyes, and I couldn't see properly for a moment or two. I rubbed my eyes and looked at my watch. It was ten o'clock. I felt as though I'd been asleep for hours, but it could only have been for a minute or two.

I got up and went into the kitchen to make myself a cup of tea. There was nobody in there. While the kettle was boiling, I thought of going in and asking Clare if she wanted a cup too, but I decided against it. I felt too disoriented to chat, and I couldn't tell her about the dream, she'd think I was mad. I needed to talk to someone who would understand, someone who knew about Kierkegaard.

Rob was a possibility, but I didn't want to phone him yet, not until I knew whether I was going to have the abortion or not. It would be confusing for both of us if I got in touch now. I didn't want to discuss it all with him. I knew it was a decision I'd have to make on my own. The only other person I could think of to talk to was Belham.

It was a bit late for phoning someone you didn't know well, but this was a bit of an emergency. Well, perhaps not an emergency, but a pressing problem, anyway. Once I told him, I was sure he'd understand how important it was. I picked up the tea, took it back to my room, put it down to cool on the desk, and checked my purse for 2p pieces. I copied down the number I'd scribbled on my file, and went down to the lobby to phone him.

When I dialled the number no one picked up. I was just about to put the phone down when a female voice came on the other end. 'Yes?' She sounded irritated.

'Could I speak to... Mr Belham, please?' I felt ridiculous calling him Mister. Perhaps I should have said James.

'Who is this?'

'Susannah Jones, one of his students.'

She sighed heavily into the phone. 'Just a minute,' she said, and went off to get him.

'Susannah?' he said when he came on the phone.

'Sorry to call you so late,' I said.

'Are you all right?' he asked.

'Yes, fine. But there's something I need to talk to you about.'

'OK,' he said. 'What is it?'

'I've had a dream about Kierkegaard. I need to find out what it means.'

He laughed. 'Well, I'm not a psychoanalyst.'

'I think it's about the...' My voice trailed off.

Belham's voice became serious. 'Ah, the...'

'Yes. I can't talk about it over the phone. Could you meet me somewhere tomorrow morning?' I was surprised at how straightforward my request sounded.

'OK,' he said, picking up my matter-of-fact tone. 'Let's go to the Mock Turtle, shall we? Morning coffee? Say eleven o'clock?'

'Fine,' I said. 'See you there. Thanks.'

I thought of adding, 'It won't take long,' but then I thought it might, so I didn't.

'Bye, then.'

'Bye.'

I put the phone down and went upstairs to drink my cup of tea.

chapter 25

I GOT INTO BRIGHTON A BIT EARLY next day for my meeting with Belham. When I got to the Mock Turtle I peered in through the window, over the cake display. I couldn't see him but I went in anyway. I sat down at a table near the window and ordered a large pot of tea, and a slice of home-made chocolate cake to go with it. I should really have waited for the cake until Belham arrived, but I was starving.

I took off my jacket and scarf while I waited for the tea to arrive, and looked around. I'd never been to the Mock Turtle before, but it was quite a well-known tea shop in Brighton. It was a brightly lit, bustling place, with strangely shaped teapots and rococo cake stands everywhere. It was quiet, but not too quiet, with a comforting background hum of voices and clattering cutlery. Belham had made a good choice. It was the sort of place where you could take your time and have a private talk, and no one would make you feel rushed or listen to your conversation.

Just as the waitress was bringing the tea and chocolate cake, Belham came in.

'Hello,' he said, taking off his coat and sitting down. 'Sorry I'm a bit late.'

'Hi,' I said. 'You're not, really.'

The waitress set down the tea things and waited.

'Do you want one of these as well?' I pointed at my cake.

'Why not,' he said, and asked her to bring him one.

I poured a cup of tea for each of us. I added milk to mine, and then put in three sugar cubes. He drank his black with no sugar. He lit a cigarette and offered me one, but I shook my head. I'd completely lost the taste for nicotine these days.

'You're looking well,' he said.

I wished I could have said the same for him, but he wasn't. In fact, he was looking awful. There were dark shadows under his eyes and he looked as though he hadn't shaved for days.

'Thanks,' I said. 'I'm not too bad. How are you?'

'Oh.' For a moment he seemed lost for words. 'Not too bad, I suppose.'

I stirred my tea. I was eyeing up my cake, but I didn't pick up my fork. Belham noticed and said, 'Go on, eat it up. You can always have another when mine comes.'

I started in on the cake. It was delicious.

'You look a bit tired,' I said in between mouthfuls. 'Did you have a break over Christmas?'

'Yes,' he said. 'Yes, I did.'

He picked up his tea and began to sip it.

'What did you do?'

'Well, I was going to… well, not much, actually.'

I looked up. Belham was shifting uncomfortably in his chair. I realised he didn't want me to enquire further.

His chocolate cake arrived and he thanked the waitress but pushed it to one side.

We chatted about this and that, and I told him I'd almost finished writing my dissertation. He asked me what it was about, and I said it was to do with Heidegger and the metaphysics of gestation. He seemed intrigued, and I said I'd hand it in at the beginning of term for him to look at. I didn't ask him to okay the subject, as I was supposed to do; there didn't seem much point now that I'd written it. I just assumed it was all right; and I noticed that he made no objection.

Then he said, 'So what about this dream then, Susannah?'

I put down my fork, took a big gulp of tea, wiped my mouth with the napkin, and began to tell him the story of the dream. I was surprised that I could remember it in exact detail. While I was talking, Belham listened carefully. From time to time he interrupted me to ask me for more details, but other than that he remained silent.

'So,' I said when I'd finished, 'what do you think?'

He looked thoughtful.

'Well, it seems fairly self-explanatory. It's a pretty good quality dream, I'd say. Philosophically speaking.'

'Thanks.'

There was a silence and then he went on, 'You know, I've never really thought about *Fear and Trembling* in terms of the abortion issue. But it's so blindingly obvious, isn't it?'

'Yes.' I started eyeing up his cake, and he pushed it over to me.

'When you think about it,' I said, starting in on it, 'that Abraham scenario is one that millions of women go through all the time.'

'Seriously, Susannah,' he continued, 'I think you're on to something here. I haven't come across any philosophical writing on this subject at all. You really must follow it up. I know you've almost completed your dissertation, and I'm sure it's excellent, but this...' There was a note of genuine excitement in his voice. 'If you could write about this...'

'Well, I'd like to,' I said. 'Maybe I will. But first of all, I've got to decide about this abortion.'

When I said the word abortion, Belham looked embarrassed and started shifting about in his chair again, but I took no notice.

'The bit of the dream I don't understand is where Kierkegaard says, "You will only be throwing your life away if you sit out the dance." What do you think that means?'

Belham frowned. 'I'm not sure. Kierkegaard talks about

the knight of faith making the movements of a dance. He says the dancer moves through pain into resignation and then somehow comes through it, landing exactly right, as he puts it. I think he's saying that if you don't do that, if you don't make the movement towards infinity and then back again, that's to say if you don't engage with life properly, you're sitting out the dance, and perhaps throwing away your true potential.'

I finished up the cake, wiped my mouth, crumpled up the napkin, and sat back. 'Yes, but what does that mean in terms of my situation? Will I be sitting out the dance if I have the baby, or if I have the abortion?'

'I don't know. I really can't advise you on that.'

'But what do you think?' I persisted. 'What's your opinion?'

Belham looked at me intently. I noticed that his eyes were a very deep brown.

'Susannah,' he said, 'I hardly know you. I can't possibly tell you what you should do. But all I can say is that you're a talented philosopher,' – I noticed he said 'are' now, and not 'could be' – 'and I think it would be a shame if you didn't continue your studies.'

'So you think I should have the abortion?'

'I didn't say that.'

'Well, how can I do both?' I realised I was sounding irritable.

'I don't know. That's for you to work out. The university is quite forward thinking about this sort of thing. We'd help you as much as possible.'

There was a pause, and then he added, 'I'd make sure of that.'

I gave a deep sigh. 'I don't know,' I said. 'I've done everything I can to think this through. But I still don't know what I'm going to do, and the abortion's fixed up for tomorrow. It's completely freaking me out.'

'Susannah.' Belham's voice was quiet. 'Don't you think

you should have discussed this with the man – I mean the men – involved?'

The men involved. It sounded terrible.

'I have,' I said. 'Well, one of them, anyway. The main one.'

'What about the other one?'

'You don't understand. He's just not in a position to help. He's too... young.'

Belham gave a wry smile. 'You're young as well. Why is that a problem?'

'It just is.' I turned my head away.

I was aware of Belham looking intently at me. He wasn't going to let this go.

'It's another student, isn't it?' he said.

'OK,' I said. 'Yes.' I was annoyed. The conversation wasn't going the way I'd planned.

'It's not...?' He stopped and looked at me quizzically.

'Yes, it is,' I said. 'It's Rob.'

Belham didn't look all that surprised.

'So he doesn't know?'

'No.'

'Well, he seems a responsible, sensitive person. I think it's only fair to tell him, don't you?'

Then he changed the subject and started talking about my dissertation again. I felt angry. It wasn't for Belham to tell me what to do. He knew nothing about my situation. He didn't know how immature Rob was. And I hadn't wanted him to know about Rob anyway. I wasn't sure why at first, but then I realised what it was.

'James,' I said, interrupting him. 'Do you mind if I call you James?' There was a note of recklessness in my voice.

'Well, I'd feel a bit odd if you called me Mr Belham,' he said, smiling but looking a little unnerved.

'I was just wondering... are you... umm?'

He waited patiently.

'Are you married?'

'Yes. But my wife and I are separated. At the moment.' He looked down at the table. I got the impression he didn't want to discuss it further.

'I just wondered,' I went on. 'I just wondered if...'

Belham was looking nervous now, but there was nothing else for it. I didn't have time to beat about the bush.

'Do you find me attractive?' I blurted out at last. 'At all?'

Belham looked as though someone had thrown a bucket of cold water over him. My heart was beating fast.

'Because it's just that...' I carried on, unable to stop now. 'If you did... I would. I would too. You know.'

Belham put his elbows on the table and began to massage his forehead, the palms of his hands shielding his eyes. He looked exhausted. Then he spoke.

'Ermm,' he said. He paused. He was trying to be kind. I knew what it was, he didn't remotely fancy me. I was just like Dennis to him. The hairs began to prickle on my scalp.

'The thing is, Susannah, you're my student. And you're... er, pregnant,' he said. 'And apart from that...' He paused. 'I'm in love with my wife.'

There was a long silence while we both looked down at the tablecloth and I tried not to squirm in my chair.

Then I said, 'Oh God. I'm sorry. I feel such an idiot.'

Belham didn't speak, but put out his hand and touched my arm.

'No, you're not,' he said at last. 'You're brave. You say what you think. Don't stop doing that.'

I pulled my arm away. 'I think I'd better go.'

'No,' he said. 'Sit down. Don't rush off. I've got nothing much to do this morning. Let's pay up here and go for a walk along the seafront, shall we?'

'I can't. I feel too embarrassed.' I started putting on my jacket and scarf.

'What's there to be embarrassed about? You're a beautiful young woman, Susannah. I'm flattered. But it's not the right time for either of us. I'm sure you know that really. So let's just forget about it and put it behind us, shall we?'

Belham was a cool guy. I got the feeling that this sort of thing happened to him all the time, and he'd learned how to deal with it. But all the same, I sensed that he wasn't just humouring me, that he genuinely liked me. He'd said I was a talented philosopher and a beautiful woman, and I felt sure he didn't say that to every second-year undergraduate who threw themselves at him. What's more, he seemed lonely and unhappy that day, and in need of company.

'OK,' I said. 'But don't ever mention it again.'

He grinned. 'I won't. I promise.'

Then he turned and waved the waitress over to our table.

chapter 26

WHEN I GOT BACK TO CAMPUS, I went straight up to my room and found Rob's phone numbers. Then I went downstairs to the phone box in the lobby to call him. I tried the first one he'd given me, but he wasn't there. The same thing happened with the second. On the third try, I finally got hold of him.

'Hi,' I said. 'It's me.'

'Why didn't you phone before?' He sounded annoyed.

'Oh, I had a few things to sort out,' I said. 'But now... could you come down and see me?'

'When?'

'Well, now really. Right away.'

He gave a sarcastic laugh. 'I might have some things to sort out myself.'

I ignored the hostile edge to his voice.

'I'm sorry, Rob,' I said. 'I'm not mucking you about. You'll understand when you get here. I'm in a very serious situation and I need your help.'

His tone changed. 'What is it? Are you all right?'

'I can't talk about it over the phone. Where are you, anyway?' I hadn't recognised the area number.

'At my grandparents'.'

'It's not in Scotland or anything, is it?' I was panicking slightly now. Maybe I'd left it too late. Maybe he wouldn't be able to get here in time.

'No, Woking.'

I breathed a sigh of relief. Woking was somewhere just outside London, as far as I knew. He'd be able to make it by evening.

'Hang on a minute,' he said, and put the phone down.

I heard some talking going on in the background and then he came back on again.

'I'll have to get the train,' he said. 'I've left the car down in Brighton. I can get in at quarter to seven.'

'Fine,' I said. 'I'll meet the train. Is it the London one?'

'Yes.' There was a pause and then he added, 'Susannah, it's not easy for me to get away today. There's a family do on here and I'm going to miss it now. My mother's furious. You'd better not be pissing me about.'

'I'm not. Honestly, I'm not. I really need you to be here.'

'OK, see you later, then.' He still sounded annoyed. 'Six forty-five. Make sure you're there. Bye.'

'Bye.' I said, and put the phone down.

I went back upstairs to my room, relieved that Rob had agreed to come down, and began clearing the books and papers off the floor. I tidied them away on the shelves above the desk, and cleared my clothes off the bed, folding each garment carefully and putting it away in the cupboard. Then I lay down and stared up at the ceiling. I needed to think.

Everything seemed to be going very fast, too fast to keep up with. In the space of just a few weeks, I'd slept with Rob, got pregnant, split up with Jason, and propositioned Belham. I didn't seem to have a clue what or who I wanted, and now, with the abortion looming up tomorrow, it was time to make some decisions. As I tried to focus on what to do, the tarot card that the Crowley freak had been playing with on the train drifted into my mind: I saw the lovers, one dark, one fair, and the baby in between them. I tried to picture the details of the card: were there two babies, or one? And was there some godlike father figure standing over them? Or perhaps a monumental, arched structure like a church window, betokening heaven or some such nonsense? Whenever I got near to seeing the image, my mind seemed to bounce away from it, which made me suspicious. There was something there I didn't want to think about. But I was going to have to now.

I started with Jason. Why had I been so in love with him? We had nothing in common. He was an ex-public schoolboy from an upper-class English family, and I was a chapel-going Welsh doctor's daughter. He wasn't remotely interested in philosophy and I couldn't stand antiques – all those awful plaster nymphs and pouting faces. True, he was an incredibly good-looking man, and to start with our sex life had been great, but there'd never been any emotional bond between us at all. Of course, now I understood why: he was bisexual, if not gay, for God's sake. All the time we'd been sleeping together, he'd been sleeping with his best friend. Any other woman would have put two and two together immediately, but not me. Jesus, what a bloody idiot I'd been. Why had I put up with it for so long? He'd treated me like a child, and I'd treated him like...

My mind bounced off the subject of Jason and on to the decor of my room. I wondered what I could put up on the wall. Perhaps one of Clare's African fabrics? Not really. Perhaps one of Rob's Indian ones? No. Maybe a print or something...

I forced my mind back to Jason. I'd treated him like... a father, perhaps? No, that was ridiculous. I couldn't think of anyone less like my father than Jason. But now I came to think of it, there was one odd similarity: they were both interested in vintage wines. And there were other, less tangible qualities: their way of organising everyone around them, making everything seem all right, safe, manageable, even when it wasn't. I let my mind wander back to the way Jason used to take me on his knee and whisper baby words in my ear when I was upset; and how, when I'd told him I was pregnant, it had – for the first time – seemed creepy and inappropriate; and I realised what I'd known all along. Jason had been a father figure to me. That was why I'd fallen in love with him. And maybe that was why, since the day he chucked me out, I hadn't given him a moment's thought – until now.

Next up was Belham. When I thought of him, my hand involuntarily went up to my face, and I covered my eyes. What on earth had possessed me to do something so excruciatingly embarrassing? Yes, I fancied him, but I wasn't madly in love with him. Why had I done it? I pulled my knees up to my chest and turned over to face the wall, shutting my eyes tight, trying to blot out the memory, but I couldn't: I saw myself sitting in the Mock Turtle and stuffing myself with chocolate cake, yapping on about my abortion, and then asking him if he fancied me. I replayed the image over and over again to torture myself until I'd had enough. Then I gave myself a break. OK, maybe it was a stupid thing to do, but I'd been tense. I had my abortion coming up tomorrow – who wouldn't be? And Belham hadn't taken it too badly. In fact, when we'd gone for a walk along the seafront on our way home, I'd got the impression that what I'd done had cleared the air between us, and that from now on our relationship would be closer.

Which left Rob. I'd hardly thought about Rob since the last time I'd seen him. In fact, now I came to think of it, I'd hardly ever given him any consideration at all. From the start, I'd never taken him seriously, even though he'd made it clear that he was in love with me. I'd kept going back to him – kept going back to his bed at least – but I'd never thought about why. He was possibly the father of my unborn child – probably, given the fact that towards the end of our relationship, Jason and I hardly ever had sex – and yet I still found it difficult to accept him as a potential mate. Perhaps it was to do with the father thing. Perhaps I still needed a father. Perhaps... oh shit, I didn't know what it was. It was all such a mess, and thinking about it didn't seem to be getting me anywhere.

I turned on to my back and stared up at the ceiling. Rob would be here in a few hours, and I still had no idea what I was going to say to him. I still didn't know whether I wanted the baby or not, and if I did, whether I wanted him to be involved or not. One thing was certain, though: if I was going to go through with this, I'd need a man. I hadn't seen that before, but if I was going to become a mother and carry on doing philosophy, the father, whoever he was, was going to have to help me.

In the early evening, I went to Brighton station to meet Rob off the train. I'd packed a small suitcase so I could stay at his place that night. My appointment at the clinic was at nine the next morning, and it would be easier to get there from Rob's than from campus. Of course, depending on what happened, I might go back to my room on campus and spend the night on my own; but at least I'd have my suitcase packed and ready for the morning.

I hadn't been quite sure what to take. The pink and blue nightdress seemed appropriate for an overnight stay in hospital, so I'd packed that, with some clean pants and socks, a towel, and a toothbrush and toothpaste. I'd had a letter from the clinic telling me to bring a pack of sanitary towels, so I'd bought some down at the campus shop and packed them as well. I'd also put in the signed forms from the health centre that Doctor Morgan had sent back to me. And nestling in a small zipped pocket on the side of the case was the milk-teeth box that Bear had given me. I'd put it in at the last minute, just for luck.

Before I left, I called in on Clare. She was in her room, but there was a guy with her, which surprised me. He was one of those tweed-jacketed, long-haired scientists with glasses that usually never ventured out of the B block, but underneath it all, you could see he wasn't bad looking.

When I knocked on the door, she asked me in, but I felt it best to decline.

'Actually, I'm just on my way out,' I said, standing at the door. 'I'm in a bit of a rush. I was just coming in to say goodbye.'

'Oh,' Clare said. 'Where are you going?'

'Umm,' I said. 'Well, you know…'

'Is it…?' she said, lowering her voice.

'Yes,' I said. 'I'll be back tomorrow.'

Clare glanced back at the guy. 'I'm just going to help Susannah down with her case,' she said, edging out into the corridor.

He smiled at me and nodded, so I smiled and nodded back.

The case was small, but Clare took it out of my hand and walked down the stairs with me.

'Will you be all right?' she said as we went. 'Is anyone going to take you in?'

'I don't know, I'm meeting Rob tonight. It depends how it goes.'

'Well, phone me if you need anything, I'll be here when you get back.'

'Thanks, I'll come by and let you know how it went.'

I didn't say I still didn't know what I was going to do.

'By the way,' she said. 'I found out about the elephants.'

For a moment, I didn't know what she was talking about.

'They do pair up for mating,' she went on. 'And they stay together for a while. But then the father goes back into the herd and the other females help the mother bring up the calf. And later, the mother may go on to become the matriarch of the herd…'

'Right,' I said, cutting her off. I didn't want to think too hard about all that just now. 'Thanks. Who's the guy, by the way?'

'Tom,' she said. 'He's a botanist. He's thinking of coming out to Kenya with me in the summer.'

'So you got the job?'

'Don't know yet, but we'll probably go out there and get some kind of work, anyway.'

'Is he... Are you...?' I asked.

'Sort of, umm I... Umm I...'

'Sorry,' I said, butting in. 'None of my business.' I wished I hadn't asked.

We stopped at the door of the lobby and she handed me the case.

'Good luck,' she said, opening the door.

'Thanks. See you tomorrow.'

I stepped through the door and out onto the road.

Tomorrow. By then it would all be over and I'd have made my decision, one way or the other.

chapter 27

I GOT TO BRIGHTON STATION just as the London train was coming into the platform. A lot of people got off the train at once, and at first I couldn't see Rob. I started panicking, remembering how annoyed he'd sounded on the phone, and thinking how stupid I'd been not to call him before. It would serve me right if he didn't turn up now that I really wanted him here. But just as I was beginning to give up hope, I spotted him, walking along at the back of the crowd, hunched forward with a rucksack on his back, wearing his big woollen sweater with the unravelling sleeves. His face had a cold, pinched look, but when he saw me he broke into an involuntary grin, then resumed his serious expression again.

'Hi,' he said when he came up to me. 'How's it going?'

I reached up and kissed him on the cheek. 'Thanks for coming.'

'That's OK,' he said, but he didn't kiss me back.

We walked down the platform together and I wondered whether to take his arm, but decided against it.

'Where are we going?' he said, indicating my overnight bag.

'To yours?' I said. 'Or we could go back to my room on campus if you like.'

He stopped walking abruptly and turned to face me.

'Look,' he said. 'Can you just explain what's going on

now? I've had just about enough of all this. Why have you dragged me down here?'

'OK,' I said, my anger rising too. 'I didn't want to tell you till we got somewhere private, but since you ask, I'm pregnant.'

He looked at me, puzzled.

'Pregnant, Rob,' I repeated. 'I'm going to have a baby.'

He took a sharp breath in.

'And I'm going in for an abortion tomorrow, unless I... unless we... decide not to,' I went on.

Rob gazed at me uncomprehendingly. 'What...' he said. 'Why...'

'I'm sorry,' I said. 'I should have got in touch before.'

Rob said nothing, so I started walking again and he fell into step beside me. When we got out of the station, he went straight over to the taxi rank, pushed me into a taxi, went round to the back to put our bags in the boot, then got in beside me. When the taxi driver asked where we were going, he told him in a clipped voice that warned off further conversation, and we sat in silence for the rest of the ride. He didn't even look at me. When we got to the house, he jumped out of the taxi to get the bags and pay the driver, still without a word to me, then handed me my bag and got out his key. He ushered me through the door into the hall and straight up the stairs to his room, where he took my bag and threw it onto the bed. Then he went over to the bedroom door and shut it with a bang.

When he turned back to me, he was shaking with rage. 'What the fuck do you mean by this?'

He came towards me and I suddenly felt afraid. I shouldn't have contacted him; I realised I didn't know him very well, and that I had no idea how he'd take the news. He didn't wait for a reply and I didn't try to give one.

'You've been pregnant all this time without telling me?' His voice was starting to rise. I hoped his flatmates wouldn't hear.

'How could you? You've been fucking me about, giving

me this and that excuse, telling me a pack of lies...'

'I'm sorry,' I said. 'I didn't know...'

He wasn't listening. 'And now you've gone and fixed up an abortion without telling me either? You knew all along, and you were giving me the run-around.' He was furious now. 'It's my child too, you know, Susannah.'

'But that's the thing...' I said. 'I don't know if...'

'Oh, great,' he said. 'You don't even know if it's mine. Well, I knew you were screwing your boyfriend as well as me, so that's no surprise. What's happened then, has he given you the push? So you've come to me as a last resort?'

'No,' I said, 'it's not like that.' But I knew it was. I'd gone to Jason first, and then even Belham, and now it was down to him. He'd been last on my list.

'At least you could have had the decency to let me know.' He walked over to the window and stared out, his back to me. 'I'd have thought that was just common courtesy.'

'I have let you know,' I said. 'That's why we're here now.'

'But you were going to go and have this abortion without telling me, weren't you?' he said, turning round to face me.

'No. Yes. I don't know.' I stood rooted to the spot, unable to explain myself.

'How could you?' he repeated, shaking his head. 'How could you?'

He covered his face with his hands and went to sit on the bed, his back to me. I didn't know what to do, so I went over, sat on the chair by his desk, and waited until he spoke again. When he did, his anger seemed to have subsided a little.

'So, why did you call me in now?' he said, his back still turned. 'What did you expect me to do?'

'I don't know,' I said. 'I just wanted to talk to you. I haven't made my mind up about what I'm going to do. I thought maybe you could... help.'

'Oh, right,' he turned round to look at me. 'Well, here I am. At your service.' He sounded bitter.

'Look, Rob.' I leaned forward, speaking as calmly as I

could. 'I realise I've made a complete mess of all this. But it hasn't been easy trying to work things out. We haven't known each other for long. You told me that you'd broken off with Beth, that you weren't into marriage and all that, so I assumed you'd be the same with me.'

'But...'

'Let me speak,' I said. 'Yes, I did go to Jason first. It wasn't a great relationship, in fact it was bloody awful, but he'd been my boyfriend for quite a while, and you and I had only just met. And yes, if you want to know, he did let me down.'

There was a pause while he took this in. 'I didn't come to you after that,' I went on, 'because I couldn't face being rejected again. I knew you weren't into marriage and that whole scene. I thought maybe you were into me just for... well, you know, a quick screw.'

It was the truth, but not the whole truth. I had sometimes wondered if it was just sex that had kept Rob and me coming back to each other. Rob had been going out for years with a girl who wouldn't sleep with him, and I'd had a gay boyfriend. In that respect, we'd both been in the same boat. But there was something else as well, something I had to approach tactfully.

'And I didn't think you were in a position to help,' I said. 'He was a bit older than you, and...'

'What, you mean, he'd got more money than me.'

'Oh, for God's sake.' There was an element of self-pity in Rob's tone that irritated me. 'Well, yes, I suppose I did think he'd be able to help more in that way. But then I realised... he made me realise... that it was a shit relationship and it wouldn't work, however much money he had.'

'So have you split with him completely?' Rob asked. He sounded suspicious.

'Yes, completely.'

When I said that, I knew it wasn't as simple as it sounded: if I had the baby and it was Jason's, we'd have to have some kind of continuing relationship with each other.

Jason had his faults, but he wouldn't ignore the fact that he was a father, and I wouldn't want him to. But there was a finality in the way I spoke about him now that rang true, both to me and to Rob, and we sat there for a while together, listening to my words reverberate around the room.

Eventually, Rob spoke. 'OK, let's work this out. How many times did you actually…?'

For a moment I didn't understand what he was asking. Then I said, 'What, you mean with Jason? Before Christmas? After I met you?'

'Yes. I want to work out the probability.'

'Let me see,' I tried to cast my mind back. I remembered the time Jason and I had had sex the morning before I was due to meet Rob for lunch. The bath water had been running and I hadn't worried about turning off the taps.

'Only once, as far as I can remember.'

'And you and I must have… I don't know, I suppose we saw each other about three times a week for five weeks, that's fifteen times…'

I wondered why I'd never done this calculation myself.

'Say twice each time, that's thirty…' Rob went on. 'Or what about that time when…'

'OK, OK.' I didn't need chapter and verse. But I could see now that the baby I was carrying was most likely to be Rob's. I couldn't imagine why I hadn't thought of doing the sums before. Anxiety, probably, or shame, or maybe that I just didn't think that way. I began to feel relieved. Whether or not I had the baby, at least I was talking to the right man.

'God,' I said suddenly. 'Just imagine that.'

'What?'

'Just imagine if the first time we'd… if the first time you'd lost your virginity… I'd got pregnant.'

Rob shook his head. 'This whole thing is insane.' His voice was quieter and calmer now.

We sat in silence, and after a while he said, 'I'm sorry I shouted at you. Come over here.'

I walked slowly over to the bed, wondering what was going to happen next. I sat down beside him, leaving a wide space between us, but he put out his arm and pulled me towards him. Then he put his other arm round me and I put my arms round his. We stayed there for a long time until I started crying.

'I've completely ruined everything,' I said, tears spilling down my face.

'Yes, you have really,' he said, wiping them away with his hand. 'You've been nothing but a pain in the arse since I first met you. But it's my fault as well. And I love you, Suse. I wish I didn't, but I do.'

We fell back onto the bed, still holding on to each other.

'I ...' I hesitated. 'I've missed you too.'

I didn't say I loved him, but I felt as though if I had, it wouldn't have been a complete lie.

He leaned over me and started to stroke my hair. I lay back and let him. It felt good, as though he could brush away all the worry of the last few weeks just by wanting to. Then he began to nuzzle my ear.

'Wouldn't it be just my luck, though,' he murmured, as though thinking to himself. 'The first time ever.'

I smiled.

'You're supposed to get a free go the first time, aren't you?' I said. 'That's what the boys in Swansea say.'

He chuckled.

'It's not fair,' he said. 'I want my free go.'

I laughed, and we rolled over on the bed together, holding each other close.

We made love slowly and carefully that night, afraid that any sudden movement would disturb the baby, even though we both knew it was still a tiny foetus far up inside my womb. I was acutely aware of my swollen breasts and the curve of my belly, and I sensed that Rob was too, but he didn't mention it until afterwards.

'Blimey,' he said. 'It's like being in bed with Raquel Welch.'

'Oh shut up,' I said, getting out of bed to put my T-shirt on.

'Don't.' He pulled me back into bed. 'I was only joking.'

'But it's freezing in here,' I said, lying back and pulling up the blankets.

He got up and lit the gas fire, shivering in the cold air. Then he lit the hurricane lamp by the bed and got back into bed. The room began to seem warmer, more from the cosy glow of the lamp and the fire than the temperature of the air.

'Susannah, why don't we go ahead and have this baby?' he said, once he'd settled back in beside me.

'It can't be that difficult,' he went on. 'Millions of people do it every day all over the world.'

'It is that difficult,' I said. 'And millions of people all over the world do it very badly.'

'Yes, but it would be different with us.' He propped himself up on one elbow and turned to look at me. 'We wouldn't do it the way our parents did, in a nuclear family. We'd bring the baby up communally, in a group of adults, with other kids around, in an atmosphere of... I don't know, freedom. Creativity. It wouldn't be like it was for us, with our fathers going out to work and our mothers being frustrated housewives; we'd have equal roles, and we'd all share in the childcare.'

'It's a nice idea,' I said. 'But it wouldn't work.'

'I don't see why not. We could start here, in this house. We already do live communally in a way, we've got a rota and a kitty and everything...'

'Oh great,' I said. 'Well, that'll be fine, then.'

Rob looked at me, puzzled. 'Well, you've got to start somewhere, you know.'

'OK.' I said. I tried to keep the sarcasm out of my voice.

'Fair enough. But does anyone take any notice of your rota and your kitty?'

'Well, we've never quite... got it together,' Rob said. 'I don't know why. I think maybe we haven't been motivated enough. Until now.'

I pictured the freezing cold, dusty toilet on the landing with the pile of newspaper on the floor to use as loo paper, the sitting room downstairs with its bare red light bulb and the blankets hanging in the windows, and the kitchen with its piles of dirty dishes in the sink and its carrier bags of rubbish stacked up by the bin that no one could be bothered to empty. I'd seen it all before, in dozens of student houses. They were all the same. They were the kind of places where you'd hesitate to drink a cup of tea, let alone bring up a baby. That was why I'd always avoided living in one.

I didn't want to be rude about Rob's living arrangements so I said nothing about the state of the house. Anyway, it wasn't his fault that the others didn't bother to clear up; his own room was always fairly tidy and welcoming.

'You mean, we could set up a commune with the people who live here?' I said. I tried to keep my voice neutral. 'With Jan and Mark and Dino? And Hervé?'

When I said Hervé I almost laughed, but I stopped myself.

'I don't see why not,' Rob said.

'But why would they be interested in looking after a child? None of them have kids themselves.'

'Well, Jan and Mark might do. Some time.'

I'd only met Jan and Mark for about ten minutes, but they didn't seem in the least likely to start a family and set up a commune with us. They had the air of a straight couple who kept themselves to themselves and were probably only sharing a house because they were too broke to get a place on their own.

'I'm sorry, Rob, I can't really see it,' I said. I was trying to be polite. These were his housemates, after all. 'I think, if we were going to do it, we'd have to live somewhere else.'

'Well, why don't we go somewhere warm, then,' he said. 'California, Spain, somewhere like that.'

I turned to look at him. His face was framed by his long, dark hair, and his eyes were lit up with excitement. He looked beautiful, the way he had that day when we'd kissed in the Meeting House, the way he had the first time we'd slept together here, in his bed, in the light of the hurricane lamp. For a moment, my heart skipped a beat and I thought, maybe he's right, maybe we can do anything we want, the two of us: have the baby, live in a commune, move somewhere sunny, somewhere far away from all this cold and damp and fog.

'But what would we live on?' I still sounded cautious, but I was beginning to be swayed by Rob's enthusiasm.

'Oh, I don't know,' he said. 'I could find work, labouring work, anything. I've done that already in the holidays, building sites, that kind of thing.'

'Really?' I looked at him with admiration. I hadn't realised Rob was capable of manual labour. I'd thought he was just a philosophy student.

'Yeah. I mean, I'm not all that keen on it, but I can do it.'

'Do you wolf whistle girls in the street, along with the other guys?' I asked. I was going off the point, but I was intrigued.

'No,' he said, 'Of course I don't. I can't stand all that male chauvinist bollocks. I mean, I must admit, I did join in at first. The brickies call you a poofter if you don't. But then they found out I was doing philosophy at college, so they called me a poofter anyway, and I stopped bothering with the wolf whistles.' He laughed.

There was more to Rob than I'd imagined, I realised. Maybe he wasn't quite as young and inexperienced as I thought. Maybe he did know how to handle himself in the real world.

'But if we did that...' I got back to the point. 'If we did

move away, we'd have to chuck in our degrees, wouldn't we?'

'Well, only for a while,' he said. 'Just for a couple of years or so.'

'But that's how it starts,' I said. 'It's only for a while, until the baby grows up, and then all of a sudden it's too late. You never get back to it.'

He sighed and turned away from me in the bed.

'You know, you're a very negative person in some ways, Susannah. You always find ways to bring me down. Of course living differently isn't going to be easy, but if we really want to we'll find a way.'

With that, he got up out of bed and put on his jeans. I looked at him in the light of the hurricane lamp. His body seemed to have filled out slightly since the last time I saw him.

'Have you put on weight?' I said.

He patted his belly. 'Christmas,' he said. 'These jeans are killing me. I'm going downstairs to make us a cup of tea. And when I come back, you'd better have come up with a plan of action.' He sounded irritated, but he leaned over and kissed me, and then went off to get the tea.

I got out of bed, found my T-shirt, and scuttled back in under the blankets to put it on. The room was warming up, but it was still cold. I propped myself up against the pillows, looked at the ceiling, and started thinking again. Rob had been joking, but I wanted to come up with some kind of plan before he came back. Nothing too airy-fairy; something concrete, workable.

In a few minutes, Rob came back with two steaming cups of tea and a packet of chocolate digestives. He put the cups on the side table by the bed, put on a record, and got back into bed beside me with the biscuits. We each took one, and then another, and then another, munching in silence. We were both starving but neither of us wanted to go out and get anything to eat.

John Martyn drifted into the room. *Curl around me like a fern in the spring...*

'I saw Belham in the holidays,' I said.

'Oh,' he said. 'How come?'

'I rang him up to ask his advice about my dissertation. And he suggested we meet in town for a coffee.'

It was a small lie, but I wished I hadn't said it. I didn't really enjoy lying these days, not the way I had when I was with Jason.

'Really?' he said. 'Do you think he's trying to get off with you?'

'No,' I said. ' Don't be ridiculous.' That wasn't a lie, but it was pretty near one.

'Actually, it might have been me who suggested it,' I went on. 'I can't remember. Anyway, I told him I was pregnant, and he said the university was quite... forward thinking about this sort of thing. He said he'd help as much as he could.'

'How?' said Rob. 'How could he help?'

'Well, they have family accommodation on campus, you know.' I realised the words 'family accommodation' didn't sound very inspiring, but I carried on. 'I'm sure Belham would help us get a room there. They even have flats, I think. That way we could continue our degrees, maybe get some part-time work to pay the bills, and look after the baby together.'

I stopped. Rob said nothing. 'It's a possibility, isn't it?' I added.

'I don't know,' he said. 'Sounds a bit grim.'

'And there's one other thing,' I said. I might as well give him the works, I thought. Now we're on the subject of grim. 'I'd want us to get married. If we have the baby, that is.'

Rob reached over me to pick up his cup of tea. I noticed that he was keeping his arm well away from my body. He said nothing, so I reached over too and picked up my cup, blowing on the tea to cool it down. He offered me another biscuit from the pack, but I shook my head. Suddenly I wasn't hungry any more.

'Well, what do you think?' I said eventually.

He didn't take a biscuit out either.

'I'm sorry, Susannah,' he said, looking straight ahead. 'But I can't do that.'

I took a sip of tea and swallowed it. It tasted bitter and brackish in my mouth. So I'd been right all along, I thought. Rob was just a boy, a dreamer. When it came down to it, he wouldn't be able to make the commitment to me, or to the child. To him, the world of being a parent, of hard work, of marriage, was 'a bit grim'. It wasn't his fault: he was only just out of his teens. He wasn't ready for any of this, I should have known that.

'OK,' I said. 'Fine.' I got up out of bed.

'Where are you going?' he said.

'Don't worry,' I said. 'Just to the loo. I'm not about to walk out on you.'

I put on my jeans and pulled Rob's holey sweater over my head. Then I remembered the cold, dusty floor in the toilet and went over to get my socks and boots. While I was putting them on, Rob spoke.

'Look, just give me some time,' he said. 'I need to think...'

'There's nothing to think about,' I said, walking over to the door. I tried to keep my voice light and steady.

'You're not going to run off, are you?' There was a note of panic in his voice.

'No,' I stopped myself from adding 'not yet'. Then I opened the door and walked down the corridor.

I stayed in the toilet on the landing for a long time, remembering the night I'd felt sick in there before, the first night I'd slept with Rob. The window was still jammed open and the pipes were still dusty, and it was even colder now than it had been that night, but I didn't want to go back into the bedroom just yet, so I sat down and tried to think.

I could understand why Rob didn't want to marry me: it was against his politics, against his ideals. He'd held out against Beth all these years and now he had me hassling him, this time with a baby involved. We'd only just met, and I wasn't even sure that I wanted to marry him, but I knew that if I was going to have this baby, I wanted to be married. Here at Sussex I could persuade myself that I was a liberated single parent, but back home it would be different. I'd be an unmarried mother, to be pitied and despised by all the girls I'd been to school with, girls who'd got married and had kids straight out of school; girls that, up until now, I'd pitied and despised myself. And I couldn't imagine explaining it to my family. My mother would be devastated – she was in a fragile enough state as it was; and Auntie Luned and Uncle Ifor would be shocked out of their minds, ashamed to show their faces ever again in the congregation. Rob just didn't understand. Wales wasn't the same as England, as Woking; down in Swansea, we were still living in the fifties, if not the nineteenth century – at least in my family, anyway.

After a while, I heard the sound of voices downstairs and a bunch of people let themselves noisily into the house, crashing down the corridor into the sitting room. I quickly let myself out of the toilet, praying that none of them would come straight up to the loo, and went back into Rob's room. He was fast asleep, so I went over to the record player, turned it off, and got back into bed quietly, so as not to wake him. I didn't feel like talking to him any more; whatever we had to say to each other had been said. So I lay awake beside him, staring up at the shadows the hurricane lamp cast on the ceiling, and listening to the sound of music thumping down below.

chapter 28

I HARDLY SLEPT THAT NIGHT, not even when the music downstairs stopped and the whole house became silent in the early hours of the morning. As I lay awake in bed with Rob breathing peacefully beside me, the tears came back again. I wanted to sob my heart out, but instead I lay there crying silently in the dark, looking up at the ceiling into nothing. When the pillow got wet, I turned it over and lay back, wiping my eyes and cheeks dry and pushing the hair off my face. Then I found myself patting my head and stroking my hair, and I almost had to stop myself from murmuring, there there, don't worry, everything will be all right. I kept stroking my hair, though, and as I did the tears subsided and a calm descended, and I realised what I had known all along: that, when push came to shove, I was on my own with all this. The question of whether to have the baby or not was mine: it was me having a sleepless night, not Rob. I knew he cared about me, but in the end it was me that was responsible for my body, for my baby, not him. He was trying to do the right thing, with his labouring job and his rota and his kitty and his commune in California, but he obviously hadn't got a clue what was involved in bringing up a child; he wasn't in a position to help me, however much he wanted to. And I couldn't do it all on my own, I knew that. Or if I could, I didn't want to. I didn't want to go back home to Swansea and live with my mother and be pitied by everyone; and I didn't want to stay here at Sussex either, and spend years struggling to get my degree, bringing up my child alone in the family accommodation section on campus or in some damp, cold little flat in Brighton. I was going to have to have the abortion. It would be sad, but it wouldn't be the end of the world. Maybe one day, when Rob and I were older, we could have a child. But for now, I'd have to go through with this abortion, and the sooner I got it over with, the better.

At around seven o'clock I got up and got dressed, tiptoeing round the room as quietly as I could so as not to disturb Rob. When I was ready to go, I woke him up to say goodbye. He'd been confused, and told me to wait, and tried to persuade me to phone the clinic and postpone the operation. He'd even offered to marry me if that was what I really wanted, but I told him I'd changed my mind, that I didn't want to marry him any more. I was going to the clinic, and that was that. When he realised he wasn't going to talk me out of it, he'd offered to get up and try and get his car started and drive me in, or at least come with me on the bus, but I said I'd prefer to go on my own. Before I went, he held me close for a long time, but I noticed that as I left, he turned over to go back to sleep with a look of relief on his face.

I was sitting in the waiting room of The Arbours, wondering when I would be called for my examination. It was a windowless room with chairs around the edge of it and a low table in the middle covered in well-thumbed women's magazines. There was a vase of artificial flowers on the mantelpiece and a David Hamilton-style print on the wall, of a girl in a big summery hat standing in a meadow blowing a dandelion in the wind. The pink-and-white wallpaper was of the wipe-down variety, and there was a plastic chandelier over the light bulb. Someone had been trying to brighten the place up, but not very hard.

The other women in the room were either middle-aged

or very young; there seemed to be no one else in their early twenties there. None of us spoke. Most of the women had their heads buried in the magazines, though they seemed to be leafing through the pages rather fast; there were only a few of us looking at the floor, gazing at the girl with the dandelion, or counting the rosebuds on the wallpaper.

'Mrs Jones, please come this way.' A nurse was standing at the doorway of the waiting room.

I got up. 'It's not Mrs, it's Miss,' I said as I walked over to her.

There was a rustle of magazines.

'This way please, Mrs Jones,' she said, ignoring me.

'Miss,' I said. 'Not Mrs, Miss.'

There was a shifting of bodies on seats. Somebody coughed.

'Or Ms, if you like,' I added.

The nurse glanced at the rows of women and raised her eyes heavenwards. Then her face fell and she clicked her tongue. I didn't dare look at the women but I knew, from the scowl on her face, that they hadn't responded. They remained dead silent, but there was something in the air that made me feel they were on my side, rooting for me, for Miss, or even Ms.

The nurse marched me off down the corridor without looking at me. She was small and sallow-faced, not much older than me, with her hair scraped back in a ponytail. As we walked along the corridor, her nylon uniform rustled and her shoes squeaked. I glanced sideways at her, and saw that her expression had darkened to one of fury.

The nurse stopped outside one of the doors in the corridor and knocked.

'Mr Skinner?' she said, poking her head round the door.

There was a murmur from inside.

'Mr Skinner will see you now, Mrs Jones,' said the nurse. Then she turned on her heel and walked back off down the corridor.

Inside the room, the doctor was sitting at a desk beside an examination couch with a little curtain around it. He indicated a chair without looking up, so I sat down and waited for him to speak.

Eventually he turned to me. 'So,' he said, 'we've fallen by the wayside, have we?'

For a moment, I was nonplussed. I stared at him. He was a florid man with a big, meaty face and fat, stubby fingers.

Then I said, 'No. We haven't.' I was about to say more, but I stopped myself.

There was a silence. Now it was his turn to look nonplussed. To cover his embarrassment, he coughed and began to read the notes on his desk.

'Ah, I see,' he said after a while. 'Sussex University.'

I was expecting a comment about women's libbers and burning my bra, but instead he said, 'Would you mind drawing the curtain and hopping up onto the couch, young lady, so we can have a look at you?'

He spoke with exaggerated politeness now. 'You need only take your lower garments off.'

I walked over to the couch and pulled the curtain around it, then took off my jeans and pants. There was a long piece of paper stretched over the middle of the couch so I lay down carefully on top of it.

The doctor came in with a pair of plastic gloves on and a silver instrument in his hand. He asked me to put my feet flat on the couch with my knees up in the air and open my legs. Then he inserted the instrument into my vagina. It was cold and it hurt.

'Try not to tense up,' he said.

I shut my eyes and attempted to relax. I told myself this was just a routine examination, that there was nothing to worry about.

'Yes,' he said. 'About eight weeks, I'd say. No more.'

Then he pulled the instrument out, wiped it, told me to put my clothes back on, and walked out of the cubicle.

When I was dressed, I went out to see him. He was writing at his desk and didn't look up.

'Right ho, my dear,' he said. 'Off you go, then. See you later.'

I walked over to the door and let myself out.

Back in the waiting room, I sat down again and glanced at my watch. My operation wasn't due for another hour, but I knew I'd be called before that to get changed and go down to the theatre. This was my last chance: if I was going to leave, it had to be soon.

I picked up an out-of-date magazine with a picture of Miss World on the front. I remembered her now. Helen Morgan, from Barry. One of her cousins was a friend of my mother's, but that was nothing unusual in Wales: it was a small place, and everyone there seemed to be related, or had gone to school together, or shared the same hairdresser, or something. There'd been great excitement back home when Helen Morgan had won; my mother had even rung me up to tell me. And then someone had found out that Helen was an unmarried mother, and she'd had to hand back her crown. Miss Venezuela had taken over, making some remark about how Miss World ought to be pure and undefiled, and how in her country, bad girls like Helen would never have been allowed to win.

My mother had been confused, because she was sure that Helen was married; and then it transpired that she was – she'd got married after she'd had the baby. But as it turned out, that was another reason to sack her; apparently, it was also against the Miss World rules to be married. So whatever Helen did, short of being a virgin and parading around in front of a bunch of men in nothing but a swimsuit and high heels and a tiara, she was always going to be in the wrong.

I put down the magazine and picked up another, but the words seemed to slide about in front of my eyes. The moment had come: it was time to choose. I looked up at the women, as if they could give me some kind of sign. We all ignored each other, yet I could see the tension etched on their faces. I wondered what they'd been going through in the last few hours, days, months. I wondered what their stories were, and if they could tell me, whether it would help me to decide what to do. We could have talked to each other, perhaps, to ease our fear, but none of us spoke. Or maybe this was the best way to deal with it: each of us in silence, alone. Because, when it came down to it, we all had to face this business of having – or not having – babies on our own. There was no escape. Something Kierkegaard had said about the Virgin Mary in *Fear and Trembling* came back to me:

Yet what woman was done greater indignity than Mary, and isn't it true here that those whom God blesses he damns in the same breath?

I glanced at my watch. Another quarter of an hour to go, and I still hadn't made up my mind. The hairs on my scalp prickled again. Perhaps it really was a question of either or. Perhaps the truth of it was that I'd either have the abortion and have a career, or I'd have the baby and drop out of doing philosophy for good. I thought of the biblical quote in *Fear and Trembling*:

And Abraham said, My son, God will provide himself a lamb for a burnt offering.

I hadn't really understood it, but now I did. There would have to be a sacrifice: my child or my work. My child or my self. But perhaps I couldn't be the one to choose which it should be. I remembered the voice, the man's voice, that used to call me in my nightmares. Perhaps I'd have to wait for it now. Perhaps it would tell me what to do.

The nurse came into the room with a list on a clipboard, and the surgeon put his head round the door.

'Now then,' he said, his red face beaming as we looked up at him. 'Who's next for the chop?'

chapter 29

Let us go further. We let Isaac actually be sacrificed. Abraham had faith. His faith was not that he should be happy some time in the hereafter, but that he should find blessed happiness here in this world. God could give him a new Isaac, bring the sacrificial offering back to life. He believed on the strength of the absurd, for all human calculation had long since been suspended.

The nurse read off my name from the clipboard.

'Susannah Jones.'

I waited for the voice. But none came.

Why wasn't there a voice, the man's voice, God's voice? *Do not lay your hand on the child or do anything unto him.*

It didn't come. And now I realised why: the man's voice in my dreams had only ever called my name. He had never told me what to do, and he wasn't about to now. I was going to have to decide for myself.

'Jones, please?'

I stood up. There was a silence around me that seemed to stretch into eternity. The room suddenly looked vast, and everyone in it very far away.

I took a deep breath.

'Yes,' I said. I heard my voice echo around the room.

I said it again, just to be sure it was me who had spoken.

'Yes.'

I'd done it. For better or for worse, I'd done it.

I walked over to the nurse. She glanced at me, sniffed,

and ticked me off her list.

The surgeon had already gone off down the corridor. The nurse and I fell into step behind him. Then we turned off and stood in front of a door.

'Could you please change in there,' she said. 'You'll find a gown to put on. Make sure you take off all your jewellery and put it in the tray provided. When you've finished, I'll come and collect you.'

I went inside, took off my clothes, and put on the theatre gown. The back kept opening, so I held it closed with my hand. I took off my watch and the silver bangle that Rob had given me and put them on the tray, then sat on the chair and waited for the nurse.

She came back wheeling a trolley bed and I climbed on to it. We went into another, larger room where there was a man in the corner preparing a needle.

'This won't hurt,' said the nurse, which made me think it would.

He came over and injected the needle into my arm.

I stared up at the ceiling. There were some polystyrene tiles on it. They didn't look as though they'd been put on very straight, and one of them was yellower than the rest. I wondered why. Perhaps it was older than the others, or perhaps someone had used the wrong glue. It was hard to tell.

Abraham had faith…

I began to feel sleepy and the tiles began to swim before my eyes. I closed my eyes and saw myself looking through a window at the black cars travelling down the white road, so fast that they became a blur.

…He believed on the strength of the absurd, for all human calculation had long since been suspended.

'I think she's out now, doctor,' said the nurse.

When I opened my eyes, I expected to find myself on the trolley bed, waiting to have my operation. No time seemed to have passed. But I found myself in a darkened room with a door that opened out onto a brightly lit corridor. There was a cramping pain in my belly and I felt nauseous. I could feel a sanitary pad soaked with liquid between my legs. I must have had the operation, I thought. It must all be over.

I leaned over and turned on the bedside light. On the bedside table was my watch and the silver bangle, still on the tray. I picked up the watch and looked at the time. It was 5.30 a.m.

A nurse walked in, one I hadn't seen before, and turned on the main light in the room. It was a fluorescent strip, and it flashed like a strobe before it came on. She was a pretty woman in her twenties with one of those carefully flicked back hairdos that you saw on singers like the Nolan Sisters.

'Right, Mrs Jones, we just need to do a few checks, and then we'll let you go home,' she said.

I couldn't be bothered to correct her about the Mrs. She came over and took my temperature, checked my pulse, then carefully pulled down the blankets and inspected the pad between my legs.

'That's fine,' she said, pulling the blankets back up. 'Now if anything unusual happens, if you start bleeding profusely or your temperature goes up, then come back and see us.'

'OK.' I was still groggy from the anaesthetic. I could hardly follow what she was saying.

'There's a toilet and a bathroom down the corridor where you can change your pad. Have you got one handy?'

'I don't know.' Then I noticed my suitcase in the corner. 'Yes, I think so.'

'You'll need to be ready to go by six.'

'Six?' I said. 'Why the big rush?'

'Well, normally it's seven,' she said. 'But today's a public holiday.'

'Is it?'

She looked at me, surprised. 'Yes. New Year's Day, of course.'

Of course. Last night must have been New Year's Eve. I'd completely forgotten.

'You couldn't get me a cup of tea, could you?' I said. 'I still feel half asleep.'

'Sorry,' she said. 'Against the rules. But I can bring you some water.'

'Thanks,' I said. 'Great.' There was a sarcastic edge to my voice but I was too tired to make much of a fuss.

The nurse left and I lay back for a minute. I felt exhausted. All I wanted to do was to go back to sleep, but I had to get up. I looked at the window. The curtains were drawn, but I could see from the gap in the middle that it was still pitch black outside. I'd be out there with my suitcase in a minute, hobbling about with a pain in my belly trying to find a bus. God, what a way to celebrate the new year.

I heaved myself out of bed and stood in the middle of the floor, my legs still wobbly from the anaesthetic. I was still wearing my theatre gown. I went over to the suitcase, found my washbag and towel and a pair of woolly socks, put them on, and shuffled down the hall, trying to hold the gown shut at the back. I cleaned myself up, then came back and got dressed. A cup of water was waiting for me on the bedside table. I drank it, then put my watch and bangle back on. I was glad they'd got me up early now; I couldn't wait to get out of the place.

I picked up my suitcase, and then I remembered something. There was a little pocket inside it where I'd packed the milk-teeth box Bear had given me. I took it out now and held it in the palm of my hand. *Dents de lait.* The little white stones in the lid sparkled under the fluorescent light. I opened it, and there inside were Princess Charlotte Augusta's little blackened teeth. What was it Bear had said to me? You can keep it for the next one. That was it.

I put the milk-teeth box in the pocket of my jacket, zipped up my suitcase, walked out of the room, and went over to tell the nurse I was going. She asked me to sign a form, then held the door open for me.

'Bye, then,' she said as I walked through. 'Good luck.'

I turned to her and nodded. 'Thanks,' I said. 'Happy New Year.'

Then I walked down the stairs and out into the street.

It was dark and cold outside, and the streets were deserted. I wished I'd brought something warmer to wear. I hadn't realised I was going to be out here at this time of the morning. I put my bag down and stood on the steps of the clinic, not sure what to do next. I had a throbbing headache, and there was still a cramping pain in my belly. I needed to find a phone box. I needed to phone Rob and tell him what I'd done.

Just then, I heard a sound. I turned my head and noticed a small, brown bird in the hedge beside the steps, only inches away from me. Dawn was a long way off, but for some reason the bird had started to sing already. I watched it hopping about, and then it flew away, still singing.

I put my hand in my pocket and closed my fingers around the milk-teeth box, feeling the sharp stones set in the smooth ebony wood. *You can keep it for the next one.*

Then I picked up my bag and walked back down the road the way I had come.

Fiction
Non-fiction
Literary
Crime

Popular culture
Biography
Illustrated
Music

dare to read at serpentstail.com

Visit serpentstail.com today to brow~~se~~
books, and for exclusive preview~~s~~
interviews with authors and forth

NEWS — cut to the literary chase with all the latest news about our books and authors

EVENTS — advance information on forthcoming events, author readings, exhibitions and book festivals

EXTRACTS — read first chapters, short stories, bite-sized extracts

EXCLUSIVES — pre-publication offers, signed copies, discounted books, competitions

BROWSE AND BUY — browse our full catalogue, fill up a basket and proceed to our **fully secure** checkout - our website is your oyster

FREE POSTAGE & PACKING ON ALL ORDERS ANYWHERE!

---

sign up today and receive our new free full colour catalogue